THE
STARS
ARE
TOO
HIGH

.

Agnew H. Bahnson, Jr.

THE STARS
ARE TOO HIGH

THE SCIENCE FICTION BOOK CLUB

LONDON 1962

Since the events described in this novel take place
in the future, all of the characters are imaginary and
have no relationship to any person, living or dead.

First Printing

© Copyright, 1959, by Agnew H. Bahnson, Jr.

All rights reserved under International and Pan-American Copyright Conventions.
Published in New York by Random House, Inc., and
simultaneously in Toronto, Canada, by Random House of Canada, Limited.

Library of Congress Catalog Card Number: 59-5720.

*This Science Fiction Book Club edition was
produced in 1962 for sale to its members only
by the proprietors, Phoenix House Ltd., at Aldine
House, 10–13 Bedford Street, London W.C.2 and
at Letchworth Garden City, Herts. Full details
of membership may be obtained from our London
address. The book has been reprinted by offset
by A. Wheaton & Co. Ltd., Exeter, Devon. It has
not previously been published in England.*

To my children, Karen, Hunter and Frank, in the hope that their generation may make greater strides toward peace and understanding than our generation has.

It was 7:23 A.M. At nine Dr. Henry Alvin was to have an urgent conference with General Waverly, but the thought of going to the Pentagon appalled him. How can I tell Waverly that bombers, rockets and guided missiles are obsolete? he asked himself.

Alvin watched the big black car from which he had alighted lose itself in the early-morning traffic. Then he began moving somewhat like a man in a dream, toward the nearest corner. The street sign told him he was on Stanton Square at the corner of Massachusetts Avenue and Fourth Street, in the Northeast section of Washington. He walked with a limp in his left leg, the remnant of a wartime injury, his body bent slightly forward from the waist, as though he were eager to reach his destination. But he moved slowly, reluctantly.

I'll have to avoid doing anything that might make them suspicious, he thought. If I act too quickly we may lose everything.

He hailed a cab coming down Fourth and directed the driver to his apartment in Georgetown. The scent of spring flowers came through the open window of the car. As they crossed the sunny Union Station plaza and started down Constitution Avenue, Alvin gazed admiringly at the Capitol, as he always did. The great dome rose cleanly, majestically, above the newly green trees. The cab moved in and out of traffic, past the sprawling government buildings, toward the stark spire of the Washington Monument.

"Rome at the height of its glory couldn't touch this city," Alvin said to the driver, as though to add a human contact to these familiar surroundings. He smiled and crow's-feet of wrinkles flashed along the sides of his face. The driver remained silent. Perhaps he has his worries, too, Alvin thought. "I've lived here all my life and I'm still amazed at it," he added, almost as though talking to himself.

"Hell," the driver finally replied, "cities are all the same when you're pushing a hack."

Alvin gave up the conversation, thinking how gladly at this moment he would trade his burden for the mundane concerns of the driver. He looked out of the window again, straining to keep his mind free. But even the beautiful Washington spring could not long distract him. He pulled off his thin-rimmed spectacles with a whipping movement of his hand. It was a gesture he made in those moments when he felt the pressure of responsibility. In the presence of other people he would often gaze upward as though to avoid distraction, his glasses dangling from his fingers. But when alone, he would look steadily at nothing, putting the brown plastic tips of the bows between his lips.

The cab stopped for a traffic signal. Starlings were fretting among the trees lining the avenue but traffic coming steadily in from Virginia dimmed their chatter. Alvin found this tangible, familiar world suddenly unreal, almost frightening. He glanced uneasily at his watch. The whole thing had started just seven hours ago. Seems more like a year, he mused.

He knew quite well that the days ahead would be trying. It would not be easy to keep a secret that must eventually be told, particularly a secret hovering on the borderline of treason, involving at least a technical dereliction of duty. It's a matter of timing, he thought, biting down hard on the bows of his spectacles. If only I could turn them in and still be sure we could capture it intact . . . But he shut his mind against this easy way out. The light changed and the taxi moved forward again.

They arrived at his apartment shortly after eight o'clock. Alvin paid the driver and walked to the elevator, ignoring his mailbox. There was a sign which read: "Out of Order." As he started up two flights of steps he showed none of the bounce and vigor that usually made him seem younger than his fifty-two years. His features were normally composed but

4

when he was worried, as he was this morning, his face lengthened, his eyes seemed more deeply recessed in his skull, and
there was a vague sadness about him, a sort of grief at man's
imperfection, particularly his own.

The apartment had been shut up all week end, and he
moved about methodically opening windows and emptying
ash trays into the fireplace. He went into the bedroom and
carefully laid out fresh clothes. Then he hung up his somewhat wrinkled suit. He drew a bath, climbed in and lay back,
luxuriating for a moment. He had had only an hour or two
of sleep and his tired body soaked up the warmth and relaxed.
But only for a moment. Time was still pressing for action.

Alvin was tall and in the full-length mirror on the bath-
room door he could clearly see his head, his long neck, his
somewhat narrow shoulders above the rim of the tub. Streaks
of gray had made substantial inroads into his almost black
hair but his eyebrows were thick and dark. His ears were
large but lay tightly against his head. He had been told that
his eyes, a rich brown, were his best feature but now they
looked tired, disenchanted.

Finishing his bath quickly, he dressed in the usual dark
suit with a white shirt and a subdued tie. It was a neat, suit-
able and perfectly inconspicuous attire—the kind he liked
best. He searched a moment for a collar pin before he remembered it was in the toilet case that had been left behind at
Crestview Inn. And that, he thought, is the first of many
things I'll have to blame on last week end.

As he came out on the street, blinking a bit in the sun that
struck brilliantly down on Georgetown's cobbled streets, a
huge airliner roared overhead, seeking the altitude that would
take it out of the traffic clustering around National Airport.
He stared up at it, hearing the labored beat of the engines,
almost able to see the heads of the passengers through the
windows.

What an ancient thing it is, he thought; what a noble mon-

5

ument to bygone days! He shook his head, feeling his secret hard and terrible in his throat, like a lump of ice swallowed the wrong way.

Before leaving for his week end at Crestview, Alvin had cleared his desk. When he reached his office in the Pentagon at 8:50 on this bright Monday morning, burning-eyed from lack of sleep, and vaguely expecting accusing fingers to point at him from every door, he found his mail with an important-looking memo: "General Waverly's nine o'clock conference has been canceled for today. Please be in Projection Room Victor at ten."

The scientist was puzzled. Victor was the private projection room for top-secret films. Perhaps Waverly finally had pictures of the new Russian ICBM in flight. He had thought something important would come out of the tremendous push for the May Day review of military power held in Moscow, and had been fuming about slow service on the films from Turkey.

But as soon as Alvin arrived at Projection Room Victor, he knew that Russian rockets would not be on the agenda. As Waverly's personal scientific consultant, he had worked at one time or another with most of the people present, but he had met with them as a group only once or twice in his entire Pentagon career. There were representatives from Joint Chiefs and Air Force Staff, of course, but most were connected with the Washington Defense Area Organization. One was Colonel Holcum, the ranking Air Force specialist in Unidentified Flying Objects. There were intraservice representatives from a committee that kept all defense warning services under continuing study. And there were unknown faces. Worry began to gnaw at Alvin again. It was going to be a long, hard pull on his nerves, he thought. The mere convening of such an unusual group made him uneasy.

General Waverly walked in at 10:10, exactly ten minutes

late, as he always was. Everyone in the room was attentive as he stalked portentously to the end of the room below the screen. Alvin was faintly amused at the interest, amounting almost to awe, he read on the faces of some of those not used to Dick Waverly's presence. The man knew how to cut a dramatic figure, he thought, admiring at least the usefulness of such theatricality. It gave the Air Force's ranking general a third dimension of power, a sort of commanding air that seized a listener even when words and deeds were ineffective. His bulldog features and his brilliant eyes were topped by a shock of copious white hair and, in anger, his jawbones would jut like rocks from his cheeks.

"Gentlemen, I'll ask that you be seated and the lights turned out." When he had been obeyed, he continued. "Most of you know that all search radar screens of our defense network are monitored by movie cameras whenever we pick up an unidentified object. You also know that we can speed up the rotation of the sweep or lock it to track any such moving object, without the sweep pattern but with a rapid, oscillatory motion in one quadrant or in any given arc of the circle. That's how we have these films of an unidentified flying object detected at 02:20 this morning within the radar search area of Patuxent Naval Air Base."

Dr. Alvin felt as though a heavy blow had been landed in the pit of his stomach. Panic gripped him and made his head whirl for a second, but he forced himself to look steadily at General Waverly.

"Picture, please," the general said. The first flicker on the screen showed a normal radar sweep pattern, with a tiny dot appearing at its periphery. On the next ten-second sweep, the dot had moved considerably. It seemed to be descending rapidly but showed little lateral motion. Quickly the radar detector had been locked into its vertical oscillatory motion, with the dot in the center of the sweep. The cameras had been speeded up to give a slow-motion picture of the object, which seemed to be falling. General Waverly indicated the moving dot with a long pointer. "For those of you who do not read the radar screen, I'll explain that this object was picked up at about seventy thousand feet in the air. It was falling vertically at approximately fifty thousand feet a *minute* at that time. Mark that now, fifty thousand feet. I know that figure is fantastic but that's what the radar showed. At around fifteen thousand feet, the fall slowed sharply, as you can see. The object seemed to be preparing to land on the earth. At fifteen hundred feet it fell out of view because of obstructions in the low angle of sight from the radar installation, which was approximately ninety miles away. That put the object about twenty-eight miles off the Maryland shore. Navy search planes were immediately alerted at Patuxent and arrived in the area fifteen minutes later. Flares were dropped over a wide area but no evidence of any sort was found."

It's come, Alvin thought. Sooner than I believed. He could not take his eyes from the treacherous screen. The palms of his hands were moist. With disgust he identified fear among the other emotions this sudden news had aroused—dismay, surprise, avid curiosity, and a sort of house-against-itself concern for his new associates on the one hand and his established loyalties on the other. He found himself in the intolerable situation of wanting both those associates and his government—even the brilliant Waverly, his exasperating superior —to win this game. He was bound by differing responsibilities to both. He saw the situation with clarity but he could not tell how much that clarity depended on the fear he had to keep swallowing like phlegm. He fought fear of discovery, fear of disgrace; fear, most of all, of failure at this infinitely dangerous moment.

But somewhere deep in Henry Alvin's quiet nature a streak of daring lay hidden. A gentle upbringing in a scholarly home and an early devotion to a scientific education had concealed it even from himself. It had been only during the war that he had felt the first hot rush of blood that he attributed to pioneering ancestors on his mother's side—ancestors who had been among the original settlers of Colorado's Cripple Creek mining area. He was secretly proud of that blood, proud of the abandon it rarely loosed in him.

He felt it now, the old pioneer blood surging in his quiet veins, blessedly springing from fear to save him. For a moment his brain spun recklessly. And as the lights came up and the picture faded from the screen, it was almost with eagerness that he made the first move of duplicity in a career that had been based on honor and integrity.

"General," Alvin said, proud of the calm he maintained in his voice, "was there any trace of departure?"

"Well—Baltimore radar messaged a blip when they heard the Patuxent report, but it was far out to sea, almost out of range. They probably wouldn't even have reported it if they hadn't heard Patuxent. The radar people say we'd better discount it."

"Then this is a true UFO?"

"I don't know anything better to call it," Waverly said, his brows knitting together. Alvin sat down, satisfied that he had shown enough interest and concern but no knowledge. He noted that the general was exhibiting his usual impatience with phenomena he could not call upon some aide to explain.

"What did Annapolis radar report, General?" The question came from a thick-necked, square-shouldered Navy captain who had been introduced to Alvin, just before the meeting, as the Navy's new representative on the Defense Warning Service Continuing Study Committee. It was a committee with which Alvin had been closely associated and he was interested in this new member.

"Captain—ah—Johnson, there was an unfortunate situation at Annapolis at that particular time," Waverly said. "The stand-by radar had been out of commission for three days, as you no doubt know. Because of the Navy's coastal exercises

9

last week, Annapolis couldn't find the manpower to fix it until an hour or so ago. On top of that, the main radar unit sheared a pin in the tracking device just fifteen minutes before this sighting. A sea gull flew against it at a critical angle. We know that because the dead bird was found near by. Gentlemen, this day and time, that's the sort of damn thing that can lose you a war before breakfast."

"Somebody will walk the plank," Captain Johnson said. "I'll guarantee it."

General Waverly looked stunned. Heads turned to look at Johnson. In a Waverly conference, the only words spoken were supposed to be questions and answers. Alvin marked Johnson automatically as a type who wouldn't make the Pentagon grade. He had seen the impulsive ones come and go before.

General Strahan of the Air Force stood up, glaring at Johnson. Alvin thought that he was probably ruffled at the mere presence of the Navy in what he would consider an Air Force affair; and he would be ready to boil over because it had been a Navy sighting. Strahan, a lanky Texan with a better combat than staff record, would not even have permitted the Navy to have radar if he had had his way. He was a bore but he was a fighter, too, and his slow Panhandle drawl could build into a hammering staccato.

"General Waverly," he said, "I seriously doubt if Annapolis would have reported anything unusual even if the radar out there had been properly maintained. They should hardly have been concerned with this object unless it had turned toward the coast. No flight plan is necessary to penetrate the Defense Zone for planes under a thousand feet of altitude and traveling at less than a hundred twenty-five miles per hour. May I ask what was the speed of this thing, General?"

Waverly finished lighting a huge cigar and took it from his lips. "It was reported as falling vertically with no apparent forward movement. The distance measuring equipment would have shown such a forward movement, even if it had struck a course directly toward the Patuxent radar before it disappeared at approximately fifteen hundred feet."

"And it was still falling at that altitude?"

"It was."

"Well, then, it's a foregone conclusion that if the object had turned toward the coast, it would have been below a thousand feet and probably moving at less than a hundred twenty-five miles per hour, from this report."

That sort of hair-splitting can lose you a war before breakfast, too, Dr. Alvin thought, wondering how often he had heard these discussions—frightening as they could be—disintegrate into jurisdictional squabbles between petty men. He watched Captain Johnson rise again.

"General Waverly, I don't represent the Navy officially but I am the senior Naval officer present. I think I can safely say —guarantee it—that despite the speed and altitude, the Navy would consider most gravely any unidentified flying object within fifty miles of Annapolis."

Waverly rapped on a table with his long stick, his jawbones beginning their famous jut. "The defense of Annapolis may prove, sir, a minor concern to what could be on our hands." Alvin could see Johnson stiffen, open his mouth, remain silent only with an effort. Guts, he thought, but no discretion. Won't last a month.

"Gentlemen, we've come here to consider this thing deliberately." General Waverly pointed his cigar first at Strahan, then at the redfaced Johnson. "Let's not get sidetracked. I don't like my conferences to get sidetracked. Ordinarily I don't get excited about you flying-saucer people and your goings-on. I've got too many things I know something about to deal with. But I have to admit that this particular sighting is one of the best evidences yet that at least some UFOs are controlled by intelligent beings. This object was not slowed by accident as it approached the earth. The very fact that it

11

came closer than fifteen hundred feet to the sea is of concern, particularly since it *was* less than fifty miles from Annapolis. We don't know where it went from that point and that's obviously another matter of concern. At the same time, I'm not going to let this particular sighting take on too much significance. It's only one of many, and none of them have been very threatening. Colonel Holcum, I have ten more minutes, and I'd like to hear your—ah—interpretation."

Colonel Holcum, used to Waverly's slurs on his specialty, stood up. "All I have to say is what I've said many times, General. I've been intimately associated with these UFO reports during the last five years. I agree that this latest one indicates a guiding intelligence. But I must confess that even those of us called specialists don't understand these objects nor can we recommend any kind of certain defense against them. Our pilots and planes would be no match for whatever it was that radar picked up this morning. Other UFOs have caused the deaths of several men who were chasing them and couldn't stand the pace. They've flown rings around many others, if we believe some pretty reliable pilots. I'd frankly be reluctant to pick an argument with the thing you had that radar locked on. It showed no enmity—none of these UFOs have. And if we start the fight, we're likely to find we don't have the means to finish it."

"Well, of course, that represents a point of view, Holcum." General Waverly began the restless pacing which the cartoonists had made his trademark. Cigar smoke came in regular blue jets from his clenched jaws. "I don't know that the Air Force Staff can subscribe to all of that."

Just most of it, Dr. Alvin thought, aware of the many hours he had put into the study of the same subject, trying to make Waverly take it seriously. His first reaction of near panic had passed, particularly since it was clear that the craft had merely been sighted, not identified in any way. He had even begun to listen with the cold calculation of a conspirator, alert for any chance to help set the stage for the disclosure he must surely make someday.

"There is one thing here that particularly interests me," Colonel Holcum continued. "This sighting does not follow any known UFO pattern. We may have detected a new menace in this vertical-fall tracing. And we already had enough troubles." A murmur of laughter rippled over the room, but quickly died as General Waverly regarded Holcum without a smile.

"I'll sum up quickly, sir. Most of these UFOs have demonstrated a maneuverability, speed, acceleration, and power to hover motionless or rise vertically with terrific velocity that we can't even measure accurately, much less match. But here we have this vertical fall to add to the list. No known aircraft could have done that, under control. It just isn't conceivable to anyone who studies these things that they could be from the earth. Their capabilities surpass even the possibilities of the most advanced concepts in our secret laboratories, to say nothing of our planes and rockets in the making. And, if we assume that the Communists have got that far ahead of us—well, if they had twenty flying saucers, as you called them, and if each could carry three H-bombs, they could wipe us out in a night. And not lose a ship doing it."

Holcum's voice broke off sharply. In the sudden quiet of Projection Room Victor, General Waverly's brisk, precise steps were loud and clear. His hands were clasped behind his back. When he spoke, there was disbelief in his voice. "Do you surmise seriously, then, that these objects must come from outer space?"

Holcum had been through this often enough to recognize defeat. He spoke wearily, already groping behind him for his chair. "I surmise, sir, that they appear to surpass any scientific concept we have and that they would probably have been used against us long before now if they had been the product of any other nation on earth."

13

Waverly turned toward Dr. Alvin.

"What do you think, Hank?"

Alvin rose. He was almost enjoying himself. There was a certain wild freedom of improvisation in conspiracy that he had never found in scientific deliberation. He whipped his glasses from his face and gazed first at the ceiling, then at the general. "Sir, in all respect for the colonel, he does, as you said, represent a point of view. It's impressive. It's damn frightening, if you'll permit the word. However, it's widespread, common knowledge that the facts mitigate against other planets having the sort of climate or density which would support life as we conceive of it. Take the planet Mercury. It's closest to the sun and has a mean temperature of seven hundred degrees Fahrenheit on the side which faces the sun. The dark side is extremely cold because of the low-density atmosphere and the slow rotation of the planet. Venus, the next planet, is slightly smaller than the earth. It ought to be ideal for some form of life except that it's so close to the sun its atmosphere is fogged by boiling vapors. Venus is still many millions of years behind the progress of the earth, our astronomy people tell me, although they have never been able to look through that foggy atmosphere and actually see its surface. Mars is our most likely challenger. It's smaller than the earth but it has an atmosphere that some believe supports a form of life. We can see the waxing and waning of the polar caps, and certain configurations of the so-called canals on the surface of the planet indicate the work of intelligent beings. But Mars is quite cold, compared to the earth, and its atmosphere would be poisonous to us. No oxygen.

"Beyond Mars are the asteroids, which have no atmosphere that could support life. Neither does the moon. Jupiter is too gaseous. Saturn, Uranus, Neptune and Pluto are too far from the sun and too fast in rotation to absorb the heat required for any conceivable beings. What I'm saying, of course, is that Colonel Holcum makes a good case that these UFOs

14

don't come from the earth. But is there any other place they *can* come from?"

He sat down, winking at Holcum. It was an old argument between them. Dr. Alvin was amused to have stolen even a secret march. After all, *he* knew where this particular UFO had come from, and it had not been outer space, unless you could consider Nevada outer space.

General Waverly paced the room like a frustrated tiger while Alvin spoke. Suddenly he stopped and stared at Alvin. Blue smoke clouded around his head. He held the pose a full fifteen seconds, savoring its shock value, its dramatic effect. "One possibility you left out, Doctor," he said, still not moving, his voice low and pleasant. "How about the more temperate climate of a planet of some other star?"

Dr. Alvin never ceased to be fascinated by Waverly's carefully planned attempts to confound him—or by a mind that could range far enough ahead in a theoretical situation to be able so often to pull rabbits out of such unlikely hats. He wondered what junior officer had dug this out of the *Encyclopaedia Britannica* for him. He stood up again, growing faintly angry at this new evidence of Waverly's one-sided battle of wits with him, but he was even more amused at the sheer vanity it concealed. "The nearest star is four light-years from the earth," he said, trying not to sound schoolmasterly, knowing how vehemently Waverly could react to mockery. "We don't know whether it has planets or not. But if there should be a star out there somewhere which does have a planet that could support a superior being, that being would have to charge himself with an inconceivable amount of resolution and energy to make many trips through space—for years at a time —even to discover our inoffensive little planet, much less return to the earth as many times as UFOs have been reported with reliability. Frankly, sir, I like to keep an open mind to the most fantastic possibilities, but I can't go along with that one."

"Ha-hum," General Waverly said. "Well, gentlemen, as usual you can give me nothing concrete to take to the Joint Chiefs, I suppose? You have no recommendations? No deductions even?"

No one spoke. They had all been through it too many times, Alvin thought. Even the unknown was losing its shock value. He felt a growing confidence. Perhaps he and his strange, new-found associates could pull something off; perhaps their combination could truly be more effective than this collection of puzzled yes men and frustrated professors and hidebound subordinates; perhaps their very freedom from preconceptions, from protocol, from channels, was their strongest weapon.

"Very well." General Waverly glanced at his watch. "You gentlemen may occupy this room thirteen more minutes before some rocket people take it over. Run the film again and kick it around." He paused, grinning for the first time. "Maybe you can be a little more frank without the old man here." He walked rapidly toward the door, his military aides springing to their feet and following him. "I may convene this group again any time," he said, without looking back, and went out.

Henry Alvin walked uneasily down the long corridor toward his office. Nothing had happened during the last eight minutes following General Waverly's departure to help or hurt his dilemma. Nothing ever happened in Waverly's conferences after he left, although it was frequently his custom to leave before the business was finished, quite confident that it would be in precisely the same state of action and resolution when he reconvened the group. Waverly's confidence that none of his pawns would move to change or amplify a situation without his guiding hand was a source of irritation.

Alvin reached his office and slumped wearily into his desk

chair. He pressed a button and his secretary appeared at the door.

"Miss Saunders, would you please get me a chicken salad sandwich and a glass of milk from the canteen?"

"Yes, sir." She turned to go.

"By the way," he called, "if you don't mind going to lunch as soon as you return, I'd appreciate it. I should have something for you to start typing within an hour—that report we didn't finish last week."

"Yes, sir. I'll be glad to."

But Alvin could not concentrate at once on the report. Scientist that he was, he tried to take stock of the situation. The fundamental fact could not be ignored. It was imprinted on the screen and on the mind of General Waverly and his entourage. But what lay behind that fact? First, Jack Baker —a young man, impetuous, idealistic, determined—and somehow distracted. Next, John Sloan, a seasoned man of sixty or slightly more, stable, the real boss of the enterprise, the source of revenue and ultimate command—but a man who usually deferred to his associates, perhaps in respect for their awesome accomplishment. And, lastly, Max Schoeller, the genius who had led the effort into fantastic reality, a man who had nothing to lose. This was the strange variety of personalities and pressures that Henry Alvin had to deal with, in addition to that unearthly, fantastic fact itself.

His duty had required that he rush to the Pentagon the moment John Sloan had released him and tell the whole, incredible truth. But he had not done so. Sitting wearily at his desk, he stubbornly resolved again to keep the secret, despite his personal danger. He thought back to the moment when Jack Baker, a friend with whom he had served in the war, had called upon his sense of duty to enter and inspect the strange craft; of how the door had closed behind him and he had been, at least technically, kidnapped. Maybe I'm a damn fool, he thought. But Jack Baker could get the Devil himself to go along with one of his schemes. He shook his head, staggered at the immense possibilities Baker and Sloan had shown him. Reluctantly he turned to the unfinished report.

Alvin had not seen the last of Dick Waverly for the day. Late in the afternoon, after many hours of forced labor on the report, a peremptory voice on the intercom summoned him to the general's office.

"Well, well," Waverly said, as Alvin entered the carpeted room. "My astronomy expert. Dammit, Hank, you know too much about too many things." He waved at a chair.

"I can afford to." Alvin sat down. "I don't have to buck up through the ranks."

"There you go," Waverly said. "You even know too much about how the Air Force works." He chuckled, but Alvin considered himself duly put on notice of disapproval. He had worked with Dick Waverly too long not to have expected some verbal rebuff for his successful evasion of the morning's trap; and he had expected it to be veiled in heavy humor, as it had been. Sometimes he wished he didn't understand Waverly so well. The man's very predictability made it hard to take him as seriously as he deserved to be taken.

"Well, that was some performance, wasn't it?" The general relaxed in his big chair and fumbled open the drawer where he kept his cigars. He had pulled a short tour in Korea just before coming to the Pentagon and had picked up the most characteristic habit of the flyer in that war: long black cigars, chewed and smoked to a frazzle. "Some performance."

Alvin knew that Waverly had passed on from the meeting of the morning, leaving for good the matter of stars and planets. He began to grow tense all over, remembering again that dot trapped in the blinking eye of the radarscope, almost unable to believe that he himself had been aboard the craft it represented. "That Holcum is a good man," he forced himself to say. "I wish you'd listen to him a little."

"To hell with Holcum," Waverly said. "Give me a man like you, Hank. A man with his feet planted on something besides half-assed notions. Listen, I'm not saying there isn't anything in this UFO business. I'm not blind. But I tell you what I've got to worry about, Hank. I've got to worry about those people." He swung around in his chair and pointed at the vast orange expanse of the Soviet Union, outlined in red on the wall map behind his desk. "UFOs, too. But those people first of all."

He popped a cigar into his mouth. Alvin settled back in his chair, glancing surreptitiously at his watch. It was already past quitting time and he had looked forward to an early dinner and a long night's sleep. But plainly Dick Waverly had something on his mind, and it was Henry Alvin's turn to listen.

"In my opinion, Hank, they're gambling the annihilation of civilization against the eventual disruption of our economy. My money's on our economy, but suppose it does fail? The free world, such as it is, goes poof. Those bastards have a good gamble when you figure the odds. It's too good for them even to think about starting a war. Which makes our big problem—what happens to us while they wait us out?"

"I believe in our system," Alvin said. "I don't know about a war, if that comes, but if you've figured it right I say they're going to lose their gamble."

"I believe in our system, too. But how many years can we fight a delaying action in the hope of international understanding and still keep up our strength? Have you got any idea of the drain an armaments race makes on the economy? Hell, the national debt may be only two hundred and eighty-one billion dollars on the books—*only* two hundred eighty-one billion—but the total extension of credits and obligations exceeds six hundred billion dollars. Six *hundred* billion. Great God, I can't even think of a figure that big."

"What we need," Alvin said, feeling the ironic edge of his words, "is a flying saucer of our own."

"What would we do with it?" General Waverly shook his head. "I tell you, Hank, we're in a box. This country is too soft to fight a preventive war and that's all you could do with a flying saucer, or with any superweapon that you had exclusive possession of."

What would we do with it indeed? Alvin thought. He looked at the bulldog features of General Waverly, the flashing eyes, the dramatic hands, with a queer, sympathetic contempt. He knew suddenly that he would never again be able to look at any of the men to whom a nation had entrusted its life without that feeling; for while they wrestled with survival in theory, he would have to deal with it in fact. While Dick Waverly called in his subordinates in rotation to listen to his long-winded ideas and inspirations and theories, he, Henry Alvin, would have to make an actual, responsible decision on what to do with a superweapon that was possessed exclusively. And while that decision would force him to look into the dreadful pit he had already glimpsed, it would also lift him, in a sense, beyond other mortals; it would set him apart from them forever. He felt a slow thrill moving along his spine.

"I'll tell you what we need," the general said. "We need a sign up in that old sky. We need something to put the fear of God in us. Something we can't explain, like your UFOs."

"And obvious," Alvin said. "Obvious to everybody."

"Obvious as God himself."

"Do you believe in God, General?"

"Damn right I do." Dick Waverly bit off the end of his cigar and spat it into a wastebasket. "Trouble is, I don't believe He paints signs."

2.

The telephone seemed to stare at Dr. Alvin when he opened
the door to his apartment that evening. Almost to the minute
five days before, it had rung to invite him into what had
turned out to be a fantasy, which had ended less than fourteen hours ago.

At first he had hardly remembered who Jack Baker was.
And when Baker had asked him to spend the week end at
Crestview, a little inn in the Poconos, near an Air Force base
where both had been stationed during the war, Alvin's reaction had been vehement.

"How the hell do you think I can get out of Washington for
a week end at a place like that?"

"Listen," Jack had said, "we got out of that mess over
Düsseldorf, didn't we? You ought to be able to get out of anything after that."

Those words had been the first step in the plot, Alvin
thought, pinching his tired forehead under his hand, conscious now of the skillful way his old acquaintance had played
his hand. Baker must have known quite well that the mere
mention of Düsseldorf would cause far more than memories
of wartime camaraderie. It had been on that historic bombing raid—with the scientist along in his usual role of observer,
this time to judge the effectiveness of the new radar techniques—that First Lieutenant Jack Baker, bombardier, had
become an official hero. Flak had got them just before the
run, a sudden burst right under the ship's nose. Both Baker
and Alvin had been badly wounded, but not only had the
young lieutenant remained at his bombsight and sent away
his bombs with precision; he had also rendered first aid to
Henry Alvin so effectively that the observer had survived a
wound which should have killed him.

21

There had been a long moment of silence—after the mention of Düsseldorf—over the wires connecting Washington with Los Angeles, while Alvin, just as Jack Baker must have known he would, relived those terrible minutes in the death-filled air over the German city, and the agonized flight home.

"Dammit, boy," he said finally, and the words crackled and snapped over the long wires like gunfire. "It's good to hear your voice. It's been a long, long time."

"Right," Baker said. "Hank, I've got to see you. I don't come East very often. Don't go red tape and brass hat just because you're a big man now."

"All right," Alvin said. "I'll rent a car and drive up. It'll do me good to get out of this madhouse."

It had been as simply arranged as that. And it had been a good week end, too, Alvin thought, right up until the moment when they were leaving and there had been that sharp, cracking sound from the rear of the rented car. It had taken no expert mechanic to see that the differential was out of commission.

Had there been a flight or a train—even a bus—back to Washington, the scientist would have been obliged to take it because of that important conference scheduled with General Waverly at nine A.M. Monday, a conference Alvin did not feel he could possibly miss. The only hope had been to have the car repaired, and they had spent most of the afternoon finding a mechanic who could, and would, do the job on Sunday. It was slow work, and at five minutes past midnight the job had not been completed.

"Let's take a walk," Jack had said. "We're doing no good sitting here."

Alvin looked at his watch, then at the mechanic. "We'll be back in twenty minutes. Try to finish up by then, will you?"

"Yeah," the mechanic said. "Sure thing."

Jack's gait had been brisk and jaunty as they walked out of the tiny business district of the little Pocono resort. He was

22

humming tunelessly and his hands were jammed deeply into his pockets. A drifting ground mist swirled about them from the cooling earth, but patches of the heavens shone through from time to time, clear and brilliant.

"Look at that sky," Jack said. "You could count a thousand stars and see a billion of them in a telescope. You know, this is just the kind of night to see a flying saucer."

"Flag it down if you do. Maybe we could bum a ride to Washington."

Jack stopped, his hands still in his pockets. "Look, Hank, I guarantee I'll have you back in Washington for that conference. I feel responsible. After all, I lured you up here."

Alvin punched his shoulder with a friendly fist. "I've had a hell of a good week end, Jack. I've been working so hard I'd forgotten all the old times. Don't you worry about me and Washington."

"I'll get you there, Hank. We may even detour by way of Pittsburgh, Chicago, Detroit, Cleveland, Buffalo, Boston, New York, Philadelphia and Baltimore. That would make a nice sightseeing trip on a clear night, wouldn't it?"

Alvin laughed. "You'll need more than those theories of modern flight we've been kicking around, if we're going to make a trip like that. You'll need some real hardware, Jack; something I wouldn't want to check out in for the first time."

Baker walked along silently. Their week end of talking had shown Alvin that this was a somewhat older version of the impetuous, indomitable youth who had saved his life over Düsseldorf. His mind was as quick, as challenging as ever, and now it was firmly grounded in an excellent education. Seldom did Alvin, even at the Pentagon level, come across such incisive and encyclopedic knowledge of aeronautical engineering.

More striking than that was the constant theme of idealism that seemed to run through Baker's ideas. What had been in the youth a callow touch of the do-gooder now seemed to be a mature realization of independence and destiny. It was a combination at once appealing and effective—the air of impetuosity combined with the dogged assertion of principle, and both backed by his impressive intellect.

Baker took his hands from his pockets and through the thin gray mist Alvin saw him move them in a single, dynamic gesture.

"If such a thing were possible, Hank—if you could rise from the White House lawn and settle down gently in Red Square an hour and a half later, that would change our whole concept of human relations, wouldn't it?"

"Certainly it would. Of course, we can toss a guided missile over there in less time than that but it's hardly the same thing."

"No, I'm talking about you or me going over there one day for a business luncheon or for a big party some evening. Or the President of the United States flying over before breakfast to talk about an international crisis."

"If the world ever gets that close together, I don't believe we can afford to have international crises."

"Neither do I."

They walked on. Alvin saw by the radium dial of his watch that it was a quarter past midnight. They were well beyond the little village. The night was quiet. Frogs and crickets sounded their easy song and a gentle breeze rustled in the trees. A red light winked through the fragmentary mist at the top of a radio tower near by. On some far-off highway, they heard the faint, indignant complaint of a Klaxon.

"I was walking out here with Sandy this morning," Jack said.

"You liked her, didn't you?"

"Didn't you?"

"Who wouldn't?"

Alvin sighed. The blond girl had been a good match for Jack—so much so that the older man was frankly envious.

I haven't looked at a girl since the war, he said to himself. Not until this one.

But even a youngster would have trouble competing with Jack Baker, Alvin thought. He was not only a fascinating person. He also had arresting blue eyes under his close-cropped blond hair and a deep, healthy tan on his face. His smile was quick and ingenuous; he stood six feet tall and his shoulders were as broad as a football star's. In fact, he had been just such a star in college and had a broken nose to prove it—the only flaw in his cheerful features.

"She was all right," Jack said. "I found her quite a gal but she's gone. Back in Cleveland by now, and when do I ever get to Cleveland?" He was walking more slowly. The red light of the radio tower was less than a hundred yards away, blinking rhythmically. Jack pushed up the cuff on his left arm and glanced at his watch.

They walked in silence for a few moments. Alvin felt an atmosphere of tension and looked at Jack through the flashes of mist that were brightened from the light of the stars in the clear heavens above. That old attitude of determination had settled on his face—the same lines of determination he had seen one night long ago over Düsseldorf. Jack's lips were tense. Alvin became more attentive. Finally Jack spoke, his voice quavering a bit.

"Fifty yards on the other side of that radio tower is the most advanced flying machine in the world. At least I hope there is nothing else like it around. If I had described it to you in detail earlier this week end, you would have thought I was crazy, particularly if I had talked you into waiting with me until now and it didn't show up. You would have had to drive to Washington tonight after the car was fixed, the way the mechanic is going to drive your car, and hope to God you could make it in time for Waverly's conference at nine."

They heard the low rumble of an approaching automobile. Jack looked at his watch again.

Alvin stopped walking and turned toward him. A sheet of light was thrown on his puzzled face as the automobile rounded a bend behind them. A horn sounded and they stepped quickly onto the shoulder of the road.

"Great God, Jack! That's my car."

The automobile came to a halt for a moment at a dirt road which led to the radio tower less than two hundred feet in front of them, then drove off down the main highway at high speed.

"Looks like the mechanic wants to get as far along as he can before the early-morning traffic slows him down."

"Must be checking out the differential. When's he coming back?" Alvin was disturbed. For a moment he had feared that Jack was pulling some ill-advised practical joke. He tugged at his glasses as though to remove them but took his hand away.

"He's not coming back," Jack said casually as they started walking again. "He dropped our luggage off by that little road."

Alvin did not want to seem foolish and be taken in by this joke but he started moving more rapidly toward the place where the car had stopped. When they arrived, their luggage was piled on the shoulder of the highway just before the turn-off. He looked at it astounded; then he turned to Jack in alarm.

"Are you serious? It's too damn late to be playing jokes." There was a touch of anger in his voice.

"I'm serious," Jack replied, picking up his bags. Alvin looked at him for a moment, then did likewise, almost mechanically.

"Let's move along, Hank. We must get the ship out of here as quickly as possible."

"But how in the hell did it get in here? There's certainly no airport this close to town and hardly a level spot." He felt

26

a little foolish by even admitting this much reality to Jack's crazy comment.

"There's a small field up front to your right that's level enough."

"It might be level enough but there's certainly no field around here big enough to land a plane in. Anyhow, Jack, it would be murder to take off in this ground fog and no lights." In spite of himself his curiosity was aroused.

"How about a vertical take-off type of ship?"

Alvin stopped to shift his bags from one hand to the other. "I've never seen even a VTO I would bring into a place like this." He set his bags down. They were quite close to the radio tower now. He heard a slight breeze whine faintly in the steel structure. A shiver went along his spine. "I still think you're kidding. You would be a damn fool to bring the world's most advanced aircraft into a public place like this, even if you could do it." There was a slight sneer in his voice. "Why, they didn't even shut this radio station down until twenty minutes ago."

"I know. The ship was about fifteen miles straight up at midnight. They got a fix on the radio before it closed down."

Alvin whistled, still incredulous. "Fifteen miles straight up! How do you know?"

Jack set his bags down and reached into his coat pocket. He pulled out an ordinary-looking transistor receiver and handed it to Alvin. "Put your ear to this and turn up the volume."

Alvin obeyed but heard nothing. Just as he started to take it away he heard a sharp click. Twenty seconds later he heard it again.

"The transmitter is intermittent," Jack explained. "No use to provide a radio fix for somebody else."

"Where is it coming from?" Alvin asked weakly.

Jack picked up his bags. "Follow me," he said and walked

27

off the road to the right. Alvin took three steps and stumbled on a rock. Jack walked on ahead. The scientist struggled to his feet and picked up the bags from the soft, sticky earth. Jack was out of sight in the mist but he could hear his footsteps and walked toward them. This is becoming ridiculous, he thought. But curiosity drove him on. The fog seemed thicker as they climbed higher. It had a wet smell. The devilish red glow from the blinking light on the radio tower was weird and unearthly but did not light the way. Alvin panted as he walked over the rough field. He had spent the last year and a half in the halls of the Pentagon where all a man needed for walking was endurance, not agility. His arms ached and he set the bags down for a moment, listening for the movement of Jack's feet on the damp soil. He heard nothing. An unfamiliar feeling of panic gripped him. His mind resolved a jumble of thoughts quickly and he realized that only now had he seriously believed that there was something unknown out here, something beyond theory and speculation, something that sounded a click every twenty seconds in the tiny receiver Jack had taken from him less than a minute ago. He started to call, then wondered if he should make his way back to the road and run for it. Henry Alvin was not a fearful man but more than fear was involved in this situation. He was not sure that he wanted to accept the responsibility of being introduced to this unknown and unseen thing Jack was leading him toward, at least not under these circumstances. He was not sure that he should let Jack go through with this. He was not sure that he would be taken back to Washington at all, even if some incredible ship awaited them. And yet curiosity drove him on—curiosity and a realization that if such a craft existed, it was his duty to look at it. I must get a close look at it, he told himself.

The sound of moving feet broke the stillness. It was quite near. A searching beam of light swept through the mist. It came to rest on him.

"We are over here," Jack said as he cut out the light. The footsteps moved closer.

"You know what you are doing, Jack?"

"I think so."

"You are not only inviting Hank Alvin to look at this thing; you are hijacking the Scientific Adviser to General Richard Waverly."

"I didn't think you and I were involved in such technicalities."

"I wish we weren't, but in this situation there's more involved than you and I. If anything goes wrong, that's the way the facts will be read. I may have a duty to you not to go on with this."

Jack was beside him now. "I'll take my chances, Hank. And I assure you that your duty is to see it through. Here, take this flashlight and I'll get the bags."

"Where do we go?" He was too puzzled to distrust any longer. Perhaps it was only a foolish prank after all.

"Straight ahead twenty feet or so. Cut the light on for a second after six paces."

They moved forward. Alvin flashed the light. A large obstruction blocked his path, extending into the thick mist on either side. An open door was just to the left of them. Jack walked through it with the bags, then turned back to help him in. Alvin hesitated a moment but moved forward. He snapped off the flashlight when one foot was securely in the ship. The feeling of panic returned. This was no prank.

He could see almost nothing, but anxiety made his senses acute. The unknown lay all about him like the midnight ground mist outside. His shoe scraped on a metal floor but it seemed to him that a step forward would take him over a dark rim, into some fearful depth. The door closed behind him. A buzzer sounded briefly and there was a sudden, quiet hum; then he felt himself being borne aloft—vertically.

"You'd better step forward into the cockpit," a voice said.

"When we start our forward acceleration, it's going to be hard to move around."

There was a tight constriction in Alvin's throat. "Jack?" he said. "Is that you, Jack?" He was not sure his legs were going to work.

"Jack's gone aft," the voice said. A gentle hand took Alvin's arm, just above the elbow. They moved forward in the direction of a sickly green glow. The hand guided him through a small door. His fingers touched its frame, found it made of metal. Alvin had to stoop to go through, brushing his graying hair against the top. He entered a cockpit that resembled those of many transport planes in which he had flown during World War II. A pilot was strapped into one of the two small seats.

"You will notice first," the pilot said, not looking up, his voice as quiet and uninflected as though he were merely thinking aloud, "that we have no control wheel or pedals to move ailerons, elevators or rudder, as with a conventional plane. The buttons in front of me control the electrical impulses to our gravity reactors and to the four rockets in the nose and tail. They appear to be long tubes protruding about six feet. The length of these tubes minimizes the brilliance from the rocket engines as we accelerate or brake the ship. Two more rockets in each side, flush with the outside shell, give us directional control. It is so simple a child could fly it. Won't you sit down, sir?"

The gentle hand, reaching through the door, directed Alvin into the other seat. It was deep and comfortable; yet it seemed to him as hard and evil and threatening as the great black electric chair he had once seen at a state prison. He sat straight up, his head jerking hard, as though he were coming out of deep sleep. No one stood over him. There was only the one silent figure strapped in the other seat. He was small but created an air of tension as real and pervasive as the constant hum of the strange, unseen engines.

All right, Alvin thought, it's just another problem. It's just something else to be evaluated. He tried hard to rid himself of the pending nausea, of the unscientific tinge of terror that had been on him since he had entered the door of this strange craft.

Vaguely, beyond the narrow windshield, he was aware of the bulk of the Pocono Mountains, those quiet Pennsylvania hills that had seemed so peaceful and friendly.

"You aren't going to be harmed, you know." The pilot's voice was irritating. I'd damn well better not be harmed, Alvin thought. General Waverly would . . . But a fresh flow of unreasoning, shaming fear chilled his spirit and he knew instinctively that General Waverly would do nothing—could do nothing for him. Ever since the car had broken down, he had been walking, unknowingly, into this situation. It had seemed simply an exasperating accident when it had happened, but Alvin knew from the tense silence of the man beside him, from the disquieting green glow of the instrument panel, from that strange engine hum—unlike anything known to the Air Force—that none of this was accidental. It had all been executed too smartly, too boldly.

"Now if you will sit firmly in your seat and put on your safety belt and shoulder straps, we shall start an interesting journey." The voice of the little man in the pilot's seat was still unexcited. "You will be more comfortable if you also use the chin strap until we reach cruising altitude."

It was absurd, Alvin thought, how blindly he followed these instructions. But the pinch of the webbed straps was real; the sweaty odor of the chin strap was human; and as his eyes grew used to the dimness he could see the jaws of the pilot working quietly at a stick of gum.

"I will accelerate as slowly as possible, for your benefit, but there is a minimum that we consider safe. We are hovering only six hundred feet above the ground now. There are still enough mountains in this locality to shield us from radar

31

detection. This is one reason why we selected it for tonight's operation. But when we go higher, we must break fast. Radar detection is our great fear. We can only hope to be written off, if noticed, as an unidentified flying object."

For the first time the pilot looked at him. He was middle-aged, a wizened, ugly little man with a sharp beak of a nose and eyes that flashed fiercely in the gentle light.

He reached to the instrument panel and touched a button. A buzzer sounded to alert the others, and the little pilot tightened his own chin strap. He waited about five seconds, then touched another button. Immediately the low hum of the engines became more intense. The craft leaped toward the stars. Alvin could feel a strong downward drag on his body. He was glad to have the chin support. The pilot pointed to a rate-of-climb indicator. The scale was graduated to one hundred thousand feet a minute. The needle rose rapidly toward ten thousand feet a minute within seconds after they had started to climb.

There was no moon, but the velvet mist on which the stars were placed seemed to glow with a subdued phosphorescence. They were alone in the vastness of the dark heavens. The hum of the engines was hypnotizing. The scientist, staring grimly ahead, was powerless to fight the dreadful sag in his body as the craft climbed toward the zenith. For a few minutes he was occupied with this motion. Then he grew used to it. He could not move his head but he could turn his eyes upward through the narrow, slanted windshield. Despite their terrible rate of climb, the stars did not appear to be coming closer. Suddenly Alvin lost the sense of speeding away from the earth. He was free in his imagination, traveling from the star Sirius to the star Altair. The journey would take twenty-five years. He had passed into the planetary system of the sun and was experiencing a moment of welcome relief from the intense heat by dodging behind the shadow of the planet Earth.

At this terrific velocity, which he assumed to be close to the speed of light, he would leave the long, tapering shadow of the planet in a few seconds and would speed out again into the brilliance of the sun. The slight opening in the heavy cockpit curtains must be closed until he had passed beyond the solar system and out into the darkness of interstellar space. As Alvin reached toward the curtains to close them he recognized the "break-off phenomenon" which had been discussed so often at the Pentagon—a strange feeling of separation from the earth which gripped high-flying test pilots after prolonged monotony, loneliness or strain. In its grip, it seemed almost natural that he should be where he was. He was even beginning to find a sense of comfort in the constancy of the annoying drag when the pilot waved his hand. Alvin looked down at the altimeter, moving his eyes only. The needle was swinging rapidly from one hundred ninety thousand toward two hundred thousand feet. They were nearly forty miles up in this speck of metal, sealed and pressurized to the comforts and requirements of earth. He realized that they were higher than any other men had ever reached, except in unmaneuverable rockets.

As they neared two hundred thousand feet he could feel a lessening of the drag. At two hundred thousand, the sensation stopped altogether. The pilot unstrapped his chin support and sounded the buzzer again. Alvin began to unbuckle his shoulder straps but the pilot stopped him.

"Now we will turn and start the forward acceleration," he said. "Please leave the other harness on for comfort and safety. When I press this button, a controlled amount of fuel is injected into the firing chamber of the port steering rocket. Somewhat less fuel is put into the starboard rocket. This enables us to turn on course without overturning or spinning around."

There was a loud roar and they moved forward abruptly.

Alvin was thrown heavily back in his seat. "Those were the rear rockets," the pilot explained. "We are now headed for Pittsburgh, Pennsylvania."

"But I must go to Washington," Alvin demanded nervously. It was the first time he had spoken since coming aboard, and he was ashamed of the inanity of what he had finally said.

"It is only 12:33 A.M., and we have not named this craft the *Argonaut* without a good reason. You are aware, of course"—and there was something in the pedantic voice, the tense movement of the head, that told Alvin he was in the company of a fanatic—"that the word comes from the Greek legend of the enchanted ship *Argo*, in which Jason carried some of the most noble mythological heroes of Greece to the shores of the Black Sea. Well, in one sense, this is also an enchanted ship." He looked at Alvin. "There is sufficient time for us to pass over some of your country's leading production centers before we land you in Washington. We believe you will be quite impressed if we take you within bombing range of several such centers between 12:30 and 2:30 A.M."

The precise words, spoken so exactly that they indicated English was an acquired, artificial tongue for the pilot, jolted into Alvin's ears with the force of human shrieks. A cold bath could not have lifted him as quickly from the dreamlike state into which he had slipped. What do they want with me? he thought. Instantly he knew at least part of the answer. He was the civilian scientific consultant to the ranking general of the United States Air Force. The possessors of this craft could only want him for the use he could make of that position.

"My name," the pilot said, "is Max Schoeller. You know Mr. Baker, I believe. The gentleman who welcomed you aboard the *Argonaut* is John Sloan. We have wanted to become acquainted with you for some time, Doktor Alvin." His German accent was noticeable only in the word "doctor."

34

"You could have had an appointment." But his sternness was lost on the grim, hunched man who sat at the controls of what Alvin knew from the evidence of the instrument panel in front of him must be the most advanced craft ever developed.

"We are not always available for appointments in the ordinary sense," Schoeller said. "Our home base is in Nevada. Auxiliary 'one' is in a remote valley of the Canadian Rockies, 'two' is in the Tanganyika Territory in Africa, 'three' is in the heart of Australia and 'four' is in the Antarctic. One would like to settle down, but . . ." He shrugged his shoulders and spread his hands in an expressive European gesture.

"How fast are we going?" Alvin asked. He tried to put a bite in the words. After all, these men wanted something of him; he was no ordinary kidnap victim; and in that limited sense he was of necessity in command of the situation.

"If we are accelerating directly from or toward the earth we use a radarscope to indicate velocity, which is similar to one model used by highway patrolmen, but when we accelerate parallel to the earth we cannot use it. We have no operating air-speed indicator at high altitude. We must calculate our speed from the density of the rarefied air, the directional air currents at lower levels, which are practically constant except in the jetstream area, and the amount of rocket boost. Tonight we have accelerated slowly for your comfort. I could calculate our boost against our drag to determine the speed and it would come out at about twenty-five hundred miles an hour."

"Is that maximum speed?" Such a puny question, Alvin thought, as he asked it. All questions seemed futile there on the rim of eternity.

"Oh no." For the first time the little man smiled. "The speed of this ship would be almost infinite in outer space if the new photon rockets ever became practical. You must realize that we are actually being flung from the surface of the earth

35

by the centrifugal force of its rotation because we have lessened the pull of gravity on the ship. There is nothing to create drag such as a wing which is required to lift an airplane."

"Then show me what it can do," Alvin said brusquely.

Schoeller pointed to a prominent instrument light, which had a red cover over it. "If I should sustain a speed of five thousand miles per hour even at this altitude, the stagnation temperature of the nose would reach one thousand degrees Fahrenheit from the friction of the rarefied atmosphere. This light comes on to warn of dangerously high skin temperatures."

Alvin looked more closely at the narrow curved windshield above the instrument panel. "How can glass withstand this speed?"

"It is made of fused silica, and the black nose is made of a metallic carbide which melts at seven thousand degrees and holds its strength to five thousand two hundred degrees. A contour in the hull just below the windshield deflects the air smoothly away from it. Any turbulence, as with the air foil of a wing, would raise the temperature to four thousand degrees instead of one thousand."

"Is that a radio altimeter?" Alvin asked, speaking with some difficulty even though he had loosened his chin strap.

"Yes. We have one aboard for low-level flying that is accurate to within nine feet. The one you are looking at is accurate to within three hundred feet and has a range of three hundred and fifty thousand feet. We shall hardly go above that except in emergencies."

"Why not?" Suddenly, the scientist was insatiably curious. The quality of fantasy had disappeared entirely from the experience.

"Somewhere between three hundred fifty and four hundred fifty thousand feet lies the last frontier of our rarefied atmosphere. Every minute thousands of tiny meteorites come hurtling into that barrier and are burned up by friction with the almost nonexistent air. As they burn they ionize the surrounding gas."

Alvin checked off the man's knowledge carefully; it was delivered as casually as an order for groceries.

"I may be old-fashioned, Doktor, but I don't care to take the *Argonaut* up there and suddenly find myself speeding along at several thousand miles an hour in a cloud of meteoric dust. If we flew in such a cloud at high speed, I suspect the *Argonaut* would turn into a flaming meteor itself. Of course, we could go through that layer vertically like the rocket missiles. In fact, the *Argonaut* has no 'absolute ceiling.' The principle of gravity reaction gives us a paved road to any place in the universe if we have sufficient atomic fuel and provisions —and, of course, if we live long enough." He smiled again. "I do not subscribe to the idea that acceleration will lengthen human life, even though it will slow down a space clock relative to an earth clock. I am not interested in space travel, Doktor. The *Argonaut* was designed to revolutionize transportation on earth—and perhaps human relationships as well."

"I don't understand you, sir." Alvin made his voice thunder in the old dramatic way he had once found effective in college lectures, but it produced no visible change in Schoeller. "If you have really adapted gravity to . . ."

Schoeller held up a warning hand. "I do not want to disappoint you, but this craft is actually—shall we say—a horse and buggy. It is just the first of its kind—a beginning, not a finished product designed for space travel. Let us say that we still have on our coonskin caps. We are frontiersmen, eh?"

"Can you deliver me a hundred horses and buggies like this?" Frontiersmen indeed, Alvin thought. Some frontier!

Schoeller ignored the question. "The power plant and the gravity reactors are simple to me. I have been working with them for fourteen years, while the other men in my field went in different directions. But the method of pressurization, the temperature control on long, interplanetary journeys, the terrific speed and acceleration in low-level flying, the sudden deceleration and sharp right-angle turns—these and other things that the so-called flying saucers are supposed to be capable of, if reports are even 50 percent accurate—these are beyond me. This ship"—his fingers strayed lovingly on the control panel—"it is just a beginning."

"But you are the inventor of the gravity—what did you call them?"

"Reactors. Let us say I brought their development to practicality, and the development of our power plant as well. Let us say that I have found a way, not perhaps to neutralize gravity as so many men have dreamed, but to put it to work for us."

"But that's fantastic! How could one man . . ."

"Pardon me, but if you will look down through the small window below your seat, you will see Pittsburgh coming into view. That window could be a bombsight, Doktor."

Alvin had been trying desperately to keep his mind free. A liberated imagination was the only insulation against the physical and mental shock he had been undergoing. But he had to look earthward. He had to recall that moment when Jack Baker had said they would fly over Pittsburgh, Chicago, Detroit, Cleveland, Buffalo, Boston, New York, Philadelphia and Baltimore, en route to Washington. When he forced himself to look at last, all was black on the earth except for a few scattered specks of brightness.

But in the next thirty seconds a nebulae of lights swept into the small circle of glass and out again.

"That was Pittsburgh." Max Schoeller pressed another button. There was a roar and a flash in front of them. Alvin tensed as though lightning had struck ten feet away. The sharp effect of braking threw him forward on his shoulder straps. He felt sick, not only in his stomach but in his heart. Schoeller had said: "That window could be a bombsight." What could a nation—any nation—do to protect itself against the *Argonaut;* against perhaps an armada of ships like it, or even more powerful?

"We will be over Chicago in about four and one-half minutes," Schoeller said. "I picked up the speed gradually and made a wide swing to the south in approaching Pittsburgh to show you how alert a bombardier must be to hit a target from this altitude. We were doing about five thousand miles an hour over Pittsburgh. That is too fast to make the change in course over Chicago where we must turn back almost a hundred and sixty degrees."

Alvin did not try to answer. A few seconds before, a well-trained bombardier could have wiped out Pittsburgh. In a few minutes Chicago could likewise be gone; then Detroit, Cleveland, Buffalo and all the rest, if there were only enough ships to carry one or two bombs per city—ships against which there could be no defense. He realized the terrifying story before it was told. This could be more devastating than the ICBM.

"It is fortunate that the weather is clear tonight over the entire mideastern part of the country. It is more impressive to see the lights of the cities than to see them on the radarscope." Schoeller's voice was more friendly than it had been. But Alvin was grasping blindly to restore his own presence of mind.

"I just cannot see—I mean—it must have taken a fantastic research project to complete this development."

Schoeller pursed his thin lips. "I believe Mr. Sloan intends to give you a full summary of that phase of our project when we get on the ground. At the moment you will see that we are approaching Chicago. Our turn will be quite sharp when we pass over the city so that we can get back on course to Detroit without losing several hundred miles in the skid. There will be no vertical pressure but the chin strap may be of some help in supporting your head."

Alvin could already see the lights of Chicago ahead. He adjusted his chin strap so that he could look downward without much difficulty.

Just before he tightened it he asked at last the one thing he wanted least to know. "And—what do you and your companions want of me? Why have I been forced into this situation?"

He kept his eyes on the rapidly approaching circle of brilliance that was Chicago and its surrounding towns, but he was aware that Max Schoeller had turned his head and was staring at him as he spoke.

"We thought it would be obvious. We have made the *Argonaut*. Now someone must decide what to do with it. Eh, Doktor?"

A dreadful sense of futility, of hopeless responsibility, fell on him. Ah yes, he thought, the words ringing and pounding in his head, the lights of the sleeping city slipping beneath him into darkness. Ah yes. There always comes the time when man must learn to use the things he has made.

3.

The path of flight led over Buffalo and back to the coast at Boston. There Max Schoeller turned the *Argonaut* southwest. He was carefully tracing their course on a mapboard for Dr. Alvin. Providence, New Haven, New York, Trenton, Philadelphia, Wilmington with its great du Pont factories, Baltimore and Washington passed beneath them.

By Alvin's watch, it was ten minutes past two. The whole incredible cycle had been made in far less than two hours—it had been only 12:15 when he and Jack Baker had walked along the country road at Mount Pocatelle. This single flight had been epoch-making, perhaps as important in itself as the Manhattan Project, and he knew from the instruments and from Schoeller's comment, that the ship had not been extended to its full capability. Furthermore, it had all been as casual as an airliner trip from New York to Chicago, and nearly as comfortable. Alvin pressed his hands to his tired eyes. He was used to startling possibilities becoming overnight the realities of an energetic science. He could, having experienced it, accept the fact of the *Argonaut;* but that such a fact should have sprung full-blown at him from that dark, misty field in the Poconos—apparently shaped by the hands of the silent, hunched little man at the controls, and his companions aft—was almost inconceivable. In his year and a half at the Pentagon he had become reconciled to the great masses of paper and people and procedure required for the least project; he had even, as do most bureaucratic officials, come to see a queer necessity for such complexity, to require it for its own sake; and he could not quite believe that this creature, this *Argonaut*, had been made privately, without benefit of government or consultation or security controls.

Max Schoeller touched the buzzer control again. "We're going down now," he said, in his toneless, precise voice.

"You'd better use the helmet as well as the chin strap, because we'll drop rapidly. It's alive with radar down there."

Alvin pulled on the helmet, craning to see into the blackness beneath them. Schoeller used another knob, kept his hand on it. Almost immediately they seemed to be falling in space, without control. Cabin pressurization and the strong harness of his seat kept Alvin from realizing the true acceleration of that fall; but something went winging in his mind again, as in those long moments above the Pennsylvania mountains when they had propelled themselves up and out to the perimeter of nothingness, and he held momentarily a tremendous vision—of freedom, of fetters falling away, of beauty so absolute that even man could not despoil it. Then Schoeller began to slow their precipitous tumble and Alvin knew there was no such beauty, no such freedom; in the east the glow of dawn began to wane again as they neared the earth. He looked at the altimeter. They were under fifteen thousand feet and still going down. Forward speed had been slowed almost to zero by intermittent firing of the forward rockets ever since they had passed above Philadelphia. Then Schoeller turned the ship gently and headed back to the coast, only five hundred feet above the dark, heaving sea. As they approached the first lights of the Maryland shore, he dropped to fifty feet and Alvin shivered, seeing dimly the cold, eager reach of the waves beneath them. They seemed almost to float across the eastern shore toward the great bridge near Annapolis, connecting the mainland with the Maryland peninsula. Five minutes later they came to rest in a large pasture which, from above, had the dim outline of three runways on its surface. The hum of the engines cut back to a barely audible whine.

"Well," Alvin said. Through the narrow windshield, a few feet from him, he could vaguely see tufts of grass and lumps of the earth. It hardly seemed possible, he thought, but there it was. Suddenly he knew he would be glad to walk upon it. He would be glad just to touch it.

He looked at Schoeller, who remained quietly within his seat. "Well," he said again.

Schoeller extended one hand, gingerly, as though he feared it might break off at the wrist. His thin, beaked face seemed to pull backward into the shadows of the brain behind it. "I shall hope to see you again," he said. His hand, even gloved, was limp but not weak. Alvin supposed shaking it was like grasping a length of fine rope. He drew back.

"This is our stop, Hank," Jack Baker said, behind them. Alvin looked around. His friend's handsome face was grinning down at him cheerfully.

Damn his smiling eyes, he thought; doesn't he know what he's done? Doesn't he know what we're all in for?

But as quickly as it had come, the rage was gone, and in its place Henry Alvin felt a great physical weariness. It was almost as much as his hands could do to free himself from the harness. When he stood up his knees were watery and trembling. He moved past Baker without speaking and into the cabin. Beyond the open door the faint green glow of the ship's lights spread a sickly semicircle. He went down two metal steps and walked forward, welcoming at last the earth beneath his feet. Behind him the metal door closed. He turned his head and looked back. The thing was—his trained mind estimated almost automatically—about sixty feet long. It rested on four apparently retractable legs, and the lower portion of its body was only about a foot above the ground at midship. After a minute the craft began to move forward in gradual ascent. Its guttural whine pervaded the air for a moment; then it was lost in the darkness above them.

"Come on, Hank," Jack Baker said. "We have a farmhouse near by where we can get breakfast."

Jack and the scientist walked slowly through the pasture toward a large white house. Soon they crossed a well-kept lawn, presided over by many huge trees. To his left, Alvin saw the dim outline of a swimming pool and tennis courts. They went across a pleasant terrace and entered the house through open French doors. A big, white-haired man, with an old, tired face contradicting his stalwart body, was standing just inside the room, apparently waiting for them.

"I came on ahead as soon as we landed to order us up some food and coffee," he said. "Dr. Alvin, I guess Max told you who I am."

They were in a large, rectangular living room. A tremendous fireplace of antique brick faced them across the narrow side. Above it was hung a large copy of "Washington Crossing the Delaware." This extended to the high, darkly stained plank ceiling of the room, which had six massive wooden rafters running across it. Steps led off the right side to the upstairs apartments and crossed over an opening into the front-hall area. Another open area entered this hall through mirrored doors from the left side of the fireplace.

On the floor was a large polar bear rug between two sofas which faced each other on either side of the hearth. On a heavy oak table at the end of a sofa was a lamp which Sloan turned on. A large grandfather clock on the right side of the room near the entrance to a downstairs bedroom showed 2:32 A.M.

Alvin moved immediately to take charge of the situation. "John Sloan, I believe Schoeller said. Frankly, Sloan, he told me nothing else. I don't want to sound stuffy but I demand an immediate explanation of all this."

Sloan looked a bit startled. "Vanity misleads us all, Dr. Alvin. I thought you'd recognize my name and be—ah—reassured. I'm head of Sloan Engineering, Incorporated. We do a lot of work for the Air Force and I thought . . ."

"I've heard of Sloan Engineering. A good company. That doesn't justify kidnaping."

Sloan smiled. "No, it doesn't." He indicated the luxurious sofa on the left side of the fireplace. "I'll be glad to give you a

44

full explanation, Doctor. Why don't you sit down while we're waiting for our breakfast?"

Alvin sat down stiffly, feeling somewhat foolish. Still, he was determined not to be led down any more blind streets. Sloan Engineering was indeed a high-priority, full-clearance supplier. But Schoeller had been anything but a reassuring type. Baker had always been a bit on the wild side, inclined to go his own headstrong way, impelled by the most predominant set of ideals he had ever encountered. Only John Sloan, solid, conservative, somewhat ruffled, but obviously a man of strength and reason, gave him much confidence. Sloan was a man of about sixty-three, healthy-looking and head of a successful business. He was tall, six feet or more. His hair was silver-white and combed straight back from a ruddy, slightly receding forehead. His eyes were deep-set and a prominent aquiline nose rose above a mouth that seemed full at one moment and thin the next.

"You've been pretty coöperative, Doctor," Sloan said. "Jack told us you were level-headed but, quite frankly, I was afraid we might run into a problem with Jack's plan."

Jack Baker laughed, somewhat hollowly. He sat down at the other end of the sofa. "The thing was, Hank, we had to get the *Argonaut* out of there. We just couldn't afford to have you demand a long explanation on the spot."

Alvin nodded. "I don't mean to be a bear, Jack. Obviously, you fellows aren't up to anything—anything . . ." He groped for a word, failed to find it. "Frankly, I just don't know what in hell is going on."

A sleepy-eyed man, wearing a bathrobe over pajamas, came in with a huge pot of coffee and a tray of cups. He put them down on the coffee table and went out again.

"We're going to give you the whole story now," Jack said. He leaned forward intently, putting a hand on Alvin's knee. "Hank, you know me. If we didn't need you, would I have pulled you into something like this?"

"I know," Alvin said. "There's a smear of blood on your head, boy. What happened?"

"Oh, nothing." Jack put his hand to his head, then looked at his fingers. "It's nothing."

Sloan grunted. "He nearly killed us all. He shucked his harness and went aft to the bombsight right in the middle of Max's turn for Cleveland. I thought he was going through the hull for sure."

"It was a damn-fool stunt," Jack said. "I wasn't thinking." He locked the fingers of his hands with a nervous gesture.

"Cleveland?" Henry Alvin looked at Jack, his face puzzled. "Wasn't that girl from Cleveland?"

Jack cleared his throat in obvious embarrassment. "What girl, Hank?"

"The blonde from the inn. The one you were following around like . . ."

"Well yes, she was from Cleveland." Jack looked blankly at the polar bear rug, reluctant to meet Sloan's eyes.

"You better go soak your head," Sloan said, his voice dry and, Alvin thought, a shade sardonic.

Jack stood up. Sloan was not looking at him. "Listen, Dud . . ." His voice trailed off, but Sloan failed to turn his head. "It was just a notion, Dud. It didn't mean anything." Still Sloan said nothing and finally Jack hurried out of the room, glancing in embarrassment at Alvin.

"Young fool," Sloan said. "He could have killed us all."

"Well, she was a pretty girl, I'll say that." Sloan was more upset, Alvin thought, than the thing seemed to warrant. Young men were young men, even in fantastic flying machines.

"Why does he call you Dud, Sloan?"

"Oh—it's what he used to say in place of uncle when he was a little shaver. I raised him, you know."

"No, I didn't. What happened to his parents?"

"Auto accident. He was just a year old when it happened."

Just then the man in the bathrobe brought in scrambled eggs, bacon, toast, a pot of marmalade, and the two men moved to a large oak table at the left side of the room and began to eat. When Jack Baker came back, still a bit shamefaced, Sloan was explaining to Alvin how he had purchased White Oaks Farm and made its pasture into a field for his private plane. As they ate, he went on with the story.

"We are in the strange position," John Sloan said, talking steadily, as though his speech had all been rehearsed—perhaps memorized, "of having the *Argonaut* completely at our disposal without any commitment to anything but decency.

"Others are working on gravity reaction, of course. They've got more money behind them than there is in all of my estate—which is our only resource—but we had the right idea. Max thinks they'll get it someday, maybe in eight or ten years. The Communist scientists may be closer. Who knows what those buzzards are up to? If someone gets on the right track—and Max says the answer looks very simple and logical in hindsight—it could come quickly. But so far we've got it to ourselves.

"The rub is that any public display of a machine like our *Argonaut* would cause as much disturbance as Hiroshima did. And remember, Doctor—nobody's figured out the right thing to do with the A-bomb yet, all these years later.

"I believe the reason you think that developing such a craft ought to have taken billions of dollars and thousands of people, like the Manhattan Project, is because we've got in the habit of thinking that way in this country—maybe thinking too big. Any enterprise as big as Manhattan would have been extremely vulnerable to espionage and leaks, and the Communists would probably be as far along by now as we are. Just like on the bombs. And all those people who're fumbling around with those goddamn bombs would be fumbling around with our *Argonaut,* too. Anyway, a very few people with enough money and the right equipment and a revolutionary idea did build the *Argonaut*. Granted we couldn't put it into mass production, or work out all the kinks. But we could build one model that works. And we did."

"It seems incredible," Alvin said, sweeping off his glasses and gazing at the rafters on the ceiling.

"I *should* say Max and Jack did it. They built it. Jack found Schoeller in a little town in Germany after the war, working as an auto mechanic. He knew of him by prewar reputation and arranged for me to bring him into this country to work for my firm. It was just blind luck because it wasn't till after he'd been here fourteen months that Max told Jack his whole story.

"You see, Max worked on a project during the war that was so secret even the German High Command didn't know in any detail what it was all about. He was one of five men who were trying to develop atomic power for rocket propulsion. The Germans had already conceived of the guided missile, as you know, and they were trying to put together a rocket-type ship that could have a tremendous range using atomic fuel and could be sent over any capital of Europe or America or Asia or any other place as a drone. Well, they never got too far along with it. Hitler was blind as a bat about anything that wasn't one of his pets, and they couldn't get priorities and so on. Same old story all over the world. But one of these guys—not Max—began to think along the lines of using a gravity adapter or reactor to support the ship. Now I know you've heard of crackpot antigravity ideas all your life. Like perpetual motion. This wasn't that sort of thing. This fellow conceived of using the gravitational force, of adapting it to work for us, not just nullifying it. While he was thinking that over, the team came up with an atomic energy motor that could convert energy directly into electrical impulse. And that pointed a new finger right at the gravity idea. They went to work on it in dead earnest."

Alvin dropped his eyes from the ceiling and looked at Sloan.

"These five men weren't Nazis, Dr. Alvin. They were scientists, and they pledged themselves never to disclose what they thought they had unless they could be sure of its use. They wouldn't even ask for extra funds for fear somebody high up would get too interested. The way they saw it, the world was in no position right then to make use of such a tremendous development. God knows if it is now or not.

"Anyway, one night when they were working on the motor, they evidently produced something like a small atomic bomb and three of them evaporated with the lab, equipment, papers and everything. Max and one other man were not there at the time. They had been shifted to what the Germans thought was a more useful assignment. Later, the other man was killed in one of the Frankfurt raids. Max worked on the buzz bombs, but only in a minor way. And when the war was over, he was lucky enough to be in the American zone, so the Russians never got hold of him. He got a mechanic's job in Grunau and that was where Jack ran into him."

"Like finding the pot of gold at the end of a rainbow," Baker murmured.

"Imagine how we felt," Sloan continued. "We had Max Schoeller right here in this country and he told us his yarn and backed it up with some information we could see was authentic. We could have brushed him off, but you don't know my nephew if you think that. We could have handed him over to the government but, like I told you, we'd seen the botch being made out of the bomb situation. It was Jack's idea for us to go ahead on our own. To tell you the truth, I thought it was a crackpot scheme at first. Jack and I are close, Doctor. The boy's a fine engineer, but he knows I can't go along with a lot of his thinking. I'm a businessman and a bit of an engineer myself. I deal in things I can lay my hands on. Aircraft instruments are my line, not daydreams. But all right, I said, I'll put up a little money. Show me what you can do with it and maybe I'll go further. Well, they showed me, Doctor. They made my eyes pop.

"The two of them set up a small laboratory in a remote little valley not far east of Los Angeles. It took eighteen months for Max to pick up the loose ends after all those years, and I was giving Jack a good ribbing every week of it. Then they began to make progress. Max had concentrated on the gravity reactor in Germany and knew the story of the atomic motor, too. When he understood the American side of the atomic energy development, which Jack and I were able to get for him piecemeal through our business and government connections, he was able to put the whole concept together. At the end of two years, they had the *Argonaut* on the drawing boards and they had me convinced.

"I set up a fake project in their lab and put out the word that we were working on a pressurized cabin for high altitudes, which could be produced at a lower first cost. My company has brought out many things that have saved aircraft manufacturers a lot of money, and they gave us every coöperation. I bought a Martin A-26 fuselage which, with certain modifications, became the hull of the *Argonaut*. Most of the other parts were made here and there in my own shops and delivered separately.

"The funny thing is that more time and money went into the task of making high-altitude flight possible than into the atomic motor and gravity reactors. The whole aluminum hull of the ship had to be coated with a mixture of gold and molybdenum and nickel alloys. We had to keep up a front that we were working on the prototype of a ship for the extraterrestrial travel everybody knows is coming someday. That way we got a lot of information and help from companies all over the country who'd been working on the same things."

Jack had been sitting on the edge of his chair. He broke in again.

"Actually, for over two years we had been working on plans for concealing the *Argonaut* when it was completed. Dud bought a tract of land in Nevada, which ostensibly was for mining uranium. Max turned out to be a damn good actor, as well as a scientist, so he played an old prospector who had inveigled us gullible city boys into working a worthless piece of property. The place is situated near one of those mesas, so we called it Mesatron. People got used to seeing Max around. As part of his mining project, we dug a good-sized tunnel into the hill with the help of some men we packed in. But the place is in the middle of nowhere, and Max made sure that everyone got to hate it. When he got through heckling them, no one would have stayed out there. Sometimes Dud and I would pack in, to see how our 'mine' was coming along. Just to confuse things, we started another mine on the other side of the property, five miles away. While we were working on that, we gradually let the one at Mesatron go out of business and sealed up the entrance. By now, most folks out there just think they're two old abandoned mines. Even prospectors don't mess around, knowing it's no use. Folks in the area see old Max every now and then but they're used to him. And what we built in that first tunnel is a perfect hangar for the *Argonaut*, just about as far from radar sweeps as any place in the whole country. It's camouflaged so that God himself couldn't find it without a chart. And we made a storeroom out of the other mine."

At this point Sloan picked up the story. "So, with the craft ready for its first flight, Max and I flew the *Argonaut* out through the roof of the Los Angeles lab one dark night about three A.M. It was a hell of a first flight for the world's most advanced flying machine. But we made it to Mesatron in Nevada without any hitch. I'll tell you that was a thrill.

"Anyhow, Jack stayed behind and set fire to the remains of our old lab and equipment. I had no insurance on it so there was no investigation except by the rural firemen, and they didn't tumble to a thing. Thus our supposed research program came to an end. The fire was put down as of undetermined origin. There were just hunks of melted metal and the charred wood of the building left. We haven't rebuilt the old lab and not many people believe we ever will get back to work. Of course, I've had to kick my own tail in public for having forgotten insurance."

"So now you've got your *Argonaut*," Alvin said, looking back toward the ceiling again. "Now you've got your Mesatron and those other bases Schoeller told me about. You've got your gravity reactors and your rockets and your high-altitude hull. And you're beginning to realize what you've really got on your hands."

"That's about it," John Sloan said. He lit a cigarette, clearing his throat after his long recital.

"I'm seeing General Waverly at nine A.M., Sloan. I could settle it all for you in two minutes. Take it right out of your hands."

"I know you could," Sloan said. "There isn't any way we can stop you from turning us in, either. But you can't turn over the *Argonaut*."

The scientist looked at him blankly.

"Max warned us not to bring you into it." Jack Baker's face was earnest, concerned. Alvin thought he looked even younger than he had on that long-ago night over Düsseldorf, even less capable of dealing with death and destruction. "He said you'd turn everything over to the Air Force. I told him he just didn't know you."

"Maybe it's you who don't know me. I work for the Air Force, Jack. I'm an American citizen. We all are. Why not the Air Force?"

52

"What is the Air Force?" Jack Baker said. "It's men. Men like you and me, Hank. Only they aren't free."

"I'm not free, either, then. I'm part of the Air Force."

"You're free, Hank. You're free in your mind, that's what I'm talking about. You know what those Air Force people would have to do with the *Argonaut*. They'd have to use it for destruction."

"That's pretty strong," John Sloan said. "I'm not sure of that."

"I don't mean a preventive war or a sneak attack. Although it wouldn't be impossible, the way some of those hardheads like to talk. But they'd—they'd brandish it. They'd threaten and talk and wave it around at the rest of the world."

A silence fell on the room, except for the fire snapping and hissing in the big fireplace. John Sloan got up and leaned against the mantel, his hands in his jacket pockets. A cigarette jutted from the corner of his mouth, its smoke curling in slow gray whorls in front of his tired face. He pulled a pencil out of his pocket and moved his thumb against the end of it. Alvin, too, was incredibly tired. Suddenly he seemed to be hearing Jack's voice from far away, as though they were at opposite ends of a long tunnel.

"That isn't what I want," Jack said. "That isn't what any of us have worked and risked our necks for. That isn't why we pulled you into a thing that could wreck your career."

"What is it then?" Alvin said. "What is it you want to do with your *Argonaut?*" It was hard to speak, he was so tired. It was an effort to control his tongue. But from that long distance he heard plain as bells ringing, the words he was afraid of hearing.

"I want to save the world," Jack said.

A log collapsed in the fireplace and sparks fanned up over the grate and out of the hearth. John Sloan carefully stepped on one that flared into a tiny flame at his feet.

"From what?"

"From itself."

"And you want me to tell you how?" Henry Alvin stared at the dying fire. Its flames seemed to stare back at him, lurid and leaping and destructive. "Is that what you want of me?"

"I'm a dreamer like Dud said, Hank. And Dud's a very practical man. I guess you can see that Max is a fanatic. We did all right building the *Argonaut* together, but we thought we needed somebody like you before we did anything with it."

"A wise man," John Sloan said. "A good man. That's what we thought we needed."

Alvin stood up. It was all too much; he could not think logically. For just a moment, while they had fallen from space toward the sea, he had had a vision, a glimpse of a grail he had never known; and now, in the quiet words of these men, that remembered vision took on reality. I want to save the world, Jack Baker had said, and no one had laughed. Was it possible? Henry Alvin didn't know. He only knew he had seen a vision and the vision had been good. It was the first dream of his ordered and sensible life that had ever seemed better than reality.

"Let me think about it," he said. "I have to think about it."

He knew that if he did not go to General Waverly immediately, he would be technically close to treason. He knew, too, that he would not be merely risking his own career but, quite possibly, endangering mankind, either by turning the *Argonaut* over to the Air Force, if he could, or by letting it slip through his fingers.

"There isn't any hurry," John Sloan said. "Take all the time you want."

No, Alvin thought, there's no hurry. And no escape, either.

4.

Jack had slept late, for it had been almost dawn before any of them had gone to bed. When he finally came down, Sloan was in the living room, sprawled on the sofa, looking very much what he was—an elderly man who had had only two hours' sleep.

"Well, I got Alvin to Washington in time for his conference," Sloan said, without preamble. "God, that traffic. I got our tickets out to the Coast, too." He reached into his inner jacket pocket, took out an airline envelope and tossed it on the coffee table.

"Good for you." Jack went to a tray in the corner and poured coffee from an electric warmer. "What'd you think of Alvin in the cold gray light of day, Dud?" He took one of the cups to his uncle, then leaned against the mantel, sipping the other.

"We talked a lot driving in. A damn good man I'd say. Level-headed. Right now, he's kind of shell-shocked. This has been like seeing a flying saucer before breakfast," he said.

Jack laughed. "The first time I heard Max hint what he'd worked out, I had to hold onto something. Isn't it funny how even the best minds can hardly ever get free of the conventional? You can't push many people out on mental limbs."

"Well, I think Alvin is just beginning to be dazzled by what we showed him. He's all hepped up to meet us here next week end, anyway. I told him we'd bring Max along and thrash something out. So—it may have been unpleasant at first but that was a good night's work you did last night."

"Glad you think so." Jack was ill at ease. He wondered when his uncle would bring up his act over Cleveland.

"I tell you what," Sloan said, "if we could just rig the

55

Argonaut to do something about this traffic problem, I could die with no regrets. I thought I'd never get back, bucking it the way I was." He took a sip of his coffee, eyeing Jack closely. "What a morning—usual airline trouble, too. They had to route us through Cleveland."

"Cleveland?" Jack looked up sharply. "Why Cleveland?"

"No seats on the through flights."

"You never had any trouble getting seats before, Dud. You could have called a dozen people to fix it up for us. Why Cleveland?"

John Sloan sat up straighter on the sofa. "Don't be a fool, Jack. We both know Cleveland is where this woman of yours lives."

"That is not"—Jack felt a quick, cold fury, which amazed him almost as much as the tickets to Cleveland—"exactly the way I would refer to Miss Carlson."

"Cool off, boy." His uncle's calm voice was the same one with which he could galvanize his office into frenzy when something went wrong; it was his action voice. And Jack had often thought that it alone would have been enough to have made him a great general. "We leave tonight at 5:15 and get into Cleveland at 6:43. You better call her up and let her know you're coming in for the night."

Jack looked at the blackened fragments of logs in the fireplace. He had expected almost anything but this.

"After you line it up with her, I want you to start thinking how you're going to give her the news."

Jack Baker put his hands in his pockets. He knew what was coming; he could tell from his uncle's set, tight lips. But I don't have to listen, he thought. He's not God. I don't have to listen to him.

"Go on, Dud. Say it."

"I want you to go out there and break it off," Sloan said. "Go to bed with her first, or whatever you want, but break it off. I don't want to argue about it."

"I don't, either," Jack said. "I'm just not going to do it, Dud. I love her. Are you able to understand that?"

"It's against the rules, boy."

Abruptly the anger and the hurt went out of him. His uncle's voice was harsh, but there was no bitterness in his eyes. And he was right; that was the inescapable truth of it. He was right and Jack could only deny it by lying to himself.

"We swore we'd put the *Argonaut* first," Jack said. "You and Max and I swore that. I haven't forgotten."

"Then how can . . ."

"A man doesn't do this sort of thing deliberately, Dud. Your wife's been dead a long time but you can remember her. It just comes and there you are and it doesn't seem to matter about some rules you've made up for another game you happen to be playing, too."

Sloan nodded, his face troubled, lined with fatigue. But his voice was still firm, decisive. "Only playing with the *Argonaut* is no game, Jack. It's life and death. Yours and mine and Max's and God knows how many other people's. Why, you said only last night you wanted to save the world. Boy, you do it and you can have that girl in Cleveland. But if you fail us . . ." He spread his hands abruptly. "You understand I'm not thinking about you so much. Or Max, or even my own hide. You're the nearest thing to a son that I've got and I suppose I could let you risk all our necks. But I won't let you risk the *Argonaut,* too, and this dream of yours that's like my own now."

They were silent for a long time. From the pantry there was a faint sound of china tinkling; far away a busy hum rose from the highway and a mockingbird sang its endless song in the rose garden.

"I'll put it to you squarely, Jack. First, you've got to throw all your energy and mind and body into whatever it is we're going to do with the *Argonaut*—if we're going to do anything. We all know we can't hide it much longer. Which means you aren't going to have time for this girl, even if Max and I could let you be that distracted.

"Second, what have you got to offer her anyway? You can't look her in the eye and say I'll see you next week, and you know it."

"All right," Jack said. "I'll tell her, Dud."

Sloan twisted his hands together. They were trembling. Jack had never seen his uncle show the slightest sign of nervousness before. They both looked at the telltale hands but neither mentioned them.

"You asked me if I could understand love. Well, I don't know if I do or not. Marilyn's been dead thirty-three years. . . ." He shook his head. "Thirty-three years! And sometimes I can reach right out and touch her. Sometimes I look in the mirror and I wonder what she would think if she could see me now. I'm the only person in the world who remembers Marilyn, really remembers anything about her." He looked at Jack. "Well, what happens when I go? Not to me but to her? We grow old and lose our lust for life and yet we remember. And in remembering, do we alone preserve those who went before us? Ten years, or a little more, and I'll be dead and gone. Will Marilyn be lost then, eternally lost to this earth? But then, perhaps this earth isn't really important in eternal things."

Jack saw the shape of oblivion and found it too moving a sight to bear. He abruptly changed his train of thought.

"It's a perfectly good question you asked," continued his uncle. "And I think I'd have to say no, I don't understand love. I just know it lasts sometimes when nothing else will. I don't know whether that's the best or the worst of it, though." He stood up abruptly. "Sometimes I wish we'd never heard of that damn *Argonaut*."

Jack stood up, "Well, we're committed, Dud. And you were right to remind me."

"I was, if you really want to save the world."

"Doesn't that sound childish?"

"It doesn't sound childish to me," John Sloan said. "I never heard of a dream a man could talk about without sounding a little childish. Not one worth having." Sloan moved toward the stairs to his bedroom. He looked back over his shoulder.

"Now you get on the telephone. I'm going to bed for a few hours."

About the time Henry Alvin entered his apartment in Georgetown that Monday evening, and began to reflect upon his strange week end, Jack Baker put down the magazine he had been reading and fastened his seatbelt. The stewardess of the big airliner in which he and his uncle were flying had just warned them through the loud-speaker that they were in the Cleveland traffic pattern and almost ready to land.

It was strange, Jack thought, how the interior of this big, cumbersome craft was so nearly like that of the *Argonaut*. The latter, though more crowded, only lacked windows and the cheerful stewardess. He adjusted the seatbelt more comfortably.

"See if you can keep that one on," Sloan said with a grin, from the seat beside him. "Don't go floundering around this ship."

"Go to hell." Jack knew his uncle was joking, but the remark made him uncomfortable. That incident less than eighteen hours ago was burned into his mind like a brand.

He thought how strange it was, how bitterly amusing that man could hurl himself with a defiant chip of metal into the great unknown ocean of space, yet remain only man, only human—that even within pressurized walls life went on quite as it did on earth with all its strains and hurts and passions.

You never get away from the ground altogether, he thought, and his mind moved back to that agonized moment the night before in this very sky above Cleveland, when he had risked the lives of all aboard, as well as his own life's dream, because of Sandy Carlson. He recalled that he had not removed his harness after the *Argonaut* changed course at Chicago. "The old ship sounds good tonight," John Sloan had said, patting the bulkhead with possessive pride. "She's giving Alvin an eyeful, eh?"

"She always sounds good." But already Jack's thoughts were moving back to Crestview and the pleasant things that had happened there. Through the long moments of silence, broken only by the steady hum, he became aware that they were approaching Detroit. Cleveland would be next. Sandy must have gotten home long ago, he thought. He shook his head, a strange sense of unreality creeping over him. The change of emphasis and tempo during the last ten hours had seemed to make their farewell that afternoon belong to a different age. He thought of how far he and his friends had gone, bringing Henry Alvin aboard this craft, which could prove a monster and destroy them all. But there could be no turning back. It was done. He suddenly felt pent-up and torn by the responsibilities he had assumed. He wanted to be released from the dark, windowless confines of the *Argonaut* cabin and see the solid reality of the earth. There was no place in the cockpit for him. The jump seat between Max and Dr. Alvin had not been set up. His only chance to see out would be from the bombardier's seat, just aft in the cabin. There he could look down through the bombsight.

The buzzer sounded, a sharp, annoying reminder that the turn could start at any time. It would be a tight one to a heading that would send them over Cleveland, only a hundred air miles away. Suddenly, he wanted to see Cleveland, to imagine her among its lights—but if he unbuckled his harness and Max started the Detroit turn before he was buckled down in the bombardier's seat, he might be thrown through the wall of the ship and bring the whole enterprise to a halt in a split second.

Jack felt cold sweat on his forehead. Normally he would never have thought of taking such a chance. But without thinking he abruptly disconnected the harness and sprang frantically toward the bombardier's seat. His first step from the couch put him just past the door and near the opposite wall. Like a flash he was exploded against the port side of the ship. There was a sharp pain in his left shoulder. A blackness came down, lightened, came down again. Great masses weighed against him. He was pinned against the wall by the terrific force of the "G" pull in the turn. He could barely hear the excited shouts of John Sloan. He fought desperately to remain conscious. If Max should overspin in straightening up on course, Jack knew he would be thrown across the cabin against the starboard bulkhead with even greater force. But even in the blackness, the thought pierced his brain that if he did not get in the seat immediately, Cleveland might sweep beneath unseen.

His shoulder felt as though it had been broken. His head throbbed madly. But now the blackness was thinning again. By pulling against a support he forced himself along the floor toward the bombardier's chair. The tubular crosswork beneath it was just in reach of his right hand when he extended his body by straightening out his legs against the port bulkhead. Thirty laborious seconds later he was strapped in the seat and looking through the bombsight. Only darkness was below.

"For God's sake!" he heard Sloan shout down the length of the cabin. "Are you trying to commit suicide?"

Something thick and wet was on Jack's forehead. Blood was flowing freely across it from a cut somewhere on his scalp. He felt drained, incredibly beaten from his struggle against the "G" pull. A lump of shame rose in his throat. If he had started that foolhardy dash a second later, he would have been hurled nearly the full width of the cabin against the door. That could have been the end of everything. At such an altitude, with a cabin pressurization of ten thousand pounds, each square inch of the hull had a pressure of about ten pounds trying to blow it out. The additional pressure of his body hurtling against it could have made them disintegrate.

"What's the matter with you?" Sloan yelled.

Just then the lights of Cleveland swept into the bombsight, and Jack knew what was the matter; all the fear and the incredulity went out of him and he was simply glad he had taken the chance, glad he was here staring at those glowing pinpoints where she lived. And he knew that as long as he lived he would remember this moment over Cleveland—gone so soon, gone already.

"Didn't you hear the buzzer?" Sloan demanded, standing over him, his own harness discarded, his lined face a curious mixture of anger and curiosity and the last lingering traces of terror. "Are you all right?"

"I'm all right," Jack said. He took a handkerchief from his pocket and dabbed at his forehead as he looked at his uncle with defiant composure. "I'm all right now."

But he was not and he knew it. How did this happen to me? he thought. How did I get in this fix?

Jack had arrived at Crestview Inn a full day ahead of his friend, Henry Alvin. It had seemed a reasonable precaution against unforeseen developments, and he had intended to use the time to locate a landing place and a mechanic who would be coöperative and not too curious. The second task was simple; the first mechanic Jack approached agreed to handle the job, after pocketing a fifty-dollar bill.

Even with that success almost immediately achieved, Friday night at Crestview Inn could have been dull going had it not been for the arrival of Sandy Carlson. Jack had been sitting in a spavined lobby chair going through a New York newspaper when she came in. She was quite obviously annoyed. He lowered the paper and watched her approach the desk clerk. She was wearing a light tweed skirt and a travel-weary gabardine windbreaker of faded tan, but it was neither her self-possession nor her blond, untended hair that caught Jack's attention; it was the small blue canvas bag in the hand of the bellboy who trotted after her. ELLIOTT FREIGHT LINES was stenciled across it in neat white letters. Jack Baker had been around aircraft and airlines all his adult life; he was a pilot himself though he preferred, and was more proficient at, the engineering part of the business. And, like most young men who frequented airports and terminals all over the country, he had heard many a tale of the luscious young blonde from Cleveland who was personal pilot for old George Elliott. But could this unkempt, striding creature really be the cool, beautiful, aloof young woman who had thrown so many airports into a male frenzy simply by landing in old man Elliott's brightly painted Twin Beech?

Jack doubted it, but there was the evidence on the handbag. The bellboy hovered behind her while she spoke to the clerk. Her voice was low and controlled. It came across the big, quiet lobby to Jack with an edge of sharpness in it, though he could not distinguish her words. Almost immediately, the clerk, who had registered Jack with a marked lack of interest, began to flutter and bustle behind the desk.

"With a shower?" Jack heard him say, his high-pitched voice breaking upward like bird song. "Oh, I'm afraid . . ." But the blond head moved a little, as if she had spoken one or two short words. The clerk's bird song broke off in mid flight and he listened a moment, smiling fixedly and anxiously. Then: "Yes, Miss Carlson," he almost shouted, "right away, Miss Carlson!"

By God, that's her, Jack thought. He watched the clerk snatch a pen from a holder and hand it to her, then pop his fingers three times at the waiting bellboy. This puts a different face on the evening; a different face indeed. His active mind began quite coldly and precisely to plot a campaign.

Jack Baker, a man of broad shoulders and powerful frame, had a face that was cheerful and ruddy and without guile. It was a face like those of the idealized young men on recruiting posters. John Sloan had once accused him of having a built-in halo. But he was too capable to be guileless or naïve and, like most bachelors who are handsome enough to attract women's glances, he had a good deal of vanity about his ability to deal with them, even if he had had little time to do so. After realizing who Sandy Carlson was, and that apparently they were to be fellow guests for at least one night at this remote inn, he definitely decided upon conquest.

He watched her turn away from the desk, where the clerk was still wringing his hands and twisting his face into preposterous smiles, and move in her determined stride toward the elevator that led to the upper floor of the Crestview. He had his first clear look at her tanned face and he was surprised by her soft, almost pouting mouth. She wore only a faint touch of lipstick, as though it might have been put on that morning and forgotten. But her features were clean and strong, and although the windbreaker concealed most of her figure, he noticed a long, graceful neck rising to a proud head. Jack dropped his paper and stood up. Her eyes turned briefly toward him without a flicker, and her chin rose a little higher. He took two steps toward her. Just as he did so he realized that he had seen her before in some far-off, unidentified place.

"Grounded in Mount Pocatelle," he said. "I'd call that a clear case of pilot error."

She stopped and the bellboy had to step around her toward the elevator with the bag and his jangling key ring. Her face and eyes were perfectly blank as she looked at Jack.

"How do you know I'm a pilot?"

Jack smiled, consciously hoisting the halo his uncle had accused him of having. He knew very well that he had a trustworthy smile.

"Pilots are like thieves. It takes one to catch one."

A fleck of amusement moved in her eyes and was gone. She looked at him intently. "Have we met before?"

Jack was racking his brain, trying to remember the answer to that question. It was embarrassing not to recall the time, place, or even the occasion—only a face. Then, like bits of mosaic falling into place, the picture began to come back to him. He snapped his fingers.

"London! I don't remember the name of the spot, but it was a little bohemian cellar. On King's Road, maybe."

Sandy Carlson nodded slowly, still a bit puzzled. "I seem to remember something—but—what's your name?"

"Jack Baker."

Sandy ignored the bellboy and the nearby elevator.

"Jack Baker," she said. "Jack Baker. I've got it now. We spent two hours saving the world over a barrel of beer. Right?"

"And I took you home."

"You tried to. You were pretty far gone."

"Well, I've heard your name a thousand times since then but I never tied it to that night in London," Jack said. "It's a hell of a small world. . . . Listen—have dinner with me, why don't you?"

"I'm really tired, Jack. Things were a little rough today. But okay for an early dinner, if that's all."

"That's a deal, Miss Carlson. I'm tired, too. Just got in from New York on a slow train."

She had started toward the elevator. "Call me Sandy," she said over her shoulder. "I'll be down in ten minutes."

She was right on time. But as soon as she came into the dining room, Jack, rising to meet her, saw that she was regretting her decision to join him. The head waiter pointed out the table where Jack waited. A faint frown crossed her face, as though she had been hoping he would not be there after all. She was still wearing the tweed skirt and windbreaker but she had combed her hair and put on fresh make-up. She moved briskly among the few occupied tables, ignoring the startled looks that other women gave her clothes.

"You'll have to take me the way I am," she said. "I don't carry much of a wardrobe in the plane. Nothing but what I've got on."

"I'll take you any way I can."

"I could hardly dodge you tonight unless I stayed in my room. Frankly, I started to do just that but it's been a long time since we met."

Jack put on a long face. "And may never meet again," he said. But she took him seriously.

"It doesn't matter—at least in one sense. What does matter when you get beyond bread and meat and some place to sleep? I guess I came down because otherwise I could only have dinner in my room. Here I can have dinner and anything you can add to it."

Jack nodded. "Sometimes you get too tired to worry about what a stranger has to add."

"I was almost at that point. Then I began to wonder about the stranger." She looked at him with open, honest eyes.

The dinner was pleasant. They tried to recall their earlier meeting.

"You talked a lot that night, Jack."

"How can you remember what I said?"

"I probably remember better than you do. You were pretty tight but you said some things that set you apart from the average guy I met during the war."

"By God, I must have been tight," Jack said. But he was pleased.

"You spoke of a love for life and of man's opportunity to give something to this world we are trapped in," she continued. "It was a little tough going but I thought you made sense."

"Sorry. That sure doesn't sound like much fun."

"Oh, you ranted on. It probably took the beer and vodka to do it."

He waited for her to finish her coffee.

"Will you take a walk?" he asked.

"O.K. if we don't stay too long."

They went out the front gate and along the edge of the macadam road without speaking. The ground mist that seemed to be the trademark of Crestview nights was drifting up to their heads, and after they had gone a few yards the lights of the hotel were lost in it. They kept well to the side of the road for fear of cars. They did not speak until they had walked quite a way. Jack strolled deliberately, his hands in his pockets. At first her plunging stride kept pulling her out in front of him. Finally she laughed lightly, stopped and turned to face him.

"You're a slowpoke. I'm walking for exercise."

Jack stopped, too. "I used to run the mile in four-fifteen or so. But I'm not on the track team any more."

"Meaning that I am?"

Jack chuckled. "Well, you're in an awful hurry to go ramming into the fog. You won't find anything out there but more of this road and maybe a broken leg."

They walked along another ten paces.

"It was quite unexpected running into you." He felt that they should speak of more than incidental things. "How do we make up for lost time?"

"Oh, I might run into you again someday thirty years from now."

Thirty years, Jack thought. What a difference that would make. Both of them would be old and tired and settled into whatever rut of accomplishment they had managed. Life would no longer be a slate to be written upon. The writing would be done.

He took her hand in his; it was warm and smooth and

67

quite firm; her fingers closed strongly. He moved a little closer, tucking her hand under his arm. They strolled on down the road. The mist swirled around them intimately. He talked of his friend, Henry Alvin, who was meeting him the next day, and she told him of her flight from Cleveland with a folder of important papers for George Elliott, who was visiting with friends near by, and of the vacuum pump which had gone bad in the Beechcraft. At Mount Pocatelle's one-runway airport—she called it "that damned goat pasture"—there had been little chance of finding spare parts, but the owner-manager had assured her he could get something up from Wilkes-Barre tomorrow.

"So here I am. Chapter twenty-eight in the adventures of Sandy Carlson, girl pilot. What's your business, Jack?"

"I work for my uncle at Sloan Engineering in Los Angeles. We make advanced accessories for airplanes."

"I've heard of Sloan. Do you make an artificial horizon that won't tumble?"

"Sure, if you've got electricity or suction for it."

"You haven't got one that will work without either?"

"Who has?"

"Well, you're no good to me without it. How did you and your friend come to pick this happy little graveyard for a reunion?"

Jack laughed. "I rather like it here. I trained at an Air Corps base not far away during the war. Hank and I met there and we'd come over here for week ends, with half the rest of the base. It wasn't so quiet then, but I like it even better now. The way I see it, if you can find a quiet place this day and time, you'd better take advantage of it."

"I don't like quiet," Sandy said. "You have to think too much when it's quiet. I'll bet you still have a crash hat like every other flyboy I ever met."

"It went through more missions with me than any airplane

68

ever did. But don't let me travel under false colors. I was a bombardier. Washed out of flight training." He let go of her hand and edged his arm around her waist.

"It must take guts to drop bombs on people. Anybody can fly."

Jack bit his lip. He thought of how he had hated the job of bombardier. The horror of dropping death and destruction on innocent people had sat with him like a specter on every mission. After the war it had touched him on the shoulder many sleepless nights, confirming each time his resolution that mankind must never again adopt such techniques of annihilation. And then he thought of Sandy, and of the incongruity of trying to save the world on the one hand and of looking at her with lust on the other.

They walked another forty feet in silence. The mist grew thicker. In the quiet countryside, their feet crunched loudly on the gravel siding of the road. "I guess we better go back," Jack said. "This fog is getting granular."

"Oh, let's go on a little way. I hate fog in a plane but it's nice to walk in."

Jack saw he couldn't rush her. What's my next move if we do go back to the hotel? he mused.

"There's such a thing as wasting time, even on a nice, foggy night," he said in a low voice.

Sandy turned toward him. Her eyes twinkled in the light of a passing car. "That depends on what you call making time."

Her lips were only a few inches from his as darkness fell upon them again. A sweet aroma mingled with the freshness of the misty night. He felt a sudden urge to kiss her and drew her to him. She seemed to coöperate with the gesture, deliberately placing her cheek against his and speaking over his shoulder.

"Don't push me around, Jack. I rather like you. Every guy

starts out like this, all sweet and gentle, but most of them turn out wrong. Try to be different. You *seem* to be different in other things."

The words cut deep. Jack felt like a thief who cringed from the searing beam of a searchlight. It was not that she had seen through his sham. Most women would have expected the worst in a situation like this, but few would have acted so decently. The thing that bore down upon him was the simple fact that he had no business being in this situation. Women are really human beings, he reminded himself, and you musn't play with them like toys. The last thing he could afford to do was to get *personal* with Sandy. Such distractions were not for him and could not be for a long time to come.

"Let's go on," he said gruffly.

"Let's go back," Sandy said. "I've changed my mind. For some strange reason you seem to have a conscience, Jack."

"I hope so," Jack said with a smile as they strolled back toward the inn. He was determined to be affable if nothing more.

He had tried to put Sandy Carlson out of his mind when he awoke Saturday morning at Crestview. He did not see her that morning or that afternoon, nor had he asked for her, though he sat for a long time in a conspicuous lobby chair. And when Hank Alvin arrived, he believed he had truly forgotten her. There had been so many old times to talk over, so many old names and faces to recall. He and Alvin had been like gluttons at an amiable orgy, serving each other the rich foods and wines of memory. But in the middle of a very good dinner that evening, Jack had looked up to see her walking across the dining room toward them in her martial, hurried stride, her blond head tipped back as he had first seen it, her firm chin preceding her like an announcement.

She came straight to their table and stopped abruptly.

Looking down at Jack and speaking quite clearly, she asked, "May I join you?"

"Good God," Henry Alvin said. "Is this going to be another one of those parties like in London?" Jack laughed.

Sandy stood looking at them, quiet, controlled, only a little tense, and Jack could almost believe that she was enjoying the joke, too.

"I'm sorry," Alvin said. "It's just—the way you said that reminded me . . ." He shook his head and struggled to his feet. Jack got up too.

"Dr. Alvin, this is Miss Carlson, girl pilot. Miss Carlson, this is Dr. Henry Alvin of the Washington Alvins."

"Please do join us," Alvin said. "We're fighting an old war, remembering old girls and so on."

"Thank you," Sandy murmured, seating herself in the chair he held for her. "I hope I won't be interrupting about the old girls."

"Not at all. I find that blondes never interrupt anything."

"Tell me about the London party."

"Henry," Jack warned, "watch your forked tongue."

"The party in London? There were so many—but there was one where Jack took the tablecloth . . ."

"Hank!"

"Bombardiers must act just like pilots," Sandy said with a laugh.

Dr. Alvin peered solemnly at his highball glass. "As an official observer, Miss Carlson, I never found much difference in the two breeds."

Then Alvin glanced up at her. "You know," he said, "that's an awfully pretty dress you're wearing."

Jack gazed in wonder at the slow flush that began to spread over Sandy's face. She was wearing a severe black dress, which came tightly to her neck. Until now he had not appreciated her figure, which in the clinging dress left little to be

71

imagined. Why, she bought that today, he thought. She must have . . . At that moment she looked up at him from eyes which were faintly amused but which still showed, like the pink flush of her skin, a shy embarrassment. His heart went out to her as she sat there, in her newly purchased finery, with her proud chin still lifted, trying for once to be entirely a woman.

5.

On that same Monday afternoon, Sandy cautiously drove toward the Cleveland airport. The traffic-jammed highway held many terrors for her, and as a huge trailer-truck roared past she found herself biting her lower lip and flinching away from the door of her car. It was unsettling to be afraid of anything, she thought, but it was almost degrading for a flyer to be afraid of something so earthbound as motor traffic. In the sky she knew an almost lyrical freedom from the cares of the world, fear included. She had often found that the most serious matters faded from her mind when she was high above the earth. It was possible to look down and get a perspective which relegated the ordinary routines of people to their mundane significance. When earthbound, one rarely had such an unobstructed view.

Sandy slowed, glancing cautiously from the rear-view mirror to the road ahead, made a precise left-turn signal and veered into the airport entrance. She crept along, scrupulously obeying the fifteen-miles-per-hour signs, until she found a parking place near the main passenger terminal. She was earlier than she had to be and sat there a moment, watching the busy terminal entrance, wondering why she had not told Jack Baker that his plan for visiting her on the spur of the moment was preposterous. Expecting her to drop everything for him. Men didn't treat Sandy Carlson like that.

No, she told herself. Not even Jack Baker. This has got to stop. She craned her neck, checking her make-up in the mirror. As she did so, she was honest enough to admit that in the last few days she was more consciously concerned about her appearance than she had been in months. That was what had led her to the exclusive little dress shop in Mount Pocatelle for the slinky black. It had been unlike any dress she had ever owned. There had been a glow in the gaze of his clear blue eyes that sparked something in her—not the usual desire to compete, to show an arrogant male that she, too, could grapple vigorously with the world. It had been a glow that had made her know that she was a woman and not a body to be wrestled into bed, or a stereotype to be locked in a kitchen, but a creature valuable in her own right, not least for the beauty of her own physical self. All right, she thought, I admit it was good for me. But it's got to stop. She got out of her car, noting without interest a taxi driver peering at her long legs. The asphalt of the parking lot was hot and she hurried toward the passenger terminal. After all, she thought, who is Jack Baker? A vague little fear swirled in her. Just a man I knew long ago and for a short while at Crestview.

She was glad Hank Alvin had been at Crestview, too. He was the owl-eyed man she had read about so often in the newspapers, somebody big in the Air Force. Sandy could never remember having a better, more unguarded time. . . . So, when Jack had walked with her to the door of her room, she had been quite unprepared for what had happened.

"G'dnight, girl pilot," he had said, leaning on one arm against the jamb of the door, smiling down at her. And Sandy had been about to answer good night when she had heard her own voice—or one that had a vague resemblance to her usual brisk tones.

"Come on in," that voice was saying, but there was nothing brisk about the words. And, looking up, a sort of quick, dismayed thrill surging along her spine, she saw his eyes widening, a faint line creasing his brow. She was suddenly weak-kneed. She thought his blue gaze came from the kindest eyes she had ever seen, and the lingering smile in the corners of his mouth was touched with an ineffable sadness. As though the gesture belonged to someone else, her hand went up and stroked his cheek.

74

"I know you are a pilot because of your bright blue eyes. Please come in," that odd voice said again, lingering on the words like a poet reading his own work.

His hand closed on her wrist and he kissed her palm. "You'd hate yourself in the morning," he said. Then his lips were on hers, and she was clinging to him, desperately, even while something in her stood aside and watched slyly and was astounded. But he had not come in.

I don't know of another man who wouldn't have, she thought, hurrying through the passenger terminal. In all these years I never met another man who cared how I'd feel in the morning. But who is Jack Baker?

She came out on the promenade from which passengers arriving would enter the terminal and moved quickly to a good vantage point by the rail separating it from the airfield. In only a few minutes, the flight from Washington would be letting down onto the runway and he would be getting out. The triphammer beating of her heart told her how glad she would be to see him. It was frightening. Three days before, the course of her life had stretched away in front of her, perhaps not entirely safe and secure, but logical, planned, sensible. Now this stranger from California had upset everything with his blue eyes and his wide smile and his simple expectation that she would be a woman.

He hasn't even told me all the truth about himself she thought, remembering how queerly he had acted on their last morning at Crestview.

They had been out long before Alvin, who had gone definitely on record for sleeping until at least noon, and they had gone for a ride in the rented car. It had been a pleasant morning and they had laughed a great deal, although both professed worse hangovers than they really had. Suddenly Jack slowed the car and turned off the road, toward a small concrete-block building with a radio tower looming over it. He stopped right by the tower. "Won't be but a minute," he said, and hurried into the little building. There was a large meadow just beyond it, almost level and pleasantly green in the morning sun. Jack came from the building and walked about fifty yards out into the field. He took something from his pocket. Sandy could tell as he looked at it, twisting from the waist, that it was a compass. He appeared to take a bearing from his location to the tower, then hurried back to the car.

"What the hell *are* you, a spy?" She smiled, but his actions seemed more mysterious than was necessary.

"I'm interested in radio. Maybe I'll buy this place someday, who knows? The engineer in there said it could be had." He drove off with a dash and she could not help noticing how quickly he changed the subject to her plans for returning to Cleveland. She told him that the Beechcraft had been repaired and that she would take off after lunch.

"Then I'm going to have to stop down there"—he nodded toward the little village which they were rapidly approaching —"and get a camera."

"Oh, I'll mail you a picture."

"Not one of you at Crestview. After all, I may not . . ." He stopped abruptly, then hurried off to another subject. He parked in front of a combination drug store and restaurant and they went in. He bought a small camera and a roll of film. Then they sat down at the counter for a cup of coffee. He fell strangely silent and Sandy wondered if she had done something to irritate him.

"Well, if you're going to make a model out of me, I'm going to pretty up." She took her handbag and walked back past a row of telephone booths to the ladies' room. When she came out, Jack was in one of the booths, his back to her. The light in the booth was not on but she could see him talking animatedly, moving his head up and down. As she drew near, he said unmistakably, "Arrive before triple zero—hold until ten after. We'll meet you there at twenty."

No, Sandy thought now, watching an airliner coming into the landing pattern, feeling a quick catch in her breath as the loud-speaker began to announce the arrival of the flight from Washington. You haven't told me much about yourself, Jack Baker.

But when the door of the plane opened and he came bounding down the steps—even from that distance she saw the wide smile on his boyish face—she knew that she had learned more than enough about Jack Baker. As she watched his long stride carry him quickly toward the gate where she stood waving to him, the old dismaying thrill made her knees tremble. He was going to upset it all. That whole, ordered, planned, logical future upon which she had counted for so long was receding as fast as he was coming. And she was not sure of what he was bringing to replace it.

They drove away from the city, laughing and talking like old friends, rather than renewed acquaintances of one week end. Jack paid no attention to where they were going, and for once Sandy gave little sign of her fear in highway traffic. Soon she turned onto a quiet country road and from that onto a narrow dirt lane. But when they swept between two large brick gates Jack suddenly began to look around him.

"We're going to Mr. Elliott's," Sandy said. "He's always got a crowd around and he said one more wouldn't hurt."

Jack groaned. "A crowd! The last thing I want tonight is a crowd."

"Uh-huh," Sandy said. "I figured that one way ahead of you. That's why I arranged for the crowd. A girl has to be foresighted."

"Well, listen. Did you tell old Elliott who you were bringing?"

Sandy frowned. "I guess so—no, I believe I just said a friend from out of town. Why?"

"He gets around a hell of a lot. Maybe it'd be better—will you just introduce me as—oh, Ray Martin from San Francisco? How's that sound?"

Sandy stepped down hard on the brakes. The car skidded to a halt on the narrow road. Through the thin trees of a well-kept private estate they could see several cars parked in front of a sprawling, rustic house.

"All this mystery doesn't go with me," Sandy said. "Just why should I introduce you as Ray Martin instead of Jack Baker?"

"Well, I'll tell you," Jack said. "Old Elliott knows my uncle, the John Sloan that I told you about. I'd just as soon he didn't connect me with him or either one of us with you."

Sandy stared at him. Through the quiet trees they could hear the sounds of men laughing and the faint, banal strains of popular music. Her high forehead wrinkled in a frown, and doubt showed obviously in her eyes.

"The truth is," Jack said, "I'm the illegitimate son of John Dillinger. I'm casing the Cleveland territory for my uncle, and old Elliott is on our death list." He opened his eyes wide in mock terror. "It would go hard with me if I were recognized."

"Listen," Sandy said, "you can fool all of the girls some of the time and all that stuff, but how long do you think you're going to be able to keep from telling me whatever it is you're hiding?"

Jack winked at her. "Drive on, girl pilot. And remember—Ray Martin from San Francisco."

"Ray Martin it is, but I don't like it. I don't like it."

They drove the rest of the way to George Elliott's house in an uncomfortable silence. Sandy parked her convertible between two large Cadillacs and they walked, without speaking, down a long flight of steps to a boathouse by a small lake.

There was a barbecue pit near the dam and quite a crowd of men and women milled around it. As they came near, a man Jack recognized from newspaper photos as George Elliott came hurrying toward them.

"Thought you weren't going to get here, sweetie," he said, seizing both of Sandy's hands. His hair was white but he was straight and slender, much younger looking than Jack had expected.

"This is . . ." Sandy started to say, but Elliott pulled her into his arms and kissed her loudly on the cheek. Then he held out his hand to Jack.

"Now you let this girl talk to the rest of us tonight," he said. "Don't you take her off for a walk, Mr. . . ."

"Martin," Jack said. "Ray Martin."

It was an uncomfortable beginning of an uncomfortable evening for Jack. Sandy was soon caught up in the crowd, most of whom were older and more flamboyant than she—the sort of society crowd, Jack thought, one reads about in the newspapers. He met many people and liked none; he heard no serious words from any of them. In the long years during which he and Max Schoeller had worked literally night and day in their remote lab and at Mesatron, Jack had virtually withdrawn from even the relatively tame social life he had once enjoyed. He had found a higher, almost supreme pleasure in his work and in his dream. Only Sandy Carlson had been able to crash through his mind and senses. Now he found he could hardly tolerate these people who seemed to have no thought beyond tonight's whiskey and women, tomorrow's business deal, next week's trip to Las Vegas. And he felt a growing puzzlement at Sandy's participation in this kind of party; at Crestview she had seemed contemptuous of such inanities. He watched her, irritated, a bit baffled, and with a dread of what he had to tell her.

He refused many drinks and much pointless conversation before he finally made his way unobtrusively from the crowded area near the barbecue pit and the portable bar, and strolled along a path that wound around the lake shore. It was a cool evening and a sizable moon was beginning to peer over the trees onto the black ruffled surface of the lake, touching it with silver. A sadness came on him. He knew that the party and the people he had left were not so bad as they had seemed. But he knew also that they were not for him—could never be for him again. So what could I offer her anyway? he thought. He squeezed his eyes tightly shut, for just a moment regretting, with a poignancy that moved him more deeply than he had once believed possible, all those "normal" ways and things he had irrevocably left behind. There were worse things than being like everyone else, and if he did not want that now he could still recognize its attraction.

But why me, he thought, why curse me with the *Argonaut?* Yet, in all fairness, he knew that no one had or would curse him unless it be himself. He and Max and Dud had built it; they had created it out of their brains and energy, put much of it together with their own hands, and almost gaily they had named it *Argonaut:* enchanted craft. They had done it knowingly and eagerly; and all the time they had realized that the day would come when the *Argonaut* would become commonplace.

I wonder, Jack thought, seeing in the brilliant circle of the moon a sudden image of his own smallness and incredible audacity, I wonder why we really did it? How much was vanity and ambition? It was an uncomfortable question and it made him flinch. Yet, as he turned and looked back toward the party for a moment, he knew it had not been done either for money or vainglory. All his life Jack had had a consuming pity for the victims of war and poverty, and now he hoped that someday things could be better, through the *Argonaut.* He recalled the many long and painful conversations he had held with John Sloan on that aspect. When their success became apparent Sloan had sketched out several plans for a merger with large aircraft manufacturers so that they could go to the government with both the ship and the means for producing it. But Max had objected, and Jack had fought it with blind idealism. They did not want it put in the hands of politicians or bureaucrats, or under the control of military cliques. At a crucial time, before John Sloan really believed that they could bring their fantastic notion into reality, Jack and Max had forced a pledge that the *Argonaut* would never be disposed of except by unanimous decision of all three. Only that pledge had constrained John Sloan as he progressively realized that Max would never consent to sell the *Argonaut* to the U. S. Air Force alone.

Jack knew that progress came slowly and he thought he knew something of the nature of man. Yet, almost to the point of an obsession, his contrary spirit had persisted in a wild hope for vital progress. It seemed to him that he lived in an era marked by a sudden, violent eruption of the human intellect, which might lead to this hope. Only sixty years had brought the airplane and the radio and the atomic reactor and more progress in conquering disease and old age than had been made in many centuries before. It was as though mankind had been revolving for eons near the hub of a slow-moving wheel and had finally reached that moment when the friction brakes on stable progress had given way to the centrifugal force of new ideas. Now, if ever, it seemed to Jack, a man of good will with power in his hands might actually prevail, might actually halt mankind short of that frightening edge where the centrifugal force could not be contained by any friction known. There was even something formidable, he thought, in the spectacle of human beings probing at the sun, into space and the unknown. They spoke for valor, hope and belief in the ultimate decency of humanity; and he was glad to be one of them.

Or I was, he thought, watching the drifting silver of the moonlight on the water. I was until I met Sandy. He shook his head in a sudden spurt of anger. Talk about controlling your mind and emotions, he said to himself. He thought of that frantic moment over Cleveland. It had been as though someone else had taken possession of his mind. The man who threw off that harness and leaped for the poor solace of the bombsight could never have been the real Jack Baker. He clenched the fingers of his interlocked hands, sincerely bewildered at the unaccountable follies of love.

Quick footsteps came along the path behind him, and he stopped, looking back. Even before he could make out her features in the dark, he knew it was Sandy. She came close to him, her soft body going up against his arm, her face touched with the moonlight. There was a faint scent of perfume about her.

"I saw you trying to get away from me, Ray Martin."

Jack chuckled. "I never was much of an actor. Frankly, this Ray Martin bozo is kind of a bore."

"He did look rather stiff-necked back there. Rather handsome, though."

"He's up to no good," Jack said. "Anybody can see that." They laughed and strolled farther from the lights and the chatter around the barbecue pit. Jack put his arm about her waist and she pressed close against him. She was tall enough to be a little disconcerting but he liked the sway of her body.

"You're wondering what's going on," he said. "About me, I mean."

"Of course," she said. "Giving false names. Making strange phone calls. Popping up out of nowhere like you did today. And going around trying to make gullible girls like me believe you're interested in buying some ridiculous radio station. You can't blame me for wondering, can you?"

"You've been a real Girl Scout," Jack said. "Many a young lady would have called for the police when I introduced you to Ray Martin."

"If I hear any more about him, that's just what I'll do."

Jack guided her toward a dark slope of grass that rose, free of trees, from the narrow path. "Maybe you've guessed this much. I didn't meet Hank Alvin up at Crestview just to exchange old war yarns."

"I hadn't guessed it. I should have, but I didn't."

"Well, you can understand why I can't tell you all about it. Hank is as close to the big Air Force brass as you can get."

"And you're working on something with him?"

Jack peered thoughtfully up at the sky. "Well, not exactly. Let's say we've worked out a little something at Sloan Engineering I wish he'd get interested in. I've been the test engineer and he was an old friend, so . . ."

Sandy made a face. "All very hush hush. You men!"

"So hush hush I'd just as soon George Elliott and people who get around a lot in the same circles I do don't tumble to who I am or even that I'm in the East. Particularly that I saw Hank."

They sat down on the grass, his arm still around her. Beneath them the lake stretched quietly, darkly to the moon-touched strip far out from shore. A sudden, high-pitched burst of feminine laughter came from the boathouse. Sandy turned her face up to his and Jack kissed her. Her lips were warm, moving. Suddenly his arms gripped her fiercely and he pressed her back to the grass. They kissed for a long time, not moving; her breasts heaving softly against his chest.

"Fight me off," Jack said, sitting up. "I give you fair warning."

Sandy smiled, her fingers straying up to his chin. "You're sneaky, getting me out here in the dark like this after I arranged a crowd."

He laughed and nuzzled his chin down into her hair; the giddy scent was like wine in his blood.

"But you'd better let me up," Sandy said. "Somebody's liable to come by any second."

Jack sat up again. He heard a faint jingle and began to

83

fumble on the grass for the key ring that had slipped from his pocket. Sandy found it first.

"Key rings interest me." She held it up in the moonlight. "I should think it would tell more of a fortune than the palm of a hand. What do all of these fit?"

Jack called them off as she separated them. "Apartment, office, desk drawer, a motorcycle I never use, Dud's house, speedboat, car, door to the lab that burned down, YMCA locker." He paused. "There's one missing."

"I'll have to get another one made," Sandy said. "What makes you so sure I'd let you have it?"

"Has anybody else got one?"

"Kiss me," Sandy said. "Kiss me hard, Jack." She lay back on the grass waiting for him. This time his hands found her breasts. She did not fight him. But after a long time he sat up again, moving away from her. A cloud crossed the moon and for a moment the night was pitch-black. He was glad she could not see the misery in his face. I can't put it off any longer, he thought, not even if she gets up and runs.

"Listen," he said. "Suppose after I leave—suppose you don't see me for a while?"

Sandy laughed; she was still lying on her back in the grass, undisturbed by her disheveled clothes. "Maybe I could stand it."

"I hate to sound fatalistic, but people have been known to get killed in my line."

"Mine, too." Sandy rolled over on her side, propping an elbow under her head. "I thought you might be in something like that. I guess test engineers test dangerous things, don't they?"

"Exactly."

"Dangerous things." Sandy leaned forward and kissed his neck, her tongue trembling for a vivid moment on his flesh. "Is your job the most important thing in life?"

"No, listen . . ." He cleared his throat and stumbled on.

"The thing is, I've—well, we're probably going to leave the country and—I just thought you ought to know."

"How long?" Sandy's voice was hard suddenly.

"Six months, maybe. A year, maybe—I don't know."

"A year?" Sandy sat bolt upright. "You aren't serious."

"I'll give it to you straight. We may not get back at all."

Sandy spoke slowly. "I begin to get the picture. I had it right the first time. I should have known it would come to this. So you aren't different, after all."

"Now listen," Jack said. "I've botched this all up but . . ."

"Botched is a mild word. Do you think I'm going to make love to a man I see once a year? I've got better things to do than that."

"Sandy—there isn't anybody else, is there?"

She grasped wildly in her mind for an answer. "George Elliott wants to marry me."

"Elliott! Why—he's old enough to be your grandfather, for God's sake!"

"Grandfather with a couple of million dollars," she said bitterly, "and lots of young ideas."

"You don't mean this, Sandy. You're just mad and upset."

"Sure I'm mad. Why wouldn't I be mad? I had it big for you. I thought, here's the real thing at last, and . . ."

"It *is* the real thing, Sandy."

" . . . and all you were doing was setting me up for the kill before you went off and found yourself another gal. Another mark on the wall, that's me."

Jack shut his eyes but he could not shut his ears. Her voice was harsh but he heard the anguish and the hurt in it; and he was astounded at the vehemence of her reaction.

"I'm going to set you straight on something," she went on. "I've been full of moonlight and roses here tonight and maybe there was a time when I wanted you. After all, I'm human. I'm human sometimes, that is. Most of the time I'm not. Most of the time I'm a girl who knows a lot about being hungry and

85

even more about being all alone and who isn't going to die the way her mother did—broke and stranded because a no-good barnstorm flyer ran off with another woman. You talk mighty sweet but if you think George Elliott doesn't look good from where I sit, even if he's a hundred years old, you're crazy."

"Then why haven't you married him before?" Jack felt the hard edge of anger. She was almost willfully misunderstanding him, he thought.

"I don't want to marry him," Sandy said. "When I saw you get off that plane this afternoon, I thought I wasn't going to have to. Now—well, I have to look ahead. A working girl has to look out for herself. Who else will?"

"Working girl," Jack said, his lip curling with emotion. "That's a laugh. Are you talking about the day shift or the night shift?"

Sandy stood up quickly, jerkily, her breath coming in broken little gasps. For a moment she could say nothing. Jack looked at her, bewildered by her attitude. He saw her try to suppress a sob and turn slowly to walk away. He rose to his feet and followed her. This time he had no trouble catching up. He put his hands on the back of her shoulders and turned her gently toward him.

"Don't go away like that. Please."

She went abruptly limp as an old cloth, falling forward against his chest. He shook her until her head moved backward. Then he kissed her, fiercely, feeling her mouth open and hot under his. She moaned softly and he picked her up, his arm going under her skirt, around the soft flesh of her thighs. He stumbled back up the grassy slope until they reached the trees. Then they went down together, clutching desperately at each other. In the darkness he could hear her crying. Then he could hear nothing but the great boom and surge of the blood in his veins.

6.

Henry Alvin moved through the week as though his feet were just six inches off the floor; no matter how hard he tried he could never touch them down to anything solid. And it seemed to him that the voices of the people he worked with— even General Waverly's booming baritone—came to him from a long way off, failing to penetrate to the center of his consciousness. So by Friday afternoon he was nervous and irritable, intensely anxious to be away from an office which had grown more and more like a prison cell as the week progressed. He had had no experience in duplicity or how it could work upon a man's image of himself. He felt unable to cope with this new dimension in his life, and it was with the determination that his dreamlike state should soon be ended that, on Saturday morning, he boarded a crowded bus for his weekend rendezvous at Sloan's country place. One part of him, even then, could look on in secret amusement as another scanned the bus-station crowd for the face of a secret agent. He knew very well that he was not under even intermittent surveillance; none of those cleared to top-secret matters were. Yet, since the moment when Dick Waverly had called for the film of that vertically falling object of which he unbelievably had been the copilot, he had felt a tinge of guilty fear.

The bus trip was short and hot, but not without profit. It was the first activity of the week that had seemed real. The man who sat next to him was concrete enough to have a bad case of B.O. By the time Alvin alighted at the Graysonville station, he was feeling almost himself again, almost unbowed. He walked casually along the street toward the big Rexall sign on the corner and found the black Ford, just where John

Sloan had said it would be, in the last parking space of the block. Max Schoeller was at the wheel.

"Well, Schoeller," Alvin said, climbing into the seat beside him, "I trust this vehicle isn't as unusual as the last one we rode in."

Schoeller looked at him blankly. "It's a Ford," he said. Alvin was carried back by that dry and pedantic voice to the green glow, the sickening sense of another world and the great black chasm of fear. But hearing the absurd words, he reached that welcomed floor he had not been able to touch all week. The weird unreality was gone and he knew that he was in great danger. They all were in danger from the unlimited power they possessed, which, misused, could ruthlessly consume them and many other people as well. And this man, turning the Ford into the light stream of traffic with the same competence he had shown in catapulting them forty miles above the earth, was at the center of it all.

Schoeller was small in frame, but agile. His face was lean and sallow. His pointed chin led to a thin, ill-defined mouth. Only when his hands were active could one detect accomplishment behind their awkward gestures. He moved his hands for a purpose, quite unlike Jack Baker who spoke in flailing symbols. The small wrists and feeble knuckles sought no success in manual achievement. Max Schoeller put his mind into his fragile finger tips and brought forth wonders.

A beaklike nose protruded from his face and barely spread his cold gray eyes. Brown, short-cropped hair bristled from his skull and eyebrows. He smoked with casual abandon in moments of tension, often cupping his left hand inversely to remove the cigarette. It seemed a specious measure of security and sureness. On his cheek there was a scar resulting from a duel he fought while at college. When Max was sorely pressed it flashed blood-red, the only note of disturbance that he exhibited.

"Are Sloan and Baker here yet?" Alvin asked, making conversation.

Schoeller nodded slightly. "They flew in this morning. I returned here yesterday from Nevada. Jonas, the man at the farm, knows me as one of Sloan's engineers. By now he thinks nothing of my visits."

"I want to have a long talk with you," Alvin said. "You've shown me what that ship of yours can do. Now I'd like to know a little more about how it works. Our best brains aren't even thinking yet about things you already seem to have solved."

"You would not understand," Schoeller said. "Einstein is dead. No one would understand."

Well, damn your hide, Henry Alvin thought. But the remark did not really anger him. He knew it was probably true, at least as far as his own knowledge was concerned.

Alvin was neither mathematician nor physicist enough to explore what he was sure was the most rarefied level of field physics. He tried never to delude himself, and one thing of which he had long been aware was that he had neither an original nor an exceptionally penetrating mind. He had a detailed educational background and a personal acquaintance with most of the truly creative intelligences of science. Above all, he had organizational and interpretive ability, and the devious persistence of a diplomat. These qualities made him a near perfect liaison between science and the military. Without ever fully grasping all its implications himself, he could make Dick Waverly see the potentialities of an idea, or the possibilities indicated by an experiment. Just as he had been a far better teacher than were many of his colleagues of international reputation in research, so he had proved, in various ways, of more value to the Air Force than men with twice his scientific ability.

"What gave that low hum to the engines?" he asked, still trying to dig for some clue as to the principle involved.

"Pulsation," Max answered curtly.

"You mean an electrical pulsation?"

"Yes."

"That's interesting, Schoeller. But all you've really told me is that you've taken advantage of gravity through electricity. I'm capable of understanding a little more than that, you know."

Schoeller nodded. "I spoke generally, of course. You could grasp the principle, Doktor. Undoubtedly, your government has certain men who might even follow such a development all the way through with sufficient notes from me if they are wise. I have given Mr. Sloan such notes in my own special symbols and drawings, but no written words. If people are not wise enough to understand this sketchy information, let them make an *Argonaut* for themselves."

Alvin was startled. "You mean, you've . . ."

"I have not consented that anyone should see them. It is simply caution, if something should happen to me. The notes are sealed, to be opened only at my death. If all of us should be killed, Mr. Sloan has instructed his secretary to send the notes to your government. He insisted on this and I consented."

Well, you can't pick your partners in this sort of business, Alvin thought, listening with distaste to the sneering quality of that voice. He gave up the effort of talking to Schoeller and gazed out at the Maryland countryside, green and lovely this far from the noisy highway and its jungle of billboards. It would have been pleasant if he had been going for a weekend holiday with good friends. Crestview had been a wonderful change for him, until the night they had gone into the field under the radio tower. It had made him newly aware of the monastic life he led in Washington—the monotonous round from Pentagon to apartment to occasional official party to infrequent inspection trips with Waverly—and of the loneliness of middle-aged bachelorhood. But instead he was faced with a difficult and distasteful job. I must get my hands on those notes, he thought.

They gathered quietly under the trees on the huge lawn of the farmhouse. They might have been four business executives, discussing a merger or last month's sales chart; and they even engaged in desultory talk about the weather before John Sloan began to take charge.

"Well, let's stop beating around the bush, boys. We all know why we're here, don't we?"

A quick silence fell across the shaded area where they sat. Jack Baker cleared his throat, relaxing deeply in his canvas chair, pressing his hands together until his knuckles cracked. Alvin, looking at Jack's blond young head, remembered how during the war Jack had been able to sleep at any given time, in any position. It was a blessed gift, he thought.

"I should like to question Doktor Alvin," Max Schoeller said, "at once."

"What about?" John Sloan frowned at him, and Alvin sat a little straighter. He was both amused and indignant.

Schoeller took a cigarette from his pocket and placed it precisely between his rigid lips. It bobbed furiously when he spoke, although his voice was scarcely more than a dusty whisper. "We should know if Doktor Alvin can accept our decision, even though it may be undesirable to him."

"We've made him one of us," John Sloan said. His white hair fell across his forehead. "We gave him no choice. I believe I'd retract that question, Max."

"No, no, John. Just a minute." Henry Alvin leaned forward intently, his elbows planted firmly on his knees. "This is more Max's baby than anyone else's. I can understand his question. And I'll say quite frankly I've put in a lot of the past week wondering how I could possibly justify, even to myself, not going to my superiors with this whole weird thing."

"You wouldn't have been human if you hadn't," Jack said.

"I suppose not. The moral and philosophical ramifications are frightening. They all come down to this: Where is duty?"

"Ah, yes." Max Schoeller's face grimaced in what, for him, might have been a smile. He touched the tips of his fingers together, peering at the scientist through the thin blue haze of his cigarette smoke. "Where indeed, Doktor?"

"I don't know." Henry Alvin shook his head. "Wiser men than I am have spent lifetimes trying to answer that. I couldn't do it in a week, that's for sure. I'll just say this, Schoeller; I can take what you call an undesirable decision. As a matter of fact, I came here expecting one."

"So?" Schoeller spread his fingers, touched them together again. "I am satisfied then." The cigarette haze almost obscured his face, but he did not move his head.

"I must remind you, however," Alvin continued, "that the most logical and proper disposition of your craft would be to sell it to the government. You have made a great discovery and it is right that you should profit from it, instead"—and his gentle brown eyes turned toward Jack—"of running the risk that you may lose everything."

"That has been my conviction all along," John Sloan said with emphasis, his chin protruding fiercely.

Max eyed Dr. Alvin and Sloan with suspicion. The scar on his cheek flushed.

"Let's get this thing over with," Jack said, impatience in his voice.

"Well now, I don't suppose it all has to be done in a day." John Sloan winked at Alvin, his lined old face breaking into a smile. "We've put in a year or so already, young fellow. Remember?"

Alvin stood up. He was an observant man and he had learned that Dick Waverly knew instinctively what he was doing when he always remained on his feet in conferences; it was difficult for those sitting to look away from him. "I think speed may be more important than any of you know," he said. "I think we must make a decision this week end and carry out immediately whatever plan we arrive at."

"What?" Sloan was shaken out of his usual composure. Even the lounging Jack sat up. Schoeller carefully took the cigarette from his mouth with his left hand, tamped it out and began to fieldstrip it.

"The *Argonaut* was detected on its flight last week. The government has monitor films of a radar sighting that couldn't be anything else."

"Great God," Sloan exclaimed. "You've seen the film, Hank?"

Dr. Alvin nodded. "It shows the *Argonaut* falling toward the ocean about ninety miles from the Patuxent Naval Air Base. The time checks, and so does everything else. And this particular sighting shook things up, I can tell you. It was too close to Washington and Annapolis."

"Was that all?" Schoeller's voice crackled for once with excitement. "Just that it was close by?"

Alvin shook his head. "That vertical fall. Our UFO experts said it was something new. While they had us on the radar, they thought they had something like a flying saucer with a power failure. And"—he spoke casually, weighing the effect of his words—"the Navy threw up a jet flight and went out after us."

Schoeller chuckled, making a harsh, unpleasant sound. "How long did it take their jets to get where they thought we were?"

"Oh—quarter of an hour from the start, I suppose."

"Hah!" Schoeller sat back in triumph. "I was two hundred miles out to sea and twenty miles up by then, Doktor."

"It's damned lucky you sneaked out over the treetops and stayed low until you got to sea." Jack Baker brushed his hand worriedly across his forehead.

"Furthermore," Alvin said, "you must not bring the *Argonaut* near here again, Schoeller. You have the Navy going quietly crazy. Not so quietly at that. You've indicated a new pattern for UFOs and you can bet your life they'll be watching for it. They're convinced whatever they saw was navigated. And just to reassure you about that adverse decision you mentioned, here's a piece of top-secret government information for you: the AD16 radar interceptive units—the latest and best we have—adjusted their sweeps up to two hundred thousand feet as of last Wednesday."

Schoeller gazed at him without expression. "Then you are correct," he said. "We must decide at once. We must act."

Jack Baker was thinking that Hank could go to jail for that disclosure of top-secret information. But it was a thought that lay like a light blanket on the cold, inner realm of his mind. A more personal problem confronted him. Once when he had been in flight training, one of his fellow cadets, a married man, had lost his nerve. In one terrible second he had become unable to bear the thought of flying again. "I had this vision," he told Jack later, his face still white and strained, a corner of his mouth lifting and jerking like an exposed nerve. "I was standing there on the line and I had this vision of Margaret standing by my coffin. Just that. She was just standing there. And I knew they were never going to get me off the ground again." But Jack had had only a vague understanding of such a fear. He had been afraid many times during the war, afraid of dying, of being maimed; still he had never known a controlling fear. So now that the great coldness was in him, almost paralyzing him, he knew he was going to have to hold tightly to his resolution, to that dream he had lived by. It was in more danger from himself than it had ever been from anything else.

Dud had been right. Dud was always right. But dammit, Jack thought, a man isn't made of clay. He can't just mold something out of himself.

He had listened to Hank Alvin's unexcited voice telling

them exactly what had transpired at the meeting when General Waverly had shown the radar interception films. But he didn't really hear the words. He realized that they had faced only the unknown before—but that now they must also, for the first time, deal with the known fears and follies of man. The first dwarfed the other; yet, as Jack knew, infinity merely waited to be conquered, while man would come looking for them.

Oh, Dud was sensible all right. This fact only made his problem more evident, only offered further proof of Dud's clear vision. "You fool," he had said to Jack, point-blank, as he would say to anyone. "You utter fool. I told you what you had to do."

"Listen, Dud," Jack had answered, carefully picking his words, holding on to the huge ballooning surge of his anger, knowing it to be as much a product of his own determination as of this blunt man's words. "I went there to do what you said. I went there to tell her it was all off."

"For God's sake!" Sloan shook his head violently, one hand bouncing a pencil impatiently against the blotter of his desk. "You're going to give me the old song and dance about you just couldn't help it. Is that it?"

"That's it," Jack said. "I counted on you to understand it."

"I never understand foolishness!"

"What about Marilyn?"

"Boy, several important lives are at stake this time. Our contraption out there is a prototype. You know damn well the next time Schoeller presses one of his buttons it might blow up all over the place. Or some eager-beaver pilot could jump us when we weren't looking or ram us or anything. To say nothing of the FBI and the whole damned armed forces getting after us. And if none of that happens, maybe we go up too high or in the wrong place and just disintegrate. And there goes your dream."

"Don't you think I know all that as well as you? I told her"

—Jack kept his voice firm, calm—"I told her I was leaving the country on a top-secret engineering job. I told her I might be gone a year. I told her something could go wrong and I wouldn't come back at all."

John Sloan snorted. "Does that make it anything but foolishness?"

"Goddammit," Jack shouted, his control deserting him as quickly as it had on that night above Cleveland, "don't keep calling it foolishness, Dud!"

"I'll call it anything I please," John Sloan said. "I know a hell of a lot more about it than you do and I'll call it anything I please. I know what a woman can do to a man. I had Marilyn and I know. Thirty-three years ago I had her and I'm still thinking about her. Still haunted by her. Does that sound foolish coming from an old hardhead like me? You're damn right it does. But it's true."

"All right," Jack said. "You ought to be able to see why I couldn't just—just tell her to get lost. Not after . . ." He stopped.

"Did you go to bed with her?"

"None of your goddamn business," Jack shouted. But he knew the answer showed on his face; that his uncle could read it.

"It's all my business, Jack," Sloan said. "I'm in this as deep as you are." His blue-gray eyes turned toward the window and he stared at the hazy sky for thirty seconds. Finally he said, "Well, if you know it isn't something physical you want . . . I said I never understand foolishness. I don't fight it, either, not after I know what it is."

Absurdly, Jack was disappointed. He knew then that he had been counting on his uncle—this hard, practical, blunt man—to find a way out for him, to supply him with an answer.

"I've been foolish myself for so long I've just finally accepted it. And I can see I'm too late to stop you."

"Too late," Jack agreed. The words rang hollowly in his uncle's big, plain, comfortable office. Beyond them, the flat roof of the Sloan assembly plant glinted in the California sun.

"You'll have to make me one pledge. You'll have to because you don't have the right not to, with Alvin and Max and me all tied up in this thing."

Jack nodded, looking past his uncle to the dull blue sky showing beyond the plant roof. "I give you my word, Dud. If it comes to a choice, I'll do my part, Sandy or no Sandy."

"What I want you to promise is that we can count on your full and undivided attention. I don't want you mooning around like a high school boy at a hundred thousand feet."

"I promise, Dud. I don't moon. I may get crazy for a moment, but I don't moon," he said, staring at his uncle across the broad, cluttered expanse of the old dining-room table John Sloan used for a desk.

"I guess I insulted your girl," Sloan said. "You know I didn't mean it that way."

"It's all right."

"In some ways, boy, you're like my own son."

"Well, you raised me, didn't you? In some ways I feel like your son."

"Maybe we're both fools. Maybe we're more alike than we know."

"Maybe we are," Jack said.

The four men sat silently, after Alvin had finished speaking. Then Sloan struck his fist on the arm of the lawn chair.

"Max, dammit, this clinches it for me. I say the *Argonaut* goes to the United States Air Force, lock, stock and barrel."

"So?" Schoeller took out another cigarette. Alvin noticed that the insides of two fingers on his left hand were stained yellow.

"Look." Sloan shook a finger at him, almost threateningly. "I've gone along with you and Jack. Neither of you could have done a thing without my money. My backing. And I'll tell you how I was able to give it to you. Because in the United States of America a poor boy can use his guts and brains and whatever else comes to hand, and build himself a fortune. He can do it because we've got something in this country—something they never heard of in Russia. Better men than me can't tell you what it is, but freedom is what it's made of. Freedom to grow."

"A very rich country," Schoeller said. "Very rich."

"Rich, hell. People always act as if that's all we are, and I'm sick of it. You're a German, Max. You're in between. Here's the damn Russians on one side of you and America on the other, at each other's throats. I ask you: rich or poor, hasn't this country proved itself the least likely of the two to go around starting wars?"

Schoeller shrugged. "Perhaps. At least, it thinks it has. But I ask you: who dropped the atom bomb?"

"Oh, for God's sake. To save lives—to end a war—yes, we dropped it. Two of them to be exact."

"Precisely." Schoeller gazed at the coal of his cigarette critically, as though it were not burning to suit him. "To save lives. To end a war. This United States of yours—it is very good at deciding what is best for people. Seventy-six thousand Japanese—poof! At Hiroshima. To save lives. To end a war."

"I think I know what Max means, Dud." Jack Baker gazed thoughtfully at the ground between his feet, his hands twisting and clasping in front of him. "God knows, I feel the same way you do about the United States. We're all brought up to feel that our country is sort of chosen. Our history is taught us that way. But Dud, we can't solve this problem by the old schoolbook. What Max is saying—and what I agree with—is that when it comes to sheer wisdom, sheer maturity—well, there isn't enough of it even in the Pentagon to trust them alone with this ultimate weapon."

"Precisely," Schoeller said.

John Sloan opened his mouth to speak but Jack hurried on. "There isn't enough in any country. God forbid that Russia should get her hands on the *Argonaut*. I don't know, maybe her intentions are as good as ours. But suppose for a minute that either country had exclusive possession. Well, we think we're right over here, don't we? And people that know say Communism is like a religion over there. I think the temptation on either side would be to deliver an ultimatum, with the *Argonaut* to back it up."

Sloan almost bounced out of his chair in his vehemence. "Well, by God, that's just what I'm saying! Turn this thing over to our people. Initiate a crash program. Build a hundred of 'em. Then call in the Russians and lay down the law."

"In the matter of ultimatums," Schoeller said, his cigarette bobbing in his mouth, "one encounters difficulties. During the time when you had indisputable superiority in atom bombs, the Soviets must have faced the possibility of such a move. They immediately locked up their country against any serious threat of espionage and began to scatter their industries and military bases. In that large country, they always have somewhere to go. In a matter of hours, entire populations can disappear into Asia. All we can threaten, even with the *Argonaut*, are known centers. So, strategically speaking, mere threats would not suffice to bring the Soviets to their knees. You would"—he took the cigarette from his mouth—"most certainly have to implement your ultimatum. This development is precisely what we propose to avoid."

"Isn't it obvious?" Jack said, looking around their circle. "The *Argonaut* must become the weapon of an international police force. There's no other hope."

"You and your United Nations," Sloan said. "Why don't you grow up?"

"Oh I know all the arguments." Jack shook his head ruefully. "It's too weak. The Russians have it shot through with spies. It doesn't have any police force or any provisions for one, and so on and so on. The fact remains, keeping peace isn't a national task. Even we Americans are not objective enough or big enough for that job. In our generation the Russians are always going to create strife and tensions. England and France are on the sideline. What's left besides the UN?"

"There is another way," Schoeller said. "Your Secretary of State—he speaks of the stalemate, does he not?"

John Sloan threw up his hands. "You see how it is with us, Hank. For two years we've been going around in this same endless circle. I'm for the U.S. Jack here is a UN man. And Max can't think of anything but giving the secret to both great powers at the same time."

"The balance of power," Schoeller said. "We of Europe respect the concept."

"It would take a fancy juggler to balance that power precisely," Jack said. "You give both sides the idea—even hold a field day and take them for a quick ride over Washington and Moscow with the presumption that each side will begin to build the same number of *Argonauts* at the same speed. We must recognize that if one side gets ahead just far enough to take a pot shot at the other, that side could wipe out the other before it could throw up any defense. Suppose we were on the short end of the stick. We could do nothing but hope that a few of our most advanced bombers could take off from some foreign base with hydrogen bombs. And that would be a rather poor idea if they had us checkmated and could destroy the industrial potential of this country in minutes after we dropped the first bomb in Russia."

"I would gamble on the fact that we could make more of them faster than they could," Sloan said.

"Okay. Supposing we did. Wouldn't we take a pot shot at them? There's that last war we are trying to avoid."

"And that's what you want to save the world from?" Alvin asked.

"That's all, Hank," Jack persisted. "Whether men are good or bad or go to heaven or hell is their own business, but I just don't want to see mankind deprive itself of that free election. Shall we call it cosmic democracy?"

"Should man continue to exist if he cannot solve his problems freely?" Schoeller spoke the words bitterly.

Henry Alvin—he was still standing—turned slowly and walked away. He leaned against one of the trees, not looking at his three companions, his glasses dangling in his fingers. "This balance of power," he said. "That is the undesirable decision of which you spoke?"

"Precisely," Schoeller said.

"Then I must argue against it until the three of you over-rule me," Alvin said. "You admit, Schoeller, that neither nation should have this weapon exclusively. As a German you must know that the Soviets have as black a record as any regime in history for absolute failure to honor commitments. How can you possibly advocate that they be given possession of this weapon?"

"They also have the H-bomb, Doktor."

"Yes," Jack Baker said, "and are you sure they aren't going to drop it on us tonight?"

Max Schoeller shrugged. Henry Alvin stared across the lawns and fields of White Oaks to the pasture where the *Argonaut* had returned him to this troubled earth. There was a stone wall between each of these men, too high to climb, too massive to break down. They would never be able to agree on anything sensible or acceptable. For a moment he thought cold-bloodedly of a gigantic steal, of playing the game as their associate, getting those notes from John Sloan and going to Dick Waverly with them. Was that where duty lay? Was it beyond integrity to his friends? Or had integrity already gone from him in deception? Was it even, in a world of sheer annihilation, an outmoded concept?

"But we have to find a way," Jack Baker said, almost as though he could read Henry Alvin's mind. "The world can't go on as it is. The Russians are smiling now all right, but there isn't any real understanding. There isn't even any real desire for understanding. People may not want to fight, but they don't want to surrender any of their notions or goods so they can get along. And either side can destroy the other. The whole world is sitting on a hydrogen bomb with the fuse hanging out, and there are plenty of mean little kids playing around with matches. We can't dodge the issue by saying there's nothing we can do, either, because we have the means as nobody else does. I don't want to keep on sounding like a Sunday School teacher, but it may be our job to save the world when nobody else has been able to."

"That's easy to say, Jack." John Sloan spoke slowly, tiredly. "But it looks like we'll need to be men from Mars to work this thing out."

Men from Mars. Dr. Alvin closed his eyes against the sudden brilliant shimmer of the sun on the glass roof of the solarium. Something tugged at the edges of his mind. Something Dick Waverly had said. *We need a sign up in that old sky— something to put the fear of God in us. . . .*

"We'll work it out, Dud," Jack said. "We've got to."

Obvious as God himself, Dick Waverly had said. Henry Alvin turned slowly to face his companions. "Gentlemen," he said, "I don't want any of you to laugh 'til you've heard everything I have to say."

"That's the damnedest thing I ever heard," John Sloan said, when Alvin had finished speaking.

"I know it." Alvin shook his head, a wry smile pulling at his lips. "I suppose it's out of the question."

"It is child's play," Max Schoeller said. "I am surprised that you should suggest it, Doktor."

The scientist shrugged. "I only thought . . . You gentlemen must remember that in the Pentagon there is a climate partially prepared for believing something exists out there." He waved expansively toward the blue sky, shadowed with the slow approach of evening. "Our flying saucer scare of several years back is responsible for that. And incidents of UFOs have been too numerous to discount completely. That's the only reason I thought this worth mentioning."

Jack Baker slid forward in his seat, his elbows resting on his knees. His voice was quiet as John Sloan looked at him sharply, recognizing the faint slur of eager words that was usually the first indication of one of Jack's enthusiasms. "Try to put yourself in the place of that odd creature, the average man. Think about him waking up tomorrow morning, opening his newspaper and seeing that men from outer space had demonstrated over Moscow and Washington. There's something in that, Max. It could throw into sharp relief the differences we have with other nations here on the earth. Maybe even politicians could see some virtue in getting along with each other under such conditions."

"It is child's play." Max Schoeller repeated, shifting angrily in his chair.

"There's one thing you gentlemen seem to have overlooked," Alvin said. "The attitude of America or Russia or any nation today would be one of self-defense. They would think of the *Argonaut* as a weapon to put in their arsenal as a weapon of war to enforce their security, or possibly their will. But they would not think of it as a means for changing the attitude of men. That would be too slow, too hazardous for any nation. And yet it is the only way to use the *Argonaut* as a weapon of peace—as a force that man must direct against his own *instincts* if he is to survive them."

"That's what we're looking for, Hank," Jack exclaimed.

"But that's not what we have been talking about, Jack. You said give it to the United Nations to *enforce* a peace. John said we should give it to the United States Government and dare anyone to come near us. Max said give it to both sides and let them stand off in mutual fear or caution, as with the atom bomb. All of you speak of military pressure and all of you know as well as I do that you can force a few men to behave but you can't force nations to anything but war unless their leaders conclude that war is an impractical alternative to some kind of compromise. The sword, the cannon, poison gas, and even the atomic bomb couldn't make them conclude this but maybe the *Argonaut* can. That is our only hope."

"I agree," Sloan said, "but what do you propose? Will our pretending to be men from the stars do that?"

"I don't know, John. I only know, in all seriousness, that if I hadn't realized the unique opportunity the *Argonaut* offers for this basic solution, I'd have turned all of you in this week. First I was afraid to because I couldn't lay my hands on the *Argonaut,* and if I frightened you off I might lose it for our government. That's where my first responsibility lies and you know it. Then I saw this chance with all its frightening responsibility."

"What did you see, Hank?" Jack looked at him intently.

"You said it, Jack. You said it that night we walked out of Crestview toward the garage, less than a week ago. You asked me what would happen if we could rise from the White House lawn and fly to Red Square for breakfast. That would literally put all nations in the same backyard."

"Bring them so close together they can't afford to fight," Jack said.

"If things get off the track," Dr. Alvin continued, ignoring him, "I'll stand by to throw my full information of the *Argonaut* to the government."

And you must have full information, Sloan thought. I will not risk it otherwise.

"This is nonsense," Schoeller exclaimed. "You may tell them of the *Argonaut,* Doktor, but you cannot tell them how to make it." He smiled with satisfaction. "Unless they are very smart they will not even do so from my notes."

"Now let's don't get excited," John Sloan said. "Let's be practical about this thing. Your 'star men' will have to get into some kind of communication with people on earth. How will you manage that, if you're supposed to be from out there?"

"Precisely." Max Schoeller nodded vigorously. "We are talking sense at last."

The four men were silent for some time. Sloan turned and looked at Jack, who was peering intently out over the restless water of the Sound. "And of course you realize there'd be a good deal of danger. Moscow and Washington aren't exactly unprotected."

Jack waved a hand impatiently. "The communication, Dud—that's big, that's important, and there's only one way. They could trace any ink or paper we could use. But if there were such a thing as a ship from outer space and if it had ever wanted to land on earth, it would almost surely have picked some remote spot like Arabia or the Australian bush or Antarctica. Why couldn't we hand-print leaflets in bad, barely readable Arabic, with ink and on paper available in Saudi Arabia? That would indicate there had been a landing for information in the Middle Eastern desert—and, for all you and I know, spaceships could have landed there."

Sloan shook his head. "It wouldn't be too convincing."

"Hell, Dud, what we're trying to do is create a possibility. The suggestion is the main thing. If it's just convincing enough so it can't be written off like the flying saucer epidemic, that's what we're after. Remember what Orson Welles did with his men from Mars?"

"Welles?" Schoeller was puzzled. "One of your university men?" They laughed, breaking the tension. But even after John Sloan had explained Jack's reference, Schoeller did not seem to be amused.

Dr. Alvin shook his head slowly, almost humorously. "Jack could make me believe my own idea isn't so crazy after all."

Max Schoeller threw down his cigarette in irritation. It was the first one he had failed to fieldstrip. "We talk of nonsense again instead of practical ideas!"

"We don't have any other practical ideas." Jack Baker leaned forward eagerly, his young face alight with enthusiasm. Alvin's idea had appealed to him like a revelation—so simple, so likely to play upon man's constant concern with the unknown, the superhuman. He believed it could lead to the dream he had pursued all his life, and behind it, with the headlong decision of youth, he was willing to place all the enthusiasm and the strength and the sheer determination he had lent to the building of the *Argonaut* itself. Even the hesitation and the dread he had felt since the entry of Sandy Carlson into his life was transformed into heady confidence.

"Grown men," Schoeller said. "Grown men talking such nonsense. I am astounded!"

Jack watched his fury with calculating eyes. Only Max Schoeller knew all the secrets of the *Argonaut*. They had to have him with them, above everything else. But Jack knew his man well—knew him as only one who had worked side by side with him for years could hope to know him. He knew that Schoeller had a mind which encompassed practically the entire range of man's physical achievements; but he knew also that outside his chosen field Schoeller had little real knowledge. The account of the "average man" reading about a demonstration from outer space had produced no effect on the grim little man because he could not possibly picture an average man; that such a creature existed had never occurred to Max Schoeller. Outside the walls of the laboratory, he lived by a small set of fixed beliefs: that the German mind was the superior of any other; that Americans possessed only wealth and physical power; that Russians were of two classes, barbarians and shrewd schemers; that one always did one's work; that there was no such thing as leisure. Because of this failure to appreciate the actual world in which he lived, Schoeller could see nothing but "child's play" in Dr. Alvin's idea. It would have to be presented to him another way.

"Max," Jack said, "you can't see the real possibilities in this just because you've been thinking so long in much bigger terms."

"So?" Schoeller lit another cigarette. There was a sneer in his voice. "Tell me the real possibilities."

"All right. I've already got an idea for the bomb. It shouldn't . . ."

"Bomb?" Alvin looked startled.

"We can't just sit there and wave at them, Hank. You've got to attract attention some way. We'll have to come in at night, of course. What I figure is that we can drop from—oh, say two hundred thousand feet—to fifty thousand and at that point release this bomb. We can prime it with fireworks—something to give us a hell of a noise and a big splash timed to go off about five hundred feet over Moscow, and then spill out the leaflets. We can tie in the detonator with a radio altimeter, packaged to be completely destroyed at the first blast. We'll make a sign in the sky like your general said, Hank. And as soon as we've made it, we head for Washington and make another just like it."

"Better make it New York," Dr. Alvin said. "That Washington radar is murder."

"Hell, men from space could be a little rusty on earth geography." Jack grinned. "We could say Washington in the leaflets maybe, but actually show up over New York. Might be safer at that."

"Men from space." John Sloan shook his head. "What a
107

damn fool thing. Would anybody really fall for that? But— Jack—that bomb idea is all right. Tell you the truth, it's hard to see where we have a thing to lose."

"Except my *Argonaut*." Schoeller's voice was thin with anger. "Except our lives, for nothing."

"We're three to one, Max." Jack moved shrewdly toward the clincher of his argument. "Don't let your lack of imagination keep us from . . ."

"Imagination! Imagination!" Schoeller almost leaped into the air, his tight Teutonic control of himself loosening in terrific emotion. "The man who built the *Argonaut*—harnessed the earth force . . . A lack of imagination!"

Jack pressed him relentlessly. "Have you stopped to think what's implicit in this idea, Max? Assume for the minute it works. That means we have imposed our will on both America and the Soviets. Now I've heard you talk about a fleet of *Argonauts*, and one side attacking the other with it. Great day, Max, here's a chance for you to handle both sides with one *Argonaut*."

"So?" Schoeller said, and the fury wavered and began to die in his eyes, as though his last, wildest outburst had found its peak.

"One sure thing," Jack said. "We can't do it without you."

"You think they—they will actually believe we have come from out there?" Max swept his hands toward the heavens.

"Maybe enough of them will. If you handle the *Argonaut* as captain. I believe you can pull it off. I'll swear I do. It'll take some expert work but hell—you built the thing, just like you said."

"The whole world," Schoeller said. "They all would believe it, eh? Believe we were something terrible from some place they cannot even imagine. Eh?"

"I think there's a real chance, Max."

"We do it my way if I am captain?"

Jack glanced at his uncle who moved his eyelids almost imperceptibly. "Of course. I'll build the bombs and you handle the rest."

"So." Schoeller pouted his lower lip. "And as you have said, if it does not work, we still have the alternatives we have discussed."

Dr. Alvin cleared his throat. "Well—of course—I don't want to be pessimistic, you understand. But if it doesn't work, it may be because somebody butts in on the act in some way we can't foresee. In that case, I doubt if there'd be any—alternatives."

"There are three possibilities of that nature." Schoeller held up one finger and again his voice took on the dry and unexcited tones of a professor. "We may be apprehended by something in the skies. Or"—he held up a second finger, his eyes peering brightly around their circle—"our bases may be discovered and destroyed. Finally, the *Argonaut* itself might fail us." He held up a third finger, then closed them all into a fist. "All are risks but not insurmountable."

"Guided missiles," Sloan said. "That's what worries me. If they pick us up over Washington or New York, wouldn't we be in the bag? And Moscow, too."

"I am not afraid of their missiles," replied Schoeller. "We have a radar perspective device that would give us a hundred-thousand-foot warning of any approaching object, and we can accelerate parallel with the earth so rapidly that no present-day rocket control could follow us. I am more worried about the *Argonaut* itself. It must have maintenance. Our other bases provide fuel and provisions, but the only real workshop is at Mesatron. If some prospector stumbles on it . . ." Schoeller shrugged. Something glinted for a moment in his eyes, and his lips moved again in that peculiar grimace that passed for a smile. "Ah, well," he said, "war is full of such risks, eh, Doktor?"

Alvin was startled. In that moment he glimpsed a quality

of reckless dash he would have least expected to find in Max Schoeller. "I don't want to speak of risks," he said. "I shall be taking none in Washington."

Alvin was fascinated at the way Max Schoeller, once confirmed as captain of the enterprise, immediately took charge of planning; at how his active mind began to nose among the problems that seemed immediately to rise like bubbles in the wake of a boat.

"Jack, we must discuss this bomb in detail," Schoeller said. "We must plan how to deliver it from the *Argonaut*. And I wonder if the rapid change in pressure when we fall from two hundred thousand to fifty thousand feet will affect your firing mechanism. We must not let the bomb fall intact if we want to maintain our disguise."

"Particularly in Red Square." Jack smiled grimly. "The altimeter I want to use is U.S. Air Force surplus gear."

"We must get to Nevada." Schoeller paced excitedly about on the edge of the shaded area beneath the trees. "We must get to the laboratory. There is much to be done."

"Hank, do you think you could write the leaflet for us?" John Sloan asked. "None of us has much access to Arabic textbooks."

The scientist nodded, slowly considering.

"I'm well known at the Library of Congress. I think I could get access to the sort of books I'd need without anyone in particular noticing. It's little enough risk to run, anyway. What shall we say in the leaflet?"

They looked at each other. "It ought to be tough-talking," Sloan said. "It ought to be scary. But rather idealistic, too."

Alvin laughed and Jack Baker winked at him. "Hell, you know more about that sort of thing than we do," Sloan said. "You write it, Hank, and send one copy to me in a plain envelope marked personal. Don't enclose a letter or anything, in case there's a slip-up. I'll get busy rounding up the paper and

110

ink. I've got some connections in Los Angeles that ought to be able to handle it with no questions asked. I suppose we'll have to hand-letter as many as we can. There isn't any safe way to bring a printer into it." He looked across at Schoeller. "Max, when do you think we can do it?"

"I will need one month." Schoeller looked at Jack. "Eh, Jack? You will have the bombs by then, if I have the *Argonaut* prepared?"

"A month ought to do it."

"Okay," said Sloan. "If you'll get me the copy within a week, Hank, I'll get enough leaflets hand-lettered to do the trick. My arm might fall off but it's the only safe way. I'll print the damn things myself."

"Now look." Jack Baker jabbed out a forefinger at Sloan. "Oughtn't we plan something beyond the first run?"

"Like what?"

"Like a second appearance. At a stated time and place. So they could be sure we're capable of carrying out any promises or threats we make."

"Well, I don't know." Alvin shook his head. "I don't think you fellows should underestimate the radar and the defensive missiles that Washington or New York is capable of employing against you, particularly if you give them a time and place to set up for you. And Moscow is probably just as capable."

"Men from space," Schoeller said, "need not be too exact about earth time. I think Jack is right. If this is worth doing, it is worth doing right. Why don't you say in your leaflet that we will appear again at some hour exactly—oh, say twenty-five days later. Then we can actually demonstrate perhaps twenty-four days later. Or twenty-six. But at the correct hour."

Jack spread his hands, looking around at his companions. "Genius," he said. "Sheer genius. I told you Max could make this thing work if he set his mind to it."

Max Schoeller laughed, but Alvin saw that he was not

amused. "It is still child's play, gentlemen. I would not be a party to it if it did not look toward a presentation of my craft to joint military representatives of this country and the Soviet Union within at least a year."

A year, thought Alvin. In this world who knows about a year from now? He listened to Jack's excited voice and Schoeller's dry one discussing the details. Above their heads, his eyes met those of John Sloan, and between them some sad understanding passed like a shared pain. They were older, less brilliant men than these other two, and perhaps because of that they saw more completely—not more clearly, but across broader fields. And life had taught them both that nothing is ever so good or so bad as it seems, so possible or impossible—that man's constant urge toward perfection is forever to be blunted by his necessity to settle for the attainable. Neither was capable of the sort of bright vision that burned in Jack Baker's eyes nor the fierce aggressiveness that motivated Max Schoeller's war against his own ignorance. Perhaps both were wiser because they hoped for less.

John Sloan blinked, his head moved almost imperceptibly; and in that moment of understanding, Henry Alvin received the signal without surprise, indeed with a sense of relief, and blinked his own eyes in return.

After a while, Sloan moved away from the others, strolling casually across the lawn toward the big white house.

"We aren't through yet, Dud," Jack called. "We haven't even started to plan this thing."

Sloan waved. "I know it. I just want to think it over alone. You and Max are doing all right so far." He walked on toward the house.

"John can't get off that easy," Alvin said. "You two keep up the good work. I'm going to get him to start working on the leaflet message with me." He walked without haste after the figure slouching across the lawn. By the time he caught up, they had crossed the front of the house and were approaching the green water of the swimming pool. They walked to its edge and stood on the slippery tile, looking down into the placid depths.

"You have a safe?" Sloan said. "A personal one?"

"In my apartment, yes." Dr. Alvin leaned against the steel diving platform. He could feel the heat of it through the thin material of his sports shirt.

"Then you'll get a package a week or ten days after the time of our first run. My secretary will send it to you, registered mail. It'll be a large brown envelope from a department store in Los Angeles and it'll be marked personal. It will be Max's notes on the *Argonaut*. Don't open the envelope. Just put it right in your safe."

Alvin nudged a brilliantly striped beach ball with his toe. It rolled across the tile to the edge of the pool and dropped with a soft plop into the still water.

"All right," he said. "What will Schoeller think?"

"Max won't know. Max is all right in his way. I trust him, even if he is a goddamn genius. But he won't know about this."

The ball floated easily away from the side of the pool. It revolved slowly as it floated, first a red stripe going under the water, then a green, then a blue one. Henry Alvin did not look away from it; he knew he was adrift, too, and out of control, and he did not like the feeling.

"A lot of things could happen," John Sloan said. "The chances are good that one of them will."

Alvin nodded. He wished, quite irrationally, that he was going with them. It would be a shedding of responsibility, a trade of care and caution for danger and decision.

"If something does happen, you take Max's notes to the right people, Hank. You'll know them better than I do."

Alvin stretched a long leg across the widening gap of water

113

and tried to kick the beach ball back into the side of the pool.

"If it comes to a choice of what to do, it will be up to you alone, Hank. There won't be anybody else to consider."

The ball eluded Alvin's foot. He watched it helplessly while it spun farther and farther out into the water.

"Hank?"

He looked at Sloan for the first time. The industrialist was peering steadily at him, eyes squinted against the glare of the dying sun on the water.

"If you say so, the package could go to your General Waverly." A muscle twitched in his neck. "I could send it to him as long as he didn't open it until something did happen."

For a moment Dr. Alvin thought he was looking upon a blessed land, where the sun shone beautifully and the sky was always blue. But the vision faded, as quickly as it had come, and he shook his head.

"You couldn't put strings on it like that, John. I'm in this thing all the way now and I'll have to take my chances. Send it to me."

Sloan nodded. Without another word they turned and went back across the lawn toward the house. They could see Max Schoeller and Jack Baker, still talking.

"Maybe you're right," Sloan said. "In some ways I'm damn glad I'm not in your shoes."

7.

Jack Baker came out of the plane that clear summer night, his sense of urgency coiled in him like a great spring, and found Sandy waiting at the Cleveland airport. Their greetings were brief and she led him quickly through the crowded lobby to where her convertible was parked.

"Are you sure you can't spend the night, Jack?"

He held the door for her on the side away from the steering wheel, then glanced at his watch. "Positive. I've got just a little less than two hours layover."

In the glow of the parking area arc lights, he could see something like a pout on her lips. It was an odd expression for this big, strong, independent girl, and for the first time since he had known her he wondered what she had been like as a child. The thought brought a sharp ache into his heart, a hurt for all that part of her life he could never really share.

They talked of that as they drove slowly through the thinning evening traffic, away from the glow the city lights cast into the sky, to a neon-lit, drive-in restaurant.

Sandy laughed, watching the carhop coming across the lot toward them. "Maybe it's better in our case," she said. "Maybe if you knew me well enough, even now, you wouldn't want me."

Fat chance, Jack thought, and like a pinthrust in the back of his neck, it came to him that he would probably never be able to put the matter to the test. The urgency rose in him powerfully, choking him for a moment, as they gave their orders. He reached blindly across the seat, groping for her hand. The day was so near at hand—it was all so close—he had not realized until this moment how much of his remaining time had flown in feverish preparations with Schoeller and

Sloan. Yet, somehow, the days were gone, the work was nearly done. And there was no way to know what lay ahead.

Dud, of course, had known that Jack would stop in Cleveland when he went east for the last conference with Henry Alvin. He had even made a wry crack about looking up some friend of his there, which Jack had thought it best to ignore. The talk with Alvin in Washington had not taken long, neither had been particularly anxious to be seen with the other or to speak of the immediate future. They had had dinner in an out-of-the-way restaurant, with Jack bringing the scientist up to date on their preparations—which were ahead of schedule—and hearing in turn that the excitement caused by the Patuxent sighting had gradually died. More to the point, Alvin had also reported that, to the best of his information, no diplomatic proceedings were scheduled which would make the "spacemen's visit" untimely or dangerous. Nor was there any indication of Soviet military activity that might include unusual air patrol or radar scanning.

"All in all," Alvin had concluded, "it looks like the time is as ripe as it's ever going to be. There's a disarmament confab opening at Geneva the day you plan your second run, but it's low level. Not more than an assistant secretary in the deal."

"That shouldn't bother us. . . . Hank, you still think it's the thing for us to do, don't you?"

"If I didn't, I'd go in and have a long talk with Dick Waverly. Damned if I wouldn't."

Jack smiled. "Don't see Waverly yet, Hank. Listen, you ought to hear about what we've cooked up. . . ." And from then until they parted, Jack to the airport and Alvin back to some late work at his office, they had talked soberly of the details of the venture.

Only when Jack was in the plane headed for Cleveland did he realize, with profound shock, that he had been secretly hoping Henry Alvin would give him some reason not to go with the *Argonaut*. Good Lord, he thought, what's got into me? Sweat popped on his forehead and under his arms, despite the air-conditioning. He had been aloft hundreds of times, yet he was suddenly as nauseated as a first-timer.

He had stared with unseeing eyes through the small window of the plane at the great banked clouds to the west, as massive and secret as his own future. And, even safe in Cleveland, he could feel strongly in his heart that unease which emerged to defy the fierce dream of a lifetime.

Beside him, Sandy settled comfortably lower on the leather seat of the convertible. "Did you know I'm an amateur astronomer?"

"Every minute I seem to find out something new about you," he said.

Sandy stretched her arms upward. "Well, that star is Arcturus in the constellation of Boötes. In 1933 they used the light from that star to cut on the power for the Chicago Century of Progress. And do you know that the pulse of light that did the trick left Arcturus forty-one years before? Think of dashing madly through space all that time. What a cold, lonely journey."

"And dashing at a hundred and eighty-six thousand miles a second. Think of that!"

"There's a light leaving Arcturus right this second." Sandy folded her arms and shivered a little bit. "It won't get here until you and I are old, old people. Another lonely journey."

Jack waved at the heavens. "We're looking right into eternity. If you start thinking about it too hard, you feel mighty insignificant. And yet some men pin their hopes on a star."

"I feel insignificant all the time." Sandy moved closer to him on the seat. He dropped her hand and touched her bare arm above the elbow, savoring the softness of her flesh. "I feel like I'm on some kind of a journey just as cold and lonely and long as that light from Arcturus."

Sandy moved her head and put her lips against his ear. "And what's your star, Jack? What's the star that takes you away from me?"

"It sounds kind of silly."

"Not to me." Sandy's lips nibbled at his ear lobe. "Nothing you say sounds silly to me."

Words were too poor, Jack thought. They couldn't express what he meant. "I mean if there's anything a man with my kind of knowledge can do that might prevent more—more wars and more suffering and more starvation and . . ."

"Do you mean to tell me," Sandy said, sitting up, "that I'm in love with a damned do-gooder?" But there was a catch, almost a sob, in her voice.

He chuckled. "Maybe that's what I am. But a man can't change the things that are right for him."

"Not even for love?"

"If even love could change it," Jack said, "I don't believe it would be right." He stared over her head into the blackness beyond the arc lights and, with his own words, the unease faded, the moment of frailty left him and he knew he would go on as he had always planned. He might have hoped in his selfishness, in his human perversity, that something would happen to stop him, but it had never been a possibility that he would voluntarily change his course. Not even Sandy— not even this love—had done that to his dream.

The carhop returned with their hamburgers and they ate in silence, sitting low in the convertible seat, looking up at the stars flung in their limitless beauty across the sky.

Sandy folded her paper napkin and brushed it efficiently across her hands and lips. She glanced at Jack. The broken arch of his nose in profile made him look rugged and determined. "That other night, I guess you could tell you weren't the first."

"It doesn't matter," Jack said.

"It's just . . . I see now that you were pretty straight

with me when you told me you were going away, that you might not be back. Don't you think I ought to be as straight as you were?"

"I think a woman should never tell too much about herself."

"Well, it was never personal anyway. Never until you came along."

Suddenly her strong arms were around him and urgency flowed through their flesh into each other. It was a siren song but even as it began, something deeper, more irresistible than blood, quieted the wild music for Jack.

"Let's go somewhere away from this light," she whispered. "Anywhere."

Slowly Jack pushed her away, his face tense. "Not now," he said. "We don't have much time left. Let's talk of other things."

Sandy drew back abruptly and stared at him for a long time; then she put her head against his shoulder.

"You lousy do-gooder," she whispered. And he chuckled into her blond hair, feeling better, feeling good, walking for that moment on the clouds—until suddenly her long hands were moving, twisting, on his back, and she was whispering again, "You'll come back!" She said it over and over, not even knowing truly where he was going. "Say you'll come back!"

But of course he could not tell her that.

A peremptory knock at his office door interrupted Henry Alvin's work on a report he had come back to his office to finish for General Waverly. He sat back in his desk chair, shaking his head. He had been completely absorbed in his work, and for a moment he felt like a stranger to the dark walls and the small circle of brightness falling on his desk. He got up hurriedly and went to the door, clicking on the main overhead light.

A Navy captain was waiting in his secretary's empty office.

"Good evening, Doctor. I saw from the log you were still in the building and I thought I'd stop by for a minute."

"Well—ah, come in, Johnson. Come in." It had taken Alvin a second or two to recognize the belligerent officer who had broken Dick Waverly's rigid conference rules.

Johnson sank down on the leather sofa. "I'll come right to the point, Doctor. I've been studying the Patuxent sighting all this month. I've run that film a hundred times and interviewed every man who had anything to do with it. I can say for sure that the vertical fall is completely unprecedented in any other well-authenticated sighting I know about."

"I thought it was." Alvin nodded calmly but his heart began to beat a little faster.

"You were very convincing about the possibilities of no human life on other planets. Of course we can't even conjecture about the planets of other stars—they're too far away. Not that I ever believed anything like that to begin with. I'm a very hard-headed man, Dr. Alvin, and the only day I'll believe in spacemen is the day I see one with my own eyes. I just don't swallow that crap like some people."

There was something brutally effective in Johnson's headlong speech. I'll bet the boys at Annapolis called him Bull, Alvin thought.

"I'm inclined to agree," he said, speaking carefully. "As a scientist, however, I do try to allow for the wildest possibilities. People once believed we'd never split the atom, you know."

Captain Johnson made a growling sound in his throat and a dismissing sweep with his thick hands. "Well, here's a wild possibility I wish you'd consider for me. We agree that there are no spacemen. But I know whatever that thing off Patuxent was, it had a pilot. It had something at the controls."

"Are you suggesting . . . ?" Alvin stopped. A cold tingle began creeping along his spine.

"I'm suggesting that this thing was a man-made aircraft,

120

Doctor. A little something the Russkys cooked up in secret."

The fear went out of Alvin like air from a punctured balloon. He smiled, tolerantly, whipping his glasses from his eyes and looking at the ceiling. "Our Intelligence people say there isn't a chance of that."

"I know what they say. But what do *you* say?"

Alvin frowned. He did not want to alienate Johnson by insulting his theory. Yet, it would be just as well to cut off such a train of thought at its source. "I admire your persistence, Captain." He looked squarely into the Navy officer's nervous blue eyes. "Too many people around here just write these things off as sunspots or something. I must admit, however, that I don't believe the Russians could possibly have an aircraft capable of doing what was done off Patuxent. Every scrap of intelligence we have argues against it, to say nothing of our own laboratory experiments."

"You really think that?" Johnson's face screwed itself up disgustedly.

"I'm afraid I do. I'm afraid—quite frankly, Captain—the spacemen idea might be closer to the mark."

Johnson stood up abruptly. "Spacemen, my ass." He pulled his white cap tightly down on his head, cocking it absurdly, like some salty chief petty officer. "I thought you'd have more sense than the other guys around here, Doctor." The frown of a martyr was on his face. "I thought you could look beyond your nose."

"I try to." Alvin held his temper carefully in check. Plainly, Johnson was not the sort of man one could simply disagree with. If one were not with him, one would be stupid or criminal or worse, in his eyes.

"Well, we'll see." Johnson marched toward the door. He whirled suddenly and held out his hand. "No hard feelings, Doctor."

"No hard feelings, Captain."

"But you mark my words." Johnson's red face worked

angrily, like the features of a hard slugger unable to reach a skillful boxer. "We haven't heard the last of the Patuxent business. Not by a long shot."

No, Alvin thought, watching the blue-clad figure lunge down the long, dim Pentagon corridor. Not by a long shot. The chill moved along his spine again, and, as he turned back to his desk, a sort of desperation seized him. In that moment he would have stopped it all, if he could have; but it was far too late. He sat down slowly, put his arms on his desk, and let his head lie wearily on them.

8.

Thirty days after the conference at White Oaks, at 2:55 A.M., the great camouflaged doors of the underground hangar at Mesatron swung open and the *Argonaut* emerged slowly into the morning blackness. A radio signal closed the doors. Max Schoeller, at the controls, carefully checked the reactors and rockets. Three minutes later the great ship moved slowly away from the earth and headed east over Nevada's desert wastes. Only a few miles from Mesatron, it started to ascend rapidly. Soon even the scattered lights of earth faded into silver blurs on a velvet setting. Jack Baker, who was in the copilot's seat, stared in fascination at the altimeter. While he watched, its indicator moved smoothly past one hundred thousand feet, then one hundred fifty thousand, then two hundred fifty thousand. Neither the *Argonaut* nor any other piloted craft had ever been so far above the earth.

"Isn't this risky?" Jack said with effort, although his chin strap was loosened. His eyes gazed steadily at the rate-of-climb indicator. "There isn't much change in air density between two and three hundred thousand feet, but even that little bit could be too much."

Schoeller shrugged, the movement almost lost in the binding of his webbed harness. What is the use of such talk? he thought. It was only the Germans and the British who could do their job without a constant babble about the risks. But he only said, "There is no alternative. The radar is scanning up to two hundred thousand feet."

"Well, you won't get a chance to regret it if the hull can't take the strain. Not this high up you won't."

Jack was not usually so cautious. Schoeller shrugged again. "Anyway, I must make a test. I will level out at three hundred thousand feet"—he pointed to a newly installed instru-

123

ment on the panel—"and this will show the relation of cabin to outside pressure. When I close off the cabin pressure tanks, the differential pressure will remain constant—unless there is a slow leakage. Of course, if there is significant falling of cabin pressure, we must go back and find the fault."

"But that could take weeks!"

Schoeller sighed but did not answer. He saw no more point in raging at the inevitable than in prattling of risks. With swift, capable hands, he leveled the craft at three hundred thousand feet.

"Wouldn't *that* be a helluva note!" Jack grumbled. "The spacemen are experiencing technical difficulties and must postpone their visit until further advised."

Schoeller cleared his throat in irritation, while he adjusted the controls for hovering. Jack was definitely not himself now, when everyone needed a cool head more than anything else.

Since his trip East, Jack had been increasingly irritable and nervous. Once Schoeller had even overheard John Sloan berating him at Mesatron for wandering off into the desert.

"Go back and watch the bomb-bay doors open and close." Schoeller spoke sharply to show his disapproval. "We must make sure they will work smoothly at this altitude and temperature."

Jack unbuckled his harness and headed aft without a word. "Send Sloan up as copilot," Schoeller called after him. "And perhaps you had better get some sleep."

After Sloan had come forward, Schoeller reached under the control panel with his right hand and closed a valve, keeping his eyes on the differential barometer. Its needle remained steady. There was no leakage, then. Schoeller sounded the buzzer to alert Jack, then rested his hand indecisively on the bomb-bay control lever. Now, when it was too late, he regretted the lack of personal attention he had given this vital equipment. They had never opened the doors at higher than one hundred thousand feet, and although their performance had been carefully checked on the ground before this flight, that was far from a real test. Schoeller was tempted to make the check while hovering. But that was only rationalization, he knew, and his hand moved quickly from the control lever to the signal buzzer. He pressed it three times. A moment later, Jack Baker thrust his head into the cockpit.

"Strap in the bombardier's seat," Schoeller said. "We are going to check the bomb-bay door operation under acceleration."

"Aye, aye, sir," Jack said with a mock salute, and went aft again.

Frowning, Max Schoeller headed north, striking a course for the polar cap. As the rear rockets were ignited, the ship lurched forward. Schoeller noted in his precise mind that one rocket fired a bit roughly, although only his sixth sense had perceived it. No instrument registered anything out of the ordinary. The acceleration was swift and their bodies were cushioned hard against the seats and headrests. When they reached about three thousand miles an hour, Schoeller cut back power to the rockets. When he found he could raise his head from the back stop, he gave the final buzzer signal. His eyes rested intently on the barometer as he slowly pulled back the bomb-bay door control. The doors opened rapidly, as shown by an indicator. The barometer needle remained stationary. He pushed the lever back to Close position; the indicator moved to show that the doors were closing. Then, just before the indicator reached Lock position, Schoeller felt a sharp pain in his eardrums. From the corner of his eye, he saw Sloan lurch forward and clasp his hands to the sides of his head. It was unnecessary to look at the barometer to know that there had been a sharp drop in cabin pressure. Despite himself, Schoeller felt the disturbing thrust of fear. But before he had time to consider the problem, he saw it was going to be all right this time: amazingly, the pressure had

125

stabilized of its own accord, well above the danger point which would have killed them in a moment.

Jack came forward again, pale but steady. From his face, Schoeller could see that he, too, had suffered excruciating pain. "The bomb-bay doors locked all right but what the hell happened to the pressure?"

"For God's sake, boost it!" Sloan shouted. "My head is blowing up."

Schoeller opened the cabin pressure air valve. "We'll have to go lower and try that again," he said. "We're far enough over Canada to be safe now."

Jack went back to the bombardier's seat as the descent began. Soon cabin pressure was back to normal. At one hundred fifty thousand feet, Schoeller leveled off. This time, when the bomb-bay doors opened and closed, the barometer needle did not move.

"So," Schoeller said, looking at John Sloan as he started a slow climb back to two hundred fifty thousand feet. "We can bomb over Moscow tonight from this altitude, but we must get higher over New York. Doktor Alvin has given us proper warning of the guided-missile radar perception. Shall we go on, you think?"

"You're the captain," Sloan said, without hesitation. "You know more about this rig than any of us. It's your decision, Max."

Schoeller nodded. "We will proceed then. Go aft and get some rest. See that our jumpy friend does the same."

Sloan unbuckled his harness. "Jack'll be all right. When the clutch is in, he'll do his part. It's just that . . ."

"In this business"—Schoeller made a delicate adjustment of the controls—"your clutch must *always* be in."

Then he was alone in the cockpit—alone with the puzzling knowledge of the mysterious leak somewhere in the bomb-bay mechanism, alone with the sixth-sense worry over the roughly firing rocket. He listened to it for a moment with that inner

126

ear only a creator can apply to his masterpiece; but even that magic ear could hear nothing. The bomb-bay door would probably hold up for this flight, but it could eventually cause trouble. It would have to be looked after in Australia—where there would be almost none of the needed equipment. Ah well, Schoeller thought, relaxing, one does what one can. He glanced at his watch. It was 3:45 A.M. Soon—too soon— they would reach the North Pole area, where the timepieces of all the world would register the same. They would pass through the everlasting summer day of the polar region and in a second from night to day. They were now passing over the billion-dollar radar defense of the Arctic Circle, unnoticed and unchallenged. Schoeller smiled with satisfaction. He thought of many years ago when the German Army had slipped around the elaborate defenses of the Maginot Line.

The sky about them had already grown bright and would remain so: they would be flying into Russia and the unknown in broad daylight. But that was a minor matter among many problems.

Those problems seemed increasingly complicated to Max Schoeller as he tuned the controls of the *Argonaut* to their correct pitch, then sat back at ease. He had no great hope for results from their project, although once his companions had recognized that only he, Max Schoeller, was likely to accomplish it, he had been willing to humor them. At least they would not be able to accuse him of having been uncoöperative when the time came to follow the only possible course he believed open to them. He would be able to say that he had gone along with them—then they would have to go along with him. Still—with a nervous and upset bombardier, an aged businessman for a copilot, and possible mechanical difficulties developing at the very outset, things could become less simple than he had expected. Schoeller thought with grim satisfaction of how he could make a certain electrical contact in a second that would turn the atomic-power reactors of the ship into destroyers if an emergency should appear. No part of Max Schoeller's *Argonaut* would ever fall into earthly hands if he were not there to deliver it in person. That had been his solemn pledge to his colleagues in Germany—long ago dead but never forgotten.

Schoeller's hands moved lovingly on the cool metal control panel of the *Argonaut*. An exhilaration began to fill him. Far below, the great Arctic wastes rolled away to the limited horizons of earth; but here on the perimeter of life there were no horizons. In that moment of freedom Max Schoeller had a vision of himself as the ultimate dictator. He was almost surprised at his subconscious instinct of beneficence toward all mankind. Before, he had looked with suspicion and disdain at man, but now he could look down at humanity with indulgence. He no longer feared the pressure of the mundane earth. Yet, in his subconscious, he sought to consolidate his position of power by telling himself that the lowly mortals beneath him could only be controlled by terror, at least until they voluntarily subscribed to an orderly existence. And, of course, *he* would have to define an orderly existence for them.

He sat patiently in the silence of upper space. Everything seemed motionless, despite their great speed, except the slow diurnal movement of the sun toward the west. Occasionally he scanned the heavens, more from habit than expectation. Both the Russians and the Americans had launched many satellites and they were moving in an orbit above the *Argonaut*. But even so, the chance of being detected was remote. Only pinpoint radar scanning from a satellite—and it was highly doubtful that the Russians had developed such a technique—would give the *Argonaut* away. Their ship was too low to attract the attention of minitrack stations which monitored the satellites.

Schoeller reflected with satisfaction—excitement still surging in his blood—that he was years ahead of them all. Now, for the first time, the world would become aware of what he had wrought. From this time on, it would know such fear as it had never imagined, whether it believed the spaceman fiction or not. Schoeller hoped the world would believe in spacemen, despite his doubts, because its fear would be the greater for being of the unknown. He wanted no personal profit or fame, and he had never considered what general knowledge of his craft could mean to him in money. He derived his satisfaction and pride not only from the great humming thing he had created but also from the terror he had always known it would bring, and from the order he believed it would ultimately create.

I believe in terror, he thought; that and order, if nothing else. He touched a control to begin his search for the powerful beam of the radio voice from Moscow.

Jack Baker tossed sleeplessly on one of the hard, narrow bunks into which the *Argonaut's* cabin seats could be converted. He heard John Sloan snoring regularly on the other. That man could sleep through an earthquake, he thought. And I used to be able to.

But there was no use thinking of such things. He made a wry face in the darkness. Nothing was the way it used to be. Here they were only a few hours from a lifetime's dream, and all he could think of was a woman. He had no regrets, not really; he was doing what he had to do, and he could not have lived with himself had he failed to do it. Still—the low, pleasant hum of the *Argonaut* was carrying him away from the sweet throb of life, toward what nobody knew. He shook his head. It was aching from his clenched jaws. Ahead of him, he realized—even in the event of success for their efforts— were long months of waiting, of loneliness, of secrecy. If for any reason they were driven into real hiding by some sort of determined pursuit, there was no telling how long their isolation might last. It was even possible—and John Sloan had not failed to point this out to him on the day of their departure—

that if things went badly, they might actually have to become "men from a star," plowing straight out into the unknown, breaking the last contact with earth. And this could mean but one thing: cold, relentless death.

Some time later John Sloan awoke, coming instantly into consciousness, with no fuzziness of the brain, just as he had waked up all his life. He knew exactly where he was, what he was doing and, before he turned his head, that Jack Baker was lying sleeplessly just across the cabin.

For a moment the old man wondered if he should have found some way to make Jack stay behind. There was a distinct possibility that his jumpiness could affect the mission. Sloan remembered with poignant force how love could pull a man about and make him at the same time more and less than he had been before.

But no, Sloan thought, he had to come. There was no other way for him. And he had good hope that in a crisis Jack would be as reliable as he had ever been. He turned his eyes beneath his bushy white brows, seeing the short-cropped blond head alert and moving on the other bunk, and he was glad that he was no longer young, even though when he was young there had been Marilyn. It was curious, he thought, how the late years brought their own compensations. For instance, he could dash impetuously into this pioneer task without a thought for his own safety, indeed with a real sense of mission. And as once he had wallowed in the miseries and glories of his own love, now he could look upon them with compassion for another.

He smiled to himself, thinking briefly of what his California clubmen friends would think of him. Only last week he had been eating creamed chicken at a Rotary luncheon and talking of the long hunting trip to Canada on which he and Jack were about to leave. Now he was one of the original men from a star, outward bound from earth. And before he plunged cleanly back into sleep, he had a warm, illusory vision of himself proudly telling the story of this exploit as a special feature of next year's Ladies Night Banquet.

Slowly they had been ascending to three hundred thousand feet, where Schoeller thought they could cruise most efficiently. His expert fingers worked swiftly with the radio controls, picking up at last a signal from Radio Moscow. Predictably enough, it was broadcasting a shrewd bit of anti-American propaganda in English. The signal was being sent out from the short-wave band on what must have been line-of-sight. As a reflected wave it would have been much stronger. It was fuzzy at first but as the *Argonaut* emerged over the Soviet land mass from the Barents Sea, the high frequency wave length broke strongly through the Heaviside layer. Schoeller chuckled grimly. He had wondered if he would be able to home on Moscow from such exceptional altitude and, ironically, he was finding that he could do so only because this short-wave band was throwing the Voice of Moscow across international frontiers. If the Soviets had been minding their own business on the lower, more local frequencies, he would have had to add navigation—one of his sketchier attainments—to his other duties. He sat back at ease, occasionally making a delicate adjustment to conform to the strengthening beam from Moscow.

In Washington, Henry Alvin found himself unable to sleep. He got up long before his usual hour, took a cold shower and went for a long walk through the streets of the city. He had breakfast in a White Tower restaurant, then caught a bus for the Pentagon.

At no time did he look at the sky, even when a flight of jets left three great streaks of white to drift like feathers above the Capitol.

It was about six P.M., Moscow time, when the *Argonaut* came to a stop above the Soviet capital. The arrival could have been made sooner but once the city was in sight, Max Schoeller adopted a cautious, circuitous route, approaching from the direction of the sun, in order to minimize the chances of discovery.

For a long time the craft hovered motionless above the sprawling city to avoid a telltale moving reflection at the moment of twilight below. Schoeller, who was still the only crew member stirring, listened for quite a while to as many radio signals as he could pick up, gleaning from them some useful weather data and the reassuring knowledge that no alert had been sounded. He had been confident that no radar would be scanning at their present altitude, but there had been no way to be certain.

The problem with the bomb-bay doors reinforced his decision to descend over the city, probably to one hundred thousand feet, before going lower to make the actual bomb drop. He thought for a moment of awakening Sloan and Baker but he decided to let them sleep on. Max Schoeller had little faith in the indefatigability of anyone but himself, and he had no desire for sleepy or tired assistants. He adjusted the controls for slow descent and settled back, alert to the radio signals, keeping a sharp watch around him.

The two-hundred-thousand-foot drop, made as slowly as his patience would allow, seemed to take an eternity. Schoeller had little fear of radar even at one hundred thousand feet but he did not wish to chance detection by the sudden, plummeting fall that was a specialty of the *Argonaut*. He took off the dark, protective glasses which he always wore while flying at very high altitudes, rubbing his eyes wearily. The windshield and the few portholes of the ship were heavily tinted and made of specially fused silica to protect them from the heat and light of the sun as well as from the ultraviolet rays, the cosmic rays, the gamma rays, and other undefined radiations of outer space. These things made the long wait over Moscow one of their most dangerous enemies. All known precautions had been taken, but there was no way to tell what was leaking through the hull of the ship. The Geiger counter registered its usual high gain but indicated nothing out of the ordinary. Radiation was not instantaneously dangerous in this situation, but they had never kept the *Argonaut* aloft as long as they would on this voyage. No one knew the effects of prolonged exposure. Yet it had been necessary. They had had to leave Nevada at the moment when discovery was least likely, and midnight was psychologically and practically the best moment for the Moscow venture. The time lag was best spent right here, where any alarm would be instantly noted, and where local conditions could best be judged. And the changing level of the Heaviside layer could have hindered the operation of the radio direction finder if they had strayed too far.

Finally the long descent was over. Schoeller could see, through the bottom window, the outline of the vast city. He could even, he thought, pick out the great Red Square. At half this altitude and at this latitude in the early summer, the sun would never set on the *Argonaut,* except for a passing twilight. To go lower would have run a greater risk of reflection from the hull, as darkness spread across the earth. He noticed that a slight drift had developed to the southeast. Schoeller adjusted the orienting rockets, bringing the *Argonaut* slowly back to the center of the city.

Still he made no move to wake up his companions. He maintained his radio monitoring and his alert lookout, occasionally noting down data for Jack's bomb run. He could have done these things as well with the others about, but he was enjoying his solitude. There was something almost indulgent in his attitude as he peered down at the great city, shimmering with light; it was as though he were deliberately withholding a heavy hand, and he found the sensation thrill-

133

ing. He was almost disappointed when Jack Baker came into the cockpit.

"Is that Moscow down there?" Jack's voice had regained some of its enthusiasm, and Schoeller's exact mind noted that as a gain. Jack was cracking his knuckles intently.

"That is Moscow," he said. "I have been monitoring the radio and you will wish to study these data before the bomb run. I learned enough Russian during the war to have complete confidence in my interpretation."

"Thanks." Jack stuck the notes in his shirt pocket. "Sorry I've been so jumpy, Max. I guess I've made it tough on you and Dud."

Schoeller pursed his lips. "It is only that we may face the emergency, my friend. We must look out for it."

"Aren't you nervous at all?"

Schoeller shrugged. "One does his work. What is there to be nervous about if one does his work?"

Jack made himself comfortable in the copilot seat and settled down for the long wait. "I used to feel the same way. Sometimes I wish I still did. It's essentially a self-centered point of view, you know."

"Essentially," Schoeller said, "people are selfish. And are we not acting on the assumption that most of them respond only to force and terror?"

Jack nodded. "I suppose so," he said. "But look down there, Max, and think of little old earth, insignificant as a light bulb in Moscow—less than nothing in this whole monstrous universe. Yet this earth is fair and green and moist and hospitable. Look at the outside temperature gauge. Sixty-seven below here at a hundred thousand feet. Most of the earth never knows anything like that. But it has oxygen to breathe, a range of bearable temperatures, green foliage and blue sky, plants that change the energy of the sun into food and beauty, rotation to give it the variety of night and day, a tilt on the axis

134

to make summer and winter. Max, isn't it hard to doubt that God singled out the earth for something very special?"

"So," Schoeller said, "if you believe in God, why do you not leave matters to him? Why are you here now?"

"Because I also believe in what God made the earth for. . . . I believe in man."

Schoeller laughed, making that high, harsh sound Jack had so seldom heard. "Then you are a remarkably persistent young man." He stood up abruptly. "I must sleep. You will call me at eleven."

"Sure. Have you decided how we'll make the drop?"

Schoeller's voice immediately became schoolteacherish, as it always did when he made explanations. "I shall drop perpendicularly to fifty thousand feet, at which point you must quickly line up your sight. When the bomb is away, we shall immediately depart west. My notes indicate that winds aloft, up to thirty thousand feet, average only about four knots from three hundred twenty degrees, so you should have little trouble."

"Good old Max. Everything's always under control, isn't it?"

"Of course! You will call me at eleven?"

"Sure," Jack said again. He took the notes from his pocket and began reading them as Schoeller left the cockpit. Beneath them the lights of the city shimmered in silent tranquility.

9.

Ten minutes before Jack was to wake up Max Schoeller, John Sloan came into the cockpit, yawning. He dropped into the copilot seat and immediately turned his attention to the lights below them, pulling a pencil from his coat and bouncing it on the palm of his hand.

"Well, take a look at that," he said. "A pretty picture, huh?"

"I haven't figured out which lights are the Kremlin." Jack tapped his notes with one finger. "But if I knew, I could drop our little surprise right in their lap with all this dope Max conned off the radio."

"You think your bomb is that good?"

"It can't miss. The first explosion will be at a thousand feet and it ought to be a humdinger. It'll also take care of the radio altimeter timer and the casing. Then the pyrotechnic capsule has a time-delay fuse to explode it at three hundred feet and release your handbills with the fireworks." He looked at Sloan. "You sure worked like hell to copy those handbills." He tapped the notes again. "Figuring from these winds, if I let her go from the northwest quadrant of the city we ought to be able to drift a leaflet or two right into the Kremlin."

"Sounds good." Sloan looked away from the lights, directly at Jack. The corners of his mouth drew down. "You all right now?"

"All right." Neither of them had to elaborate, but Jack continued. "You're a steady hand to have around, Dud. I was lying back there trying to sleep, not getting very far, and then I took a look at you in that other bunk, stretched out like a baby."

"Hell," Sloan spoke gruffly as he always did when he was embarrassed. "An old man like me doesn't have much to worry about. No wonder *you* couldn't sleep."

"Well, I don't have an awful lot to worry about either. After all, Dud, how many guys ever get to see their dream come true?"

"Yours hasn't, boy. Not yet."

"Well, it won't be my fault if it doesn't." Jack grinned at Sloan again. In that moment the old bond of affection between them was as strong as it had been before Sandy Carlson came into their lives. "That's what I made up my mind to when I looked at you sleeping back there."

Sloan cleared his throat. "Well—hump—let's get this show on the road."

Jack glanced at his watch. "Time to wake up Max anyway."

The remaining moments passed quickly in final recitals of each man's part for the coming strenuous hours, with as many operational checks as their hovering position allowed; in a close collaboration on navigation between Schoeller and Jack, and in rotational monitoring of the radio.

Then Schoeller entered the cockpit and went to the controls. He gave the signals and they strapped themselves into their seats. Schoeller adjusted the reactors. The bottom dropped from beneath them. If any Russian radar had been monitoring that high, directly above Moscow, it would have picked up what might have seemed to be a comet blazing perilously close to earth. Such drops always brought searing moments to those aboard the *Argonaut*, but this time there were more pressing things to think about, and when Schoeller halted them at fifty thousand feet, they knew the critical moment was at hand.

"The airport tower is clearing a plane in on runway thirty-three," Schoeller told Jack on the intercom. "That bears out our wind information."

"Check." Jack worked efficiently from the bombardier's seat, applying all the skill and knowledge he had developed during the war. But even as he congratulated himself on the disappearance of some broken clouds Schoeller had noted at nightfall, he thought of the irony of his "horse and buggy" bombsight installed in this craft of the future.

"A minute to go." Schoeller's dry voice crackled on the intercom.

"Check." There was not much left for Jack to do. He had long since calculated the time it would take the "peace bomb" to fall to a thousand feet above earth, thankful that he had not had to make the difficult calculation for the altitude of Moscow above the sea, since their radio altimeter told them height above ground itself.

But there was too much time for thinking. What if the bomb-bay doors, which had opened normally, had been injured by the continuous pressure in the ship during their long wait? What if the doors sprang a big leak in closing and suddenly killed them all? At least Max would have started his getaway, he thought with relief, and the *Argonaut* would become a satellite of the earth, a cosmic hearse, until, perhaps, they were cremated in space by friction with the atmosphere. But what if Max had not started his getaway? Then their grave would hang in this very spot above Moscow until some Russian spaceman brought them and their secret back to earth. And what if something happened and they fell to earth? War in its most terrible form would surely follow.

"Tower is clearing a plane for runway twenty-one," Schoeller said on the intercom.

But Jack did not answer. It was too late to change position. There were only twenty seconds to go and in his concentration he began to count them aloud. Through the glass eye of the bombsight, Moscow glittered like the dream that had brought him here. " . . . *twelve—eleven—ten* . . ." His fingers found the releasing button. ". . . *seven—six—five* . . ." Excitement clutched at his heart. ". . . *two—one*—ZERO."

A second later he shouted: "Bomb's away."

Straining his eyes earthward, Max Schoeller heard further landing instructions for the plane approaching runway twenty-one. The wind's changing, he thought, wondering briefly, in a queer, detached clarity, if it would lose their leaflets among the high buildings north of Red Square. It seemed a year—a lifetime—since Jack had dropped the bomb. Then, through the bottom window, he saw a flash—barely perceptible against the glitter of the city. Beside him, John Sloan caught his breath audibly. It was fifteen seconds before midnight.

A moment later fireworks spread out brilliantly in a tiny circle, like the wild joy leaping unexpectedly in Max Schoeller's heart. He touched the buzzer. He saw his own hands moving godlike upon the controls. The *Argonaut* headed west, rapidly increasing its speed.

Soon Max sounded the all-clear buzzer. Sloan and Jack had anxiously awaited this signal and now they scrambled to remove the restrictive harness which protected them on sudden changes of course. Jack hurried to the cockpit. He had thought, on the original acceleration, that the ship had lurched to port just as the rear propulsion rockets were fired. "Anything wrong?" he asked Schoeller.

The little pilot looked up, frowning in irritation, shifting an earphone to hear him. Jack realized he had waited longer than usual to sound the all-clear because he was concentrating his attention on Moscow radio. "Put on that headset. Slip an earphone out of the bracket and give it to Sloan." Schoeller's orders were crisp, military.

"Have they said anything?" Jack automatically followed instructions, even as a faint irritation awakened in him at Schoeller's tone.

"Not yet. So far the midnight program of recorded music hasn't been interrupted."

"For God's sake," Jack said, putting the headset to his ear, "how much dynamite does a man have to dump on a Communist before he quits listening to Tschaikovsky?"

"Maybe your firecrackers didn't look so hot from down below." John Sloan shifted the receiver from one ear to the other.

"They ought to have seen it in Leningrad."

"If they were looking. Maybe we should have warned them it was coming."

"Well, at least our leaflets warned Washington. That is, if the Russkys can translate your Arabic and *want* to warn anybody."

"Maybe they think it's an American blitzkrieg. Maybe we had them figured all wrong."

"Quiet, please," Max Schoeller said. "Sooner or later they will say something."

For another minute and a half they droned through the black Russian sky, the wild final movement of the Fourth Symphony playing them a weird accompaniment. Suddenly the radio went silent, almost at the peak of the thunderous Tschaikovskian climax.

They listened in silence for another thirty seconds. Only the faint hum of the *Argonaut's* power plant could be heard. Schoeller manipulated the receiver among several frequencies of Radio Moscow but found no response. It was almost frightening, Jack thought, this eerie silence where moments before the music had given them its exciting company.

"They must think it's a surprise attack," Sloan said.

Jack shifted nervously in his cramped position between the cockpit seats. "We've got time to go back. We can see if they've blacked out the city."

"To hell with that," Sloan said. "Let's clear out of here."

"Max can put her back up to two hundred thousand. With our differential radar they couldn't hurt us even with guided missiles."

"Nonsense," Schoeller snapped. "We must get on. Of course they have blacked out the city and we couldn't find it without radio. They are not fools."

"Well, I wish I knew what was going on," Jack said.

"Get back to your post." Schoeller traced a line rapidly on a navigational chart. "That glow of lights on the northern horizon is Leningrad. We shall make a pass over it at fifty thousand feet."

Jack went back to the bombardier's seat and strapped himself in. Schoeller had cut the intercom into the radio receiver and he could hear a swirling Slavic dance tune, presumably from Leningrad. He felt a slight acceleration of the *Argonaut*. Suddenly the dance tune went off in the middle of a shrill violin solo.

Schoeller cut in. "They're blacking out Leningrad."

"Maybe they've got us on the radar," Jack answered. But Schoeller had cut the radio back in and was tuning all around the band. Again, he found nothing but silence.

"All right," Schoeller finally said. "The city is completely dark and we are still miles away. Keep in your seat. If they have us on the radar we must give no hint of heading back to the American continent. I am going to change course radically to the east, then head south. We'll go straight for Africa. We will approach New York over the Atlantic."

When the turn and speed were stabilized, Schoeller signaled that they were free to move about. Jack hastened to the cockpit. "Leningrad reacted pretty slowly if Moscow really thought it was being attacked," he said.

"I'm beginning to believe we may have caused just the reaction we wanted," Sloan exclaimed. "If there had been none at all, we'd have failed completely. If they had reacted too quickly, it would have been evidence that they were ready for immediate trouble and our hopes for this whole thing would have been far-fetched."

"These Russians," Schoeller spoke slowly and thought-

141

fully, "are a very shrewd people. Now I think we must be sure to make our drop over New York as advertised. If we fail, they will be certain the Americans have made this demonstration over Mother Russia."

"That's right." Jack nodded vigorously. "And I'll bet they won't even be decent enough to warn New York we're coming."

"Well, how do we know they can get the leaflets translated quickly enough to warn anybody?" Sloan shook his head. "That Arabic isn't an ordinary lingo. I ought to know. I copied the blasted things until I was blue in the face. Anyhow, we told them Washington, not New York."

"At least we know the bomb went off," Jack said. "I thought it looked like a damn good show. If it hadn't, they'd have recognized the radio altimeter, or a piece of it, as American-made, and they'd probably have declared war by now."

"Well, be sure it goes off over New York." Sloan smiled. "If that one's a blank, Hank Alvin's friends won't have much trouble figuring where the UFO came from."

"At any rate," Max Schoeller said, his mirthless lips parting in his reluctant grin, "how is it you say? The fat is in the fire? No?"

Sloan nodded slowly. "The whole world must know by now that Moscow radio went off the air without warning and without explanation. That alone ought to have New York on the alert."

"They are afraid, yes?" Schoeller said. "All over the world they are afraid of us now."

"I guess so." It came to Jack that he had never seen Schoeller jubilant before, not even on the first flight of the *Argonaut*.

"All over the world," Schoeller smiled again, his grim face creasing from cheekbones to chin, his hard little eyes gleaming brightly in the green light of the cockpit. "All over the world."

They kept the *Argonaut* at a relatively low altitude above the satellite belt around Russia, in the hope that any radar tracking would divert suspicion from their American destination. Then Schoeller began a slow ascent as the craft crossed Bulgaria, to indicate that they were not heading for some African base of the Western nations. The *Argonaut* was in the deep shadow of the earth near the equator before he thought it safe to go to high altitude.

Over the Belgian Congo, Schoeller leveled off at two hundred fifty thousand feet and made a wide turn toward New York. They could take it easy then. Even though New York was on daylight-saving time, these "men from the stars" would make their run by sun time. So they had seven hours for the flight from Moscow—an easy trip. And they had used minimum rocket power, except when necessary, to conserve fuel. At last they were on final course and Schoeller throttled back even more to relax for the long run. Beside him, John Sloan napped in his seat. He punctuated the gentle hum of the reactors with a vigorous snore.

The letters on the page of the book Sandy Carlson was holding in her lap blurred into black, illegible lines. She closed it with a snap and tossed it carelessly at the hotel table where she had found it. It missed and dropped to the floor with a thud.

Some joint, Sandy thought. She looked around, wrinkling her nose at the dull furnishings of the sitting room. Ordinarily such things meant nothing to her; but George Elliott had made such a production out of his announcement that he had a suite for her, instead of the usual inexpensive room, that she had really expected something pretty grand. Hotels are all alike, she thought. Like hangars with furniture.

She got up and went to the tall double windows at the end of the room, holding her robe close about the man's pajamas she always wore. The lights of New York spread out in a constellation around her; across the canyonlike street just outside, a tall apartment building rose haughtily into the night sky. She could see people moving about in its cheerful windows. She knew they were people with homes, people with families, people with claims against them that made them integral parts of a society in which she in her solitude had never moved. Watching them, craning to see more than their vague shadows on the windows, hearing from beyond her the low, disturbing strains of some music she could not place, she thought again that she was tired of being alone. She looked up, above the tall buildings, at the black sky and at the stars lost in the glow of the great city. Somewhere in all the world's infinity was Jack Baker. Merely thinking of his name brought a small glow to her, like the effect of a fine champagne. It was his fault, she thought, his doing that her old free ways, her old independence—yes, her toughness—were gone. All those years she had been a woman after all, but only he had known how to find her. Not those other men with their hard, demanding hands, their eyes that spoke to her with abrupt desire; not even George Elliott with his easy money and his shrewd but friendly ways; not anybody. Ah Jack, she thought, clutching her arms about herself in an emotion that was almost maternal. Now she hated those lost years of constant fighting for a place in a world that yielded nothing without exacting its price in goods or honor or hope. Now she hated them, and once she had gloried in that lonely, brutal struggle—in the sense it afforded her of absolute competence, of courage, of a cynical knowledge not given to the weak and the comfortable. But she could never again be secure in that knowledge that had seemed so special. Jack Baker had shown her its limit: that it had never made allowance for love.

The phone rang, its shrill jangle causing her to jump. That

144

was another thing—she had never been nervous until the last few days, except when driving her car. She hurried across the room, wishing irrationally that it could be Jack even while cold reason told her he could not possibly know of this flight to New York. But she snatched eagerly at the phone.

"Hello?"

"I'll bet I didn't get you out of bed." George Elliott's voice was perfectly modulated, in keeping with his slender elegance. It matched him well, just as his rich ties always matched his perfect shirts.

"You didn't." Sandy fumbled in the pocket of her robe for a cigarette. "I turned in early, but who can sleep in New York?"

"I think we ought to go out on the town tonight."

Sandy was taken aback. George Elliott had always been friendly, even affectionate, but he had never mixed business with pleasure.

"Have you heard the news?" he asked.

"What news?"

"My God," Elliott said. "The whole town's on its ear, and you say what news. Don't you have the radio on?"

"I've got the Muzak on."

"Well, have you got anything else on? Because I think I'd better come down there and talk this over with you. It might keep us here longer than we planned."

Sandy was suddenly irritated. "What the hell are you talking about, Mr. Elliott? Are you staying in this hotel?"

"Next floor up. I'll be right down." The phone clicked in her ear.

The old rascal, Sandy thought, banging the receiver down in exasperation. In a place like this. She looked down at herself, wondering if she should put on more clothes. Hell no, she thought. If I can't handle George Elliott after all these years I'm in bad shape.

10.

At 11:45 P.M., Eastern Daylight-Saving Time, the *Argonaut* was about a thousand miles from New York, over the Atlantic Ocean. No known radar was adjusted to detect it at that distance and altitude. Schoeller decided to "let down" to seventy-five thousand feet to pick up American broadcasts. Soon the stations began to come in loud and clear, bringing music, speeches, hillbilly combos. Schoeller fiddled around the band, then settled on classical music from a New York station. He had no ear for music, but that particular frequency was coming in more strongly.

Without warning, the music broke off. "We interrupt this program to bring you a special bulletin from our newsroom in New York," a portentous voice proclaimed. Then, in tones dripping with the controlled excitement of the professional newscaster: "Tonight Radio Moscow went off the air at five and a half minutes after midnight, Moscow time. Within a few minutes, other radio stations in all important Russian cities were silenced abruptly. There has been no explanation monitored anywhere outside the Iron Curtain.

"Washington and all other Western capitals have issued assurances that no attack against the Soviet capital has been launched or contemplated. A State Department spokesman said the Administration is at a loss to explain this unprecedented development.

"Meanwhile, the following communiqué has been issued by the Secretary of State. I quote: 'No aggression has been or will be launched from this country against the Soviet Union. Nor do we know of any developments which would explain the sudden silencing of the Soviet radio.

" 'In the absence of any explanation for this extraordinary

146

situation, our Defense Department is assuming the strong possibility of an aggression against us by Russia. Radar screens are properly alerted and interceptor planes are aloft. Guided missile defenses are also prepared for attack. Naval vessels are on extensive patrol.

" 'It is estimated that at least a three-hour alert will be given before any attack can be effectuated by an enemy against the mainland of the United States. At that time, a blackout will be ordered everywhere it is considered necessary.

" 'The Armed Forces are on the job around the entire periphery of the nation and it is the considered opinion of the Defense Department that any aggression can be handled effectively by our forces.' End of quote.

"It is obvious that this sudden silence from the Soviet Union means a quick alert for the United States. Stay tuned to this station for further developments."

John Sloan snored on. Beside him, feeling strangely alone in the cockpit high above the Atlantic, Max Schoeller smiled as the music began again. So the Defense Department was confident! So no one could get through! He reached across to the other seat and touched Sloan's shoulder. The old man sat up immediately.

"Go wake up our young friend. They are on the alert all over your country."

Sloan immediately brought Jack forward to the cockpit. Schoeller repeated the import of the broadcast rapidly. As he spoke, he sensed an exhilaration sweeping through them. Their experience at Moscow had been dampened by the long wait in the skies. They had looked at the "sitting duck" so long that they had found little thrill in shooting at it. But this new bird would be "on the wing."

"So," Max said. "The problem is complicated. If we come in low and slow, as we had hoped, some of the coastal radar

147

on ships a hundred miles offshore may spot us and cause the alert and blackout. We would lose WCBS to range on and the possibility of surface wind reports from La Guardia Approach Control or Tower. We would have to putter around to find our target."

"Hell," Jack said. "Men from the stars can't putter around!"

"Hardly." Schoeller tapped a rapid tattoo on the control panel with his fingers. "There is only one way. I will arrive over the city at two hundred fifty thousand feet. When you give the signal, bombardier"—he shot a glance at Jack—"we shall fall straight in, to seventy-five thousand. There I will slow the fall. At fifty thousand, you can let go. We will then start a rapid climb and head for the South Atlantic, cross over the Amazon jungle and cruise across the South Pacific to Australia."

"That's the vertical fall pattern Hank Alvin warned us about," Sloan said. "If we're tracked, it'll be just like a signature."

Schoeller shrugged. "It is, nevertheless, the best approach. Men from the stars must have some flying techniques of their own. And if we do not make the vertical approach, we will have to make the bomb run at high speed."

"I don't know." Jack shook his head. "Hank said they really got excited about the vertical stuff."

"I have made up my mind." Schoeller slapped his knee for emphasis. The scar on his face flushed slightly. "I do not believe that at high speed and high altitude you could drop your bomb anywhere near the target."

They were silent for a long time.

Then: "Maybe we'd better not stick around to watch the fireworks," Sloan said. "I say let's get in there and out again and go home."

Schoeller nodded. "It will take the bomb too long to drop,

148

even from fifty thousand feet. If their radar is really good—and Doktor Alvin says it is—they would have too much chance to send up a missile. Even our differential radar would be very little protection at that altitude."

"Hell," Jack said. "Couldn't you zoom up to two hundred fifty thousand and watch from there?"

"Your firecracker would look like a glowworm." Sloan shook his head. "I agree with Max."

Jack made a face. "Okay. Line me up the way you say, Max, and I'll put it on the dance floor of the Tavern on the Green."

Within minutes after the first news from Russia, Henry Alvin had been given an emergency alert and was on his way to the Pentagon under orders to report directly to General Waverly.

The scientist had had to feign sleep and then surprise when the summons arrived. Actually, he had been awake in his darkened apartment listening to news broadcasts.

He found General Waverly striding about a big, echoing conference room, with one or two other Air Force generals sitting glumly around its table. Couriers came and went busily, but they were bringing little of importance. Waverly hardly glanced at the messages they handed him.

"Hello, Hank," he said, as Alvin entered. "You got the word?"

"Well, I got orders to report to you and I heard a news broadcast on the way down."

"Then you got the word," Waverly said. "At this point, we don't know what the hell is going on."

"All right." Alvin looked around the circle of glittering uniforms. "What do you want me to do?"

Waverly strode the length of the conference table and back. A long black cigar whipped between his handsome teeth.

"The Moscow Embassy got a message through to State a while ago. Or part of one. The damn Russkys busted them off in the middle. Code is on it now. Just sit down there and sweat like the rest of us till we get our copy of the transposition."

Alvin sat down.

"Just let the Russians start something," General Strahan said. "They'll get a surprise when they find out what's waiting for them."

"They aren't starting anything," Captain Johnson said. "They'd never give us this kind of warning if they were."

Waverly looked at him with disdain. He puffed at the cigar nervously.

"Well, if they do, they're going to get one hell of a surprise," Strahan said, his Texas drawl edged with tension. "I mean they are."

"Not if they have a bigger one for us." Waverly grinned. "The last war was a lot simpler."

A messenger entered with a big tray of cups and a coffeepot. He had started to set the cups out on the conference table when an armed courier came in.

"Here we are," Waverly said, taking a sealed pouch. "Took them long enough." Impatiently he signed a receipt, broke open the pouch. He read the message through briefly, swore under his breath. He looked up, his quick eyes settling on Alvin. "Sounds like your department, Hank. Listen to this: 'Approx 0000 Moscow standard loud explosion plus fireball over northeast quadrant Moscow. Apparent pyro display followed. No casualties reported. Blackout order soonest all principal cities west. City under strict army control, no official . . .' It breaks off there."

"What the hell?" Strahan said. "Sounds like somebody's playing games."

"Games?" Waverly strode the length of the table, reading the message again to himself. "When they black out the city and silence the radio, somebody's scared. Hank, what does this sound like to you?"

Alvin was staring fixedly at a pencil stub with which he was drawing, over and over, the initial of his last name on the waxed surface of the conference table. For a long moment he did not move, except for the slow, repetitive flexing of his fingers around the pencil. He knew that when he looked up and spoke, the game would begin in earnest. Not only would each word have to be weighed for its effect on Waverly, for guiding him along the conjectural paths Alvin wanted him to take; but each word would also have to be considered as a possible giveaway. And Dick Waverly was a tough man to fool.

"Hank?" Waverly said. "You have any ideas?"

Henry Alvin raised his eyes from the fattening *A* his calm fingers were tracing on the table; steadily they met the hard, probing gaze of General Waverly.

"That sounds like an airborne explosion to me. It doesn't make sense that anybody would set it off from ground, like a big Roman candle."

"Check." Waverly nodded. "And they probably wouldn't have taken such drastic action if it had been some local resistance move. Although that's a possibility our Intelligence people are already yelling about."

"*We* didn't cause any airborne explosion over Moscow," Alvin said, removing his glasses. "That's definite. Under the circumstances, I think we can also take it as definite the Soviets didn't do it themselves. How about our allies?"

"Even those blithering Britishers wouldn't take that on themselves without us." Waverly chewed fiercely at the cigar, then took it out of his mouth. "Not any more."

"Well then," Alvin said, "that indicates some unknown agency."

Dick Waverly chuckled and put the cigar back between his teeth. "You and your UFOs. I knew what you were going to say before you said it."

Alvin shrugged. "You said yourself it sounded like my department."

"I know I did." Waverly rocked up on his toes, back down. "I still do. I just hate to admit it, that's all. I sure do hate to admit it."

The lack of malice in this venture, Jack supposed, as he strapped himself back into the bombardier's seat, was what gave it a resemblance to a sporting event. It was like a tennis match in which they would ace their opponents on the first serve. But he still wished, in a strangely competitive way, that those opponents could be playing the game on more equal terms.

Max Schoeller's voice crackled over the intercom. "We will be lined up over the city in fifteen minutes if they don't silence their radio. Will that give you enough time?"

Suddenly Jack felt a distaste for Schoeller. He could not overlook the martinet air nor the obvious relish with which he had talked of frightening the whole world; and in this entire mission he had displayed an appetite for a terrible power the *Argonaut* gave them—more precisely, gave him, Max Schoeller—that was disquieting. Jack answered shortly.

"Time enough. Get me the winds as soon as possible." He began his calculations.

Ten minutes later Schoeller called him. "Overcast at seven thousand feet. Twenty-five knot surface wind from three hundred degrees. The airliners are using runway thirty-one at La Guardia."

"That's bad." Jack was figuring rapidly. "We'll have to drop the bomb by radar over New Jersey to put any pamphlets in the city. The Hudson River and George Washington Bridge will blip the screen, but is there something west of them we can get a good fix on?"

"If we hold over Station WRQG, would that do?"

"Let me figure it out." His calculations were becoming involved but in a minute he called back, "Hold there for the time being at least. Is the wind steady?"

"Gusting up to thirty."

That probably means some turbulence, Jack thought. The damn leaflets might float right out to sea, he said to himself.

"We can go further inland."

"That would waste the big blowoff on some farmer in Jersey. Let's gamble on WRQG. At least it's a positive fix."

Five minutes later Schoeller spoke again. "All ready here. Now I will drop in fast to seventy-five thousand, start the braking there and halt at fifty. You must take no more than a minute. That is all I can permit."

Jack's calculations were nearly complete; time of fall for the *Argonaut*, time of fall for the bomb, effect of wind on the leaflets. All this had to be squeezed into a formula that would give him sixty seconds leeway to make the drop, so that the explosion would take place over the western edge of the city at the stroke of midnight, standard time, and yet not dump the leaflets into Long Island Sound or the East River.

"One minute will do it. Move a little to the northeast, Max."

He stared intently at his radar repeater. "That'll do it. Hold it right there."

Schoeller sounded the warning.

"Okay," Jack said. "Start the fall."

There was a sickening feeling of blood rushing to his head as the *Argonaut* plummeted through space. Jack forced himself to keep watching the luminous radar screen. The straps holding him in his deeply cushioned seat seemed to cut like blades into his flesh. His teeth felt like great sharp points in his bloodless jawbones. Then the pressure slackened and he knew Max was slowing the fall. In less than ninety seconds he would have to push the button.

The *Argonaut* came to a halt and Schoeller sounded the buzzer. "Open bomb-bay doors," Jack said.

Jack's eyes moved back to the radar repeater screen.

"A fraction northeast, Max."

The whitening blobs on the circular grid of the screen moved exactly into the relationships he desired.

"Hold it right there. Easy, Max."

They had been stopped twenty-eight seconds. At this moment other eyes might be glued to other screens; other voices might be giving the commands that would send death winging at them in a screaming arc. Even if Jack's calculations had been wrong—and he suddenly had the feeling that he was working too far to the northeast—there was no time for further change.

He pressed the bomb release. "Bomb's away," he said, his voice catching nervously in his throat, rasping loudly on the intercom.

The warning buzzer sounded. He quickly tightened his harness. The *Argonaut* leaped forward. As it did so, it spun sharply to port much as it had done over Moscow, Jack remembered, but more abruptly now. He could feel the hull shudder as Schoeller applied the directional control rocket on the forward port side to correct the spin. The movement carried them far to the west. With one part of his mind, Jack noted ironically that it was good evasive steering; but the rest of his intelligence drew back in alarm from this sudden, new danger. On his compass repeater, he saw that they were headed south-southeast. They seemed to be rising rapidly. Now he could tell from the familiar, even throb of the propulsion rockets that all were firing correctly. He wished he could see the radio altimeter, and for the hundredth time he marveled at the speed with which the *Argonaut* raced up the "ladder" of gravity, a ladder that reached to the stars.

He thought he heard a pop against the hull of the ship in the vicinity of the entrance door. Without warning a sharp pain struck his ears. Instinctively, he looked out of the corner of his eye through the window at his feet and saw the bomb-bay doors, just as they closed.

Abruptly their ascent stopped. Jack clasped his hands to his ears; he did not think he was going to be able to bear the pain that twisted like a dagger in his brain.

"Are you serious?" Sandy's whole body tingled at the shock of his words. "Do they really think another war is starting tonight?"

George Elliott relaxed carefully on the sofa. "Oh, I don't think it's that bad. I hardly believe our Russian friends would give us all this warning if it were the real thing."

"But—but—shouldn't there be a—blackout or something?"

Elliott dismissed the thought with a casual wave of his hand.

"The government says they can provide a three-hour warning if anything is really coming over, unless the Russians cut loose with those ICBMs. However, as you can imagine, all civil air traffic is frozen tight. Anything that moves up there tonight is going to have to pick bullets out of its rear."

"Frozen? For how long?" The first shock of the news about the Russian radio had passed. She was still standing and she moved slowly toward the window again, anxious to see the reassuring lights of New York spread around her.

"Who knows?" Elliott got up and switched off the Muzak. He tuned in the radio to a disc jockey's chatter, then came across the room toward her. "If it's all a big-bad-bogeyman scare, probably no longer than tomorrow. If it's an attack— well, we're right in the heart of Manhattan and we don't have anything to worry about except staying alive."

Her own situation had not occurred to Sandy in the confusing welter of thoughts Elliott's news had brought. Looking out over the city's lights as they winked bravely in the night, she knew that she had good reason to be afraid. She had seen the H-bomb movies, and as a pilot she had a good idea of the inadequacies of civil defense planning in the

156

United States. Yet she was not frightened. It had been a part of her life to face death, ever since she had performed as a child "wing-walker" for her stunt-flying father; death no longer had the power to intimidate her. Nor was she greatly concerned with the horrors a nuclear war would visit upon the earth. Sandy Carlson had been too long an inhabitant of what had seemed a hostile jungle for that sort of worry—at least until recently. She was thinking, almost angrily, about what a war would do to her new outlook, how it would take Jack away for an even longer time, how it might obliterate them both, cheat them of what they could have together.

Elliott stood beside her.

"What are you doing in this hotel? I thought you stayed uptown."

George Elliott gazed out of the window. His jaw muscles tensed.

"I've had a feeling of late that life was getting away from me. Tonight I thought I ought to talk to you about it." He turned, towering above her. "Maybe you can give me some advice, even if you can't help out."

Sandy Carlson respected Elliott. She had never thought of him in an intimate sense. He had never been intimate with her, just constantly friendly.

"That news we just heard seems to pinpoint my feelings. I didn't expect that when I checked in here." He looked out of the window again.

Sandy gazed at his stolid, sunburned face. She knew the story behind it. She knew that George Elliott had started with two trucks in a small Midwestern town thirty years ago and had grown to one of the largest and most respected carriers in the whole country. She knew that his persistence and sense of fair dealing had gained him that success, even at the expense of the finer things of life. Her sympathy went out to him; yet she had no heart to give, for it was elsewhere.

He turned toward her again.

"Sandy," he said, "perhaps it is my respect for you, as well as our pleasant association, that makes me bold enough to say this." He hesitated. "I've done my duty to the world. I've got enough money to support myself and others too, but I've got little time left. There are plenty of women, sure; anyone with money can have women of a sort, but not the kind he wants to marry. And this damn thing tonight made me realize that even more clearly." He paused and placed his hands on her shoulders. "I'm going to do something, Sandy, something besides leave my hard-earned dollars to charity. Frankly, I have a friend, an older woman whom I respect but do not love. Perhaps I should take her; it's more appropriate, but I don't want her. I want you."

Sandy walked over to the couch and sat down. Here was the thing she had spoken to Jack about—not leading a careless life, not dying as her mother had died. And if it had come two months before she would have been greatly tempted. Her future and her security were at stake.

For the first time in her life terror clutched at Sandy with cold and nasty fingers, and she thought she knew what he must feel as he stared down the short span of years left to him. She was going to have to choose: the bargain or the dream.

"That news on the radio," Elliott said. "I told you it did something to me. The way things are, I can't afford to wait any more."

I can't choose, she was thinking. I can't! Jack had told her he would be a long time returning. He had said he might never return, that it was even possible she would never hear from him again. And if he did come back, wouldn't he go again, sooner or later? Some old hard-earned caution reared up softly, secretly, from the ashes of those lost, burned years. When she last saw Jack in Cleveland there would have been no choice. Now, in the light of the brutal facts, there had to be.

She turned to Elliott, tensing slightly to keep the telltale trembling from her face, trying to hide the disturbance his words had brought her. "I'm flattered, George. This calls for a big decision. Please let me think about it."

"You must, I realize. But not too long." A smile broke the hard lines of his face. "Couldn't you think better at the Stork Club?"

Perhaps she should go, but she had no spirit for it. Her eyes met his in a steady, gentle gaze.

"Not tonight, please. I'm too upset."

George Elliott moved toward the door, and even in her confusion she could not help but admire his poise and confidence. The door closed behind him. The old secret caution spoke to her again, as loudly as the cry in her heart. Listening to both, she could not hear the exciting voice breaking into the wailing song of the saxophone.

Max Schoeller clenched his jaws against the piercing pain in his ears. Automatically, his hands moved on the controls, leveling the *Argonaut* in forward flight. His eyes were squinted almost shut with the pain from the runaway pressure. Nevertheless he noted that they were at only seventy-eight thousand, two hundred feet. Then, just as it had before, something quickly stabilized the pressure without human adjustment. Fighting down panic, Schoeller immediately boosted the pressure to normal, feeling the blessed relief of the pain leaving his ears.

"Good God," John Sloan muttered through his chin support, "let's get this damn thing back on the ground."

Before Schoeller could reply, his alert eyes picked up a blip on the differential radar screen. The old dueling scar on his cheek turned blood-red. The little German moved as efficiently as he had in leveling off when the pressure drop occurred. No signal had been given to Baker or Sloan to remove their protective harness, and Schoeller threw the *Argonaut* into maximum climb and forward speed, feeling his head drive back against the padded seat with terrible force. For a moment a curtain of blackness dropped over his eyes; but Schoeller summoned all his Teutonic resolution and made his hands move blindly on the controls, boosting the rocket propulsion to full power, instinctively applying compensation for the roughly firing nozzle on the left rear. Even so the ship executed a partial spin and headed out over the Atlantic. A bright, ruddy flash from the light just below the narrow windshield signaled a dangerously high skin temperature. Schoeller ignored it. Gradually he overcame the blackout and fixed his eyes again on the differential radar. The blip was still on a collision course but it was rapidly losing ground; apparently it had got near enough for its "homing" gear to go to work and lock on the *Argonaut*. But even rocket missiles were not designed to combat the performance of this child of his brain, Max Schoeller thought, leveling out at over two hundred fifty thousand feet. He watched the screen with a grim, tight smile as he lengthened his lead until the missile exhausted its fuel. He continued to watch during its plummeting fall back toward earth. Then the blip dropped off the radar screen and Schoeller throttled back. He touched the all clear buzzer after adjusting their course southward, well out from the Atlantic seaboard.

Jack Baker came hurrying forward. "What in hell was all that about?"

"They fired a missile at us." Max sounded as though he was discussing a problem in mathematics. "I regret that it was necessary to move so abruptly."

Jack wiped sweat from his forehead. "Our damned left rocket went sour and then the pressure drop came right on top of it."

Schoeller nodded, frowning. "It was the pressure that caused me to halt our ascent. During that time the missile got too close before I could take evasive action."

"What in hell is causing that pressure drop?" Sloan demanded. Jack busily studied the control panel.

"We must find out," Schoeller said. "The rocket failure, too. But particularly the pressure. You notice it is progressive? This time it happened at less than a fourth of the altitude of the test. We almost got picked off by a guided missile because I slowed the ascent." His fingers strayed lovingly over the controls of the *Argonaut*.

"Well—don't you think we'd better go to Mesatron then?" Jack wiped his forehead a second time. "We'll have everything we need there."

Max Schoeller shook his head impatiently. "We must assume they are still tracking us. At the least, they can do so once we cross into continental United States again. No, I think we must go to Australia."

"But how are we going to fix anything in Australia?"

"One does the best one can," Schoeller said. "It will be easier to return to the United States later, if that is necessary. I think we shall cross the Gulf of Mexico tonight, rather than South America. I am growing fond of these American news broadcasts."

For a long time they listened intently to every radio signal they could pick up. But by the time they swung westward, no news broadcast had mentioned the events over New York. Quite a bit of time was still being devoted to the unexplained silence from Russia, though nothing was added to earlier information. Meanwhile, Jack looked with disfavor on the compass, as their course pointed them farther and farther from Nevada. Now that arid waste of desert and sand and brush around Mesatron seemed to him like a blessed oasis, and Australia seemed as far away as any star. But the die was cast and he could not disagree with the decision.

Schoeller looked up from some computations he was making on a pad strapped to his knee. "I am not so strong on navigation, but from what I have here, I think that missile came at us from the sea."

"You're probably right," Jack said. "Hank Alvin told us the Navy was more excitable about UFOs than the Air Force. And all they have aboard ship is short-range guided stuff."

"Hold it a minute." John Sloan held up a hand. He had been manipulating the radio dial. "KOMA is interrupting a program." He turned up the volume.

". . . At thirteen seconds past one o'clock, Eastern Daylight Time, a loud detonation, followed by a brilliant display of fireworks, took place approximately five hundred feet over the Bronx. This event, apparently a signal of some kind, caused no damage or casualties, but city authorities say they are convinced it was not a prank. It is, of course, being closely studied for any possible link to the threat of armed aggression from the Soviet Union which has been posed by the sudden radio silence and blackout beyond the Iron Curtain. . . ."

Max Schoeller chuckled, the harsh sound of his voice grating through the cabin. It was a contemptuous sound, Jack thought, and again a stir of dislike for Schoeller moved in him.

". . . A few minutes after the incident, a number of crude leaflets floated to earth over the terminal building at La Guardia Airport. A packet of similar leaflets, which had not broken apart, fell to earth in a parking lot in the Bronx. New York City police, immediately calling on Federal authorities for consultation, have released no word on the contents of the leaflets. . . ."

"There must have been winds aloft," Jack said. "The timing was right but they fell much too far to the northeast."

". . . Meanwhile, Civil Defense officials announced that New York and other principal cities were in readiness to meet a nuclear attack. However, Air Force authorities, in a late

Washington bulletin, have just denied that this event, which they termed a 'possible prank,' is connected with the strange silence previously reported from the Soviet Union. And they repeat their earlier assurances that a three-hour warning will be given if an actual attack should develop. . . ."

"Hah!" Max Schoeller sat back abruptly in his seat. "Fools. A three-hour warning. Suppose *we* had been an enemy. Hah!"

"Well, they've got to do the best they can," Jack said. "Everybody awake and listening to the radio must be plenty upset already. Why would the government want to terrify them by telling about an unidentified flying object over New York that they couldn't shoot down?"

"Terror is what we must have." Schoeller took off the radio headset. "Terror is the only thing that will bring fools and jackals to heel. Not hate, not beautiful promises, not pain— nothing but terror, my friends."

"That's a little strong for my stomach," John Sloan said.

Schoeller spread his arms in a wide gesture. "Why else are we here, risking all? Doktor Alvin's general said it—to put the fear of God in them."

"But you don't believe in God." Jack's voice was quiet, detached.

"God is for fools who need him, not for me. For jackals afraid of him. But if down there they think up here is God, dropping the leaflets on them, let them think it. I play the role. I terrify them. Let them think it."

"Is that what we're doing?" Jack looked at John Sloan. "Are we playing God, Dud?"

"What else?" Max Schoeller answered. He handed Sloan some notes on a pad, then wormed out of the cramped pilot's seat. "Here is our course, position and speed. Now I must sleep an hour. Else I cannot even find Australia." Jack moved out of his way. Schoeller stopped in front of him, grinning, his

163

sharp little teeth showing beyond the thin split of his lips. "This God business—how do you say it? Great stuff? Eh? Is it not great stuff?"

"I'll call you in an hour, Max." Jack watched the little man move aft, then climbed into the empty pilot's seat. Sloan was busy at the radio controls. They were silent for several minutes. Then Jack spoke. "So we've been playing God all along?"

Sloan pursed his lips. "Well, you said you wanted to save the world, didn't you?"

"But that *is* God's business."

"I don't know." Sloan shook his head wearily. "I'm not a thinker, boy. I'm a doer. And this seemed to me the right thing to do. But I don't know."

"Well, the fat's in the fire," Jack said. "Max was right about that."

"Wait a second." Sloan pointed at the headset. "Here's more news."

Jack fumbled with the earphones. Another excited voice tumbled across the airwaves.

"Station KRAM interrupts this broadcast to bring you further news of the mysterious explosion over New York City early this morning. Earl Cranford, a Bronx gasoline station attendant, informed police that he was just closing his establishment when the detonation took place almost directly above it—at an estimated height of five hundred feet. Mr. Cranford said that a brilliant white flash accompanied the loud explosion, at just after one A.M. Eastern Daylight Time. A few seconds later, he said, the sky was filled with multicolored fireballs, pinwheels, silver sprays and sharp reports. 'It looked like the big moment of a fireworks show at Coney Island,' Mr. Cranford told reporters.

"Meanwhile, New York City police report that Army language experts have taken over the leaflets which apparently were released by the explosion. No word as to the contents of

164

the leaflets' message, which an unidentified source reported to be hand-lettered, has been given out.

"From Washington came further assurance, just a few moments ago, that our Armed Forces believe the nation is secure from attack. 'No hostile action is considered imminent,' an Air Force spokesman said, 'and we are confident of our ability to repel any that may develop.'

"Other Washington sources indicated that the Bronx incident is probably unrelated to earlier news from the Soviet Union—news which brought the Armed Forces into . . ."

"They're playing it cagey," Sloan said, as the announcer rattled on about the Russian radio silence. "No word about the UFO they fired on. And if they know about our show over Moscow, they're keeping that to themselves, too."

"Everybody's scared," Jack said. "Just like Max said. Is that the way we planned it, to scare everybody?"

"Not so scared." Sloan bent forward to check the compass. "Our side didn't order any blackout. I guess the explosion was so local and they tracked us out of there so fast, they figured they didn't need to chase us—or they realized that they couldn't."

"Well, I'm glad of it." Jack shook his head. "I don't find scaring people any fun, Dud. I don't find any of this like I thought it would be. And there's something else I guess I ought to tell you."

Sloan raised his eyebrows.

"I think I know what caused those drops in cabin pressure. You remember the night we kidnaped Hank and made the run over Cleveland?"

"Good God," Sloan said, "you mean that night you went crazy for a moment about that woman?"

Jack nodded. "I believe I sprung the hull of the ship when I was thrown against it. The operation of the bomb-bay doors puts a slight torque on the brace that supports them as they close. That brace is anchored to the hull just about where I

165

hit it. The damage probably allows the gasket sealing off the bomb-bay chamber to be dislocated just a fraction at one position—just enough—when the doors are closing."

"Well, let me give you a piece of advice," Sloan said. "You find that leak when we get to Australia and you help Max fix it, but don't you tell him where it came from. The way he loves this damn ship, he'd probably try to break your neck." He stopped, grinned a little. "I ought to do it myself."

"I know." Jack passed a hand tiredly across his forehead and then up over his stubby hair. "The truth is, Dud, I've been a fool from the start."

"Do you suppose there's a chance," Sloan said, fumbling in the pocket of his shirt for a cigarette, "that all of us have been?"

They caught up with the sun rapidly. At their altitude, it became daylight shortly after they headed out over the Pacific. Max Schoeller took over the controls again with the Solomon Islands in sight. He immediately found the beam of Darwin radio and followed it to the Australian coast. Over the city, he made a sharp turn, picking up a heading of one-eight-one. The base was approximately four hundred miles south of Darwin, where man had no cause to venture. The last leg was run on a time basis. A clock on the panel counted the minutes to a fifth of a second, and, at the proper moment, Schoeller stopped the forward motion and hovered. Then they fell vertically to thirty thousand feet. He snapped on a switch which transmitted an impulse to a small receiving set at their secret base. This receiver, a transistor outfit that could be left in continuous battery operation for months, turned on a transmitter that sent back a guiding signal.

Fifteen minutes after Schoeller heard that signal in his earphones they were placing camouflage panels around the *Argonaut* as it nestled safely on the ground.

12.

Dr. Alvin had never seen such turmoil in the Pentagon. The morning after the New York incident passed in hurried conferences, in film screenings, in dashing from office to office, service to service. He had to accompany General Waverly to a Joint Chiefs of Staff meeting, standing by for an hour in an anteroom while the four men met in absolute secrecy. Not one Pentagon employee in six, he reflected, knew anything about what had happened, other than newspaper accounts; yet some part of the excitement of those who did know communicated itself to all. Corridors fairly hummed with activity. Alvin marveled that this vast organization could react so quickly to the energizing effects of this new peril.

From the Joint Chiefs meeting, Waverly led him swiftly back to an Air Force conference room. Gathered there were Generals Strahan and Burton, Colonel Holcum, Navy Captain Johnson and members of his defense warning committee, and other officers of all services. It was a working group, Alvin saw at a glance; one that had met often and long together, and one to which Dick Waverly would naturally turn on a matter of aerial defense policy.

"All right," the general spoke crisply, striding across the front of the room with his accustomed swagger. "I've just come from the Joint Chiefs. It's my pigeon to tell them all I can, as soon as I can, about whatever the hell that thing was over New York. You people are supposed to have been finding all that out this morning. Now—is CIA here?"

"Yes, sir!" Colonel Crockett, a balding Army officer, snapped smartly to his feet.

"At ease. All you gentlemen at ease." Waverly turned his back on them. "I heard the New York leaflet read at Joint Chiefs, Crockett. Suppose you give this group the translation."

"Right away, sir." Crockett unlocked his brief case and took a paper from it. "It reads: 'We come as friends from another star to help you if you will help yourselves. Strife must cease on your planet. If not, we come to destroy you. Earlier in this shadow we spoke to the main city of the larger continent of your planet. Twenty-six shadows will pass before we come again.'

"That's it, gentlemen. As you know, General, that's just a reconstruction based on probability. Our language people identified the hand-lettering as being very close to Arabic. It was misspelled, very ungrammatical and almost illegible. But they think it's a good rendering of the sense of the thing."

Damn good, Alvin thought, congratulating himself on successful authorship.

"What else does CIA know about the message?"

Crockett shrugged. "Nothing helpful, I'm afraid. All the leaflets were identical, written in the same poor hand. A brownish paper was used and what appears to be some primitive ink. They're being traced. No fingerprints, bond marks or the like."

"In other words," Waverly said, "just the sort of thing somebody out of this world might come up with. The evidence indicates—and I hate like sin to admit it—that there's a faint chance we *are* dealing with something out of this world."

Alvin could only half believe what he heard. He had never thought that a man of so little imagination and such mundane mind as Dick Waverly would ever accept anything so alien as other-world creatures. Looking at their ruse now, Alvin wondered what wild romanticism, what flight of dreams could ever have led him to suggest it. Yet here was the hard-eyed, tough-talking general on the verge of a mental revolution that could make world history. Sweat broke out coldly all over the scientist's body. His eyes roved slowly about the conference table. How many of the rest of them did I underrate? he thought. Did I miscalculate it all so badly?

"What's the time element in this thing, Strahan?" Waverly said.

General Strahan stood up, clutching hastily at his jumble of notes and papers. "Well, sir, the interrupted message places the Moscow incident at midnight, their time. The New York incident was at 01:00 Daylight-Saving Time, or midnight sun time. That means, if it was the same aircraft in both cases —and the leaflet indicates this—it made the flight in seven hours." He paused, his face working itself into a fine jumble of wrinkles and lines, his hands moving nervously among his rustling papers. "No jet aircraft I know of could have made such a run and had the fuel left to go where we tracked this —this thing."

"Tracked it and lost it," Waverly said. "Johnson, what's new on that?"

Captain Johnson stood up, his head butting belligerently forward. He wore his air of persecution like a medal. "We didn't lose it, sir. It simply flew out of our radar coverage. It got away from us for a while after it had made an incredible ascent to avoid a missile the Navy launched just after the New York incident. But we picked it up again heading south a hundred miles off Florida. It turned west and crossed the Gulf of Mexico. By that time"—he cleared his throat and glared around the room—"Air Force had given orders not to attack it unless it violated United States air again. We watched it cross Yucatan and Mexico, then tracked it as far out into the Pacific as possible."

General Waverly's voice was soft, almost dreamy. "If Air Force had left Navy alone, could you have shot down that craft, Johnson?"

The beefy captain turned even redder. "Well, sir, I'm on a joint mission—not Navy duty—but I think—we'd have tried, sir."

Waverly's voice suddenly snapped out like a drill sergeant's. "You did try once. In violation of standing orders about

UFOs. It had not been established that it was hostile. It has not been so established yet. You gentlemen might care to know that the President is seeing the Chief of Naval Operations this afternoon. He will have something to say about that New York missile." He paused significantly. "The one the UFO outran."

"Is there any further word from the Soviets?" Strahan asked, standing up again.

Waverly pointed at General Burton. "Your department, Burt."

Burton spoke briskly. "They came back on the air, sir, at six A.M., their time. Not a word of explanation. Just started in a normal day's broadcasting. We're monitoring the hell out of them, of course, but all we're getting is Tschaikovsky, Prokofiev, Shostakovich and the usual propaganda."

"And as far as we know," Waverly said, beginning his restless pacing again, "there were no leaflets over there?"

Burton spread his hands in a questioning gesture. "Well, we know so little, sir. They could have dropped old whiskey bottles over there and we wouldn't know."

Waverly whirled, pounding a fist into the palm of his other hand. "No, dammit, we wouldn't!" He pounded his fist into his palm again, making a flat, slapping sound. "The truth is we don't know anything, gentlemen." He took a step nearer the table. "And all we can surmise is—is flying saucers from outer space!"

"I don't believe it!" Captain Johnson said. Every head in the room except Dick Waverly's turned immediately toward him. He had come within an inch of interrupting; he had certainly spoken out of turn; he was, worst of all, being contradictory. Even Henry Alvin, torn suddenly with dismay at Johnson's exclamation, was interested to see what Waverly would do.

"You don't believe it?" Waverly said, his words as gentle as a prayer, yet as cold as gun metal.

Johnson stood up. "I beg the general's pardon for interrupting, but I feel so strongly about this thing—well, I'd like to present my views, sir."

Waverly nodded. He turned toward Johnson, moving with the threatening grace of a stalking cat. "Make it good, then, Johnson. Make it very good."

"I'll try, sir. Ever since Dr. Alvin delivered an informal little lecture to this group a few weeks ago about the possibility of life existing in outer space, I've been studying that matter. Perhaps I have no imagination, or perhaps I haven't studied long enough. But frankly I just don't believe there is anything"—he swung an arm in a wide, upward sweep—"out there. I certainly don't believe such a thing is responsible for that message Crockett read. The odds are too long for me. *I just don't believe it!*"

"I don't think this is going to be good enough, Johnson." General Waverly's voice was almost amused now. But Alvin could not look away from Johnson. Here, at last, was what he had so fearfully expected from Waverly—the hard, empirical mind of a modern technician, versed in the abilities of a science that, no matter how lofty, could always be expressed in a formula. In the absence of those marching white lines of logic scrawled in equations on a blackboard, such a man as Johnson would simply disbelieve.

"I'm far from through, sir," Johnson said. "And I hope you understand that I'm not just trying to be doctrinaire. You remember the first days after we knew the Soviets had the atom bomb? There were all those articles in the press speculating that Red spies could come freely into this country carrying parts of bombs in suitcases, in their shoe soles and so on? Then they'd assemble them, plant them around the country timed for simultaneous explosion, and be able to wipe us out all at once."

"I remember," General Waverly said. "Make this as short as you can, Johnson."

171

"Yes, sir. My point is, sir, that we're assuming the Russians can't be very far ahead of us in aircraft. Well, I'm assuming that they can be. I know it's hard to admit, but I'm assuming they've built a craft that could do what General Strahan said it could do. I'm assuming they've built it just the way those bombs were supposed to be put together—from single parts made here and there and carried individually to some assembly point. I think that's how they kept it so secret until now. And I think they're trying to bluff us into some drastic sort of disarmament with this men-from-the-stars crap. I think . . ."

"That's enough, Johnson," Waverly snapped. "Your language is as distasteful as your logic. Major, would you be kind enough to screen the New York film?"

Alvin relaxed as the lights were dimmed. It was obvious now that Johnson was the real danger, not Waverly. His obstinacy was almost appealing, perhaps because, in other circumstances, his position was the one Alvin himself might have taken. But his reasoning about the Russians was as far off base as it had been on his earlier visit to the scientist's office.

When the lights came up after the film of the radar-sighting in New York, which had led to the firing of the Navy missile, Johnson was on his feet again. General Waverly eyed him coldly but nodded curt recognition.

"Sir, I apologize for any offense I gave previously. However, I would like to point out the vertical pattern followed by this craft. It is exactly the same as observed from Patuxent Naval Air Station some weeks ago. I think it adds to my theory because it shows a definite technique on the part of the flyers. It even seems to me to reflect a method of training. I submit that that indicates a mentality at least of the same nature as ours."

"It indicates a mentality of some kind," General Waverly said, his voice dry but no longer unpleasant. "Your theory will be considered, Johnson. At the moment, I must say I lean toward something more—unusual. But it will be considered."

172

"That's all I ask, sir." Johnson sat down. Alvin looked at him with a bitter respect that was almost envy. This man alone was pushing for recognition of the earth-origin of the unidentified craft. I wish he were in my shoes, Alvin thought, and I were in his. The thought startled him so much that for a moment he put his hands to his eyes. What have we done? he thought. What have we done?

An armed sentry entered, followed by a courier with a message for General Waverly. The general read it swiftly. His lips pulled back in a tight grin.

"Well, gentlemen," he said, "perhaps we shall have us an earth-type war after all."

A strange, inarticulate sense of having committed an unforgivable offense filled Henry Alvin. He suddenly decided to confess his role in the mystery and beseech their tolerance. Then he heard the inevitable cry of treason ring in his ears. This sense of a word spoken that could never be retrieved made him feel like a man facing a firing squad. It seemed to him that Dick Waverly's cold eyes sought him out and probed his guilt.

"I have here a précis of another message to the State Department from the Soviet foreign office." Waverly paused professionally, gauging his effect. Alvin was irritated by the obvious show of excitement all around the room. Why do they fall for his affectations? he thought angrily.

"The précis reads: 'The Government of the Union of Soviet Socialist Republics most strongly protests the violation of its territorial air by craft of the Air Force of the Government of the United States of America, which took place early this morning. The Soviet Government further strongly protests the demonstration above its capital which accompanied this violation of its air. Conclusive proof that the craft involved represented the Government of the United States is furnished by a mutilated but undestroyed label from a piece of United States Air Force radio equipment found among the debris of

173

the explosion, which could have caused loss of life and great panic. Such provocative incidents cannot be tolerated by the Soviet Government. An immediate explanation and proper steps toward restitution are demanded.' "

Waverly's voice fell silent. No one spoke. All around the long conference table men sat as though stunned. Henry Alvin stared straight ahead at the white movie screen still open on the wall. Pressure rose from his chest into his head, and for a moment he thought he would lose consciousness.

Then, to his horror, he heard the sound of his own impassioned voice.

"That goddamned altimeter!"

Dick Waverly's head snapped up as though bee-stung; and in a second every eye, puzzled, surprised, beginning to be suspicious, was fixed on the scientist. The pressure was gone from his head as quickly as it had come. The sense of irrevocability vanished, lost in the challenge of his frustrated outcry.

"What was that?" Waverly said. "What did you say?"

It's all up, Alvin was thinking, his brain suddenly working as smoothly and efficiently as a fine engine. That shoots the spaceman idea. You'll just have to save what you can. Fight for what's left.

"Alvin?" Waverly's voice was as soft, as threatening, as it had been earlier with Captain Johnson. But there was no theatricality about him now. He took a step closer, his face gone stern and rigid.

"Sorry, General." Alvin stood up, careful to appear as casual as possible. "Until you read that message I hadn't quite realized that I really believed the outer space theory. I think I must have liked it." He grinned at the circle, wrinkling the sides of his face, feigning an air of relaxation. "Even at a time like this I—well, I was looking forward to meeting somebody from space. Then that message. And all I could think was just those Russians again."

"But why an altimeter?"

Alvin spread his hands. "Simple logic. A piece of radio equipment, they say. A radio altimeter could make a perfect timer for an aerial bomb."

"Hump." Waverly blinked once, twice. "Well, that makes sense. Only I believe I'd say it's just those *damn* Russians again, Hank. That's the way I'd put it."

Relieved laughter was heard as Alvin sat down, and secret exhilaration broke momentarily through his despair. How eager they were to move toward some concept their minds could accept! Even if there was to be war with Russia in an hour, that would be less terrifying to men who, a moment before, had sat face to face with the unknown.

"I'll read the rest of this now," General Waverly said, holding up another sheet of paper. "It's a transcript of the pertinent parts of a telephone conversation of less than an hour ago between the Secretary of State and the American Ambassador in Moscow. He called to give this précis of the protest the Soviets are making via regular diplomatic channels. Here's the rest of his conversation with the Secretary." He cleared his throat, swaggering once again across the room before reading.

" 'I must speak to the Secretary of State.'

" 'This is the Secretary.'

" 'I have just received a most serious message from the Russian Foreign Minister, sir. Immediate action must be taken. He cleared this call through to you himself.'

" 'What is the message?'

" 'I will read it.' " Waverly looked up from the paper, shaking it. "That's where he read the message I've just read you gentlemen. When he finished, the Secretary said:

" 'Are they taking this position in good faith?'

" 'The Foreign Minister appeared very serious and apparently quite disturbed, sir. I might say he seemed personally angry.'

" 'Do you believe this evidence is genuine?'

" 'I was presented with it. It appeared to be so.'

" 'Could it have been planted?'

" 'I have no way to tell for certain. If so, it is certainly a most elaborate deception.'

" 'Do they know of a similar episode over New York last night?'

" 'From the radio. But it merely serves to confirm their suspicions, sir. The Foreign Minister stated explicitly that no aircraft could have made such a flight so fast without refueling. He believes there were two, both of United States origin.'

" 'Were leaflets dropped there?'

" 'Apparently so, sir. The police are busy searching them out.'

" 'And do they—this may seem facetious—are they giving any credence to the possibility of—this idea of creatures from beyond the earth?'

" 'Not after the discovery of the label. I'm afraid not.'

" 'I see. I see. This is most serious then, Mr. Ambassador.'

" 'Indeed it is. In my years here I've never seen them so upset. Can you possibly give me an explanation of this matter, sir?'

" 'I cannot. Until you called we had been under the impression that an attack on us might be imminent.'

" 'Well, may I say, sir, that such a threat is now very likely. I sense a definite mood of belligerence concerning last night's incident. They're feeling their oats and they aren't likely to take lightly what they think is an insult.'

" 'We shall have instructions for you as soon as possible, Mr. Ambassador.' "

Waverly threw the papers on the conference table.

"All right, boys," he said. "Let's forget about Buck Rogers and get down to brass tacks."

"General," Captain Johnson said, "I hate to get up again but I think we're all agreed that we've got to act quickly here. We can't stand on ceremony."

Waverly glowered at him. "I suppose not. What is it this time?"

Johnson kicked his chair back and strode out into the middle of the room, his hands clasped behind his back. It occurred to Alvin, watching him apprehensively, that there was more than a little of the quality of Dick Waverly in this man. Give him years of directing men, of real power, and that belligerence might mellow into authority. If Johnson lasted at all, he might go far.

"I suppose it must have occurred to everybody here, sir, just as it did to the Secretary of State, that the label is a plant."

"I suppose it must have, Captain. Unless some shavetail has gotten out of hand, *we* certainly didn't drop it over there."

"Right, sir. We have to assume it's a plant. But carry that a step further. If it was a plant, then they really have developed a super weapon. We know that because we've tracked it on radar. Nothing we know of could match it for rate of climb and maneuverability, to say nothing of some of the maneuvers it's apparently capable of."

"Good logic," Waverly said. "However, it assumes a very complicated bit of scheming on the part of the Russians. Staging the demonstration over Moscow, the blackout, the leaflets and all that. I know they're slick as a whistle but why did they have to be? If they've got a craft like that, why not just come over here and deliver an ultimatum?"

"Exactly," Johnson said. "All their past history indicates they would do just exactly that if they had such a weapon."

The game is really up, Alvin thought. Johnson's deadly reasoning, so surprising in one who had seemed at first glance more lion than fox, could lead him only to one place.

"Are you suggesting, Captain Johnson, that this aircraft isn't Russian?"

"I'm suggesting, sir, it isn't logical that it could be Russian and we know it isn't ours. Now, how a group of private citizens could develop any such thing is beyond me, but a process of elimination leaves us with that. It leaves us inescapably with that."

"Good God," Waverly said. "I believe I'd rather have the spacemen."

Alvin went numb.

"Captain Johnson"—Waverly addressed him with military stiffness—"I must say that this is a convincing argument. I shall present it to the Joint Chiefs at once. Whether the State Department will wish to use it in their reply to the Soviets, I can't say. In the meantime, I want you to take immediate steps toward blanketing the air over this country with radar."

"Yes, sir." Johnson sat down, looking, for the first time since Alvin had known him, at least faintly mollified.

"I don't mean just the coast. Pull every portable piece of gear into use. Comb out the warehouses. I'll see that all the other services coöperate. I mean I want the sky above this country to buzz. Every last square inch of it."

"Yes, sir." Johnson began making notes.

"Because there's one thing you didn't mention, Captain." Waverly wheeled about in mid-stride, staring at the beefy Navy officer, his hand coming up, his finger half pointing.

"What was that, General?" Johnson said, almost coming to attention.

"That was a piece of American gear they found over there. *American* gear, Johnson. And if you're right, then Americans made this thing. And I'll bet my bottom dollar they made it somewhere here in America—somewhere they'll eventually come back to, before or after this second appearance they threaten to make. Do you follow me, Johnson?"

"I follow you," Johnson said. "The air's going to buzz, sir, I promise you."

"Every inch of it, Johnson. Every goddamn inch."

And there isn't a way in the world I can warn them, Alvin thought. Not a way in the world.

Yellow sand blew against the two small tents they had erected. Only a few scrawny bushes eked out a dwarfed existence on the hot, flat earth. When the *Argonaut* was away from the Australian base they never left the tents above ground. They took no chances. It was very unlikely that any man, even an Australian aborigine, would venture to this part of the vast wasteland, four hundred miles from civilization. There was no water, no plant or animal life of value; only the dreary, baked expanse of desert. That was why they had chosen this place, despite the inconvenience of bringing in all their supplies. These they hid in a large vault beneath the surface. Only a tiny wire, the antenna of their radio fix, extended above the earth when they departed.

Max Schoeller gave Jack Baker and John Sloan little chance to succumb to the inertia of this Australian back country. There was much to be done, and with German energy he directed them. Almost immediately they found that their situation was much worse than they had thought.

Jack found the faulty bracket near the bomb bay on their first day aground. Schoeller studied it carefully.

"We can fix that here, can't we?" asked Jack. Schoeller only muttered something in German and went back to his survey of the left rear rocket.

Discovery of the engine trouble was a more involved matter. It took them almost two days. In that type of rocket engine—it used alcohol and liquid oxygen—alcohol is circulated through a hollow section of the propulsion cone. This tends to heat the alcohol for ready combustion and to cool the cone where extremely high temperatures are produced. Schoeller discovered that a pinhole leak had developed in this cone, on the aft side of the throat where the thrust of the engine was produced. Under these circumstances a portion of the alcohol fuel was lost in the cone as it tapered toward the exhaust. The leak actually caused opposition to the thrust of the engine.

"And when we used full power in maximum climb and speed over New York," Schoeller said, "we compounded the damage. Without that, we would have only a minor leak. As it is . . ." He shrugged and turned away.

That night, around the fitful glow of a campfire, the three men held a council of war. It was ironic, Jack thought, that in the shadow of the most advanced aerial craft in the world, they still sat on the bare earth around open flames, as warriors had done all through history. In a sense, Jack thought, it was well that some things never changed—that age-old habits kept men in some ways the captives of their own past.

"Well, gentlemen," Schoeller said, leaning forward to light a cigarette from a burning splinter, the orange glow of the fire leaping grotesquely across the harsh planes of his face, "We have just twenty-four days. And a great deal of work to do."

"Well, now." John Sloan put his head back and talked into the sky. "A reconsideration of this whole thing might be in order, Max."

"Reconsider-a-tion?" Across the fire, Jack could see Schoeller's thin body go tense.

"You've heard the radio broadcasts." Sloan still spoke upward, not looking at them. "I don't know what went wrong, but something did, God knows. We thought we were going to force two heavyweights into getting along with each other. Instead of that, we seem to have thrown them literally at each other's throats, right now."

Jack stood up, spreading his chilly hands against the warmth of the fire. "We figured it wrong, Max. We figured it wrong from the start."

Schoeller chuckled; a dry, quiet sound not unlike the

181

crackle of the flames. "You Americans." He chuckled again. "You are incredible. One day you are all hope and energy and wearing the big smile. The next day the whole situation —it is so terrible—one wonders if one can survive."

"I don't deny that, but I'll tell you another thing about Americans, Max. We try to adjust. We try to make sense, all the time. God knows, we go wrong, but when we do we try to understand the situation and adjust."

"Precisely. But sometimes one must ignore the situation. One has something to do. One must do it. The situation is simply a difficulty."

"Not this time." Jack put his hands in his pockets. "This time the situation is one hell of a lot of responsibility."

"So?" Schoeller's voice was almost unconcerned. "In twenty-four days perhaps it changes again. Who knows?"

"What Jack's trying to say"—John Sloan spoke carefully as though he were reading the words by the firelight—"is that we don't think we ought to make that second run. We think we've done enough damage."

The silence of the great desert settled down above the waning fire like fog. It bore heavily on the three men, and it seemed to Jack Baker in that long moment when no one spoke that the fire grew dim.

"We will go," Max Schoeller said. "We must terrify them again. Again and again and again, if necessary. We must rule them with terror."

He spoke quite simply, so simply that the traces of accent were almost lost on his tongue. Each of the words, like something cold, made Jack Baker flinch. Now, at last, he knew Schoeller. He knew him too well. He turned his head, staring off into the blackness of the desert, not wanting to watch the derisive light of the fire playing on Schoeller's face.

"That's wrong," John Sloan said. "We can't do that, Max. We can't go along."

"But I am captain." Schoeller's voice was hardly audible. "I say we must go."

Baker felt the nails bite into his palms as his hands clenched into fists. There was no use arguing with Schoeller. Nor was there any possibility that he and his uncle could surrender to such ideas. He tried diversionary tactics.

"Besides," he said, "that rocket is in bad shape, Max. Even if we had welding equipment here, we couldn't do anything with it. We need an annealing furnace. And you know as well as I do that if we get over New York or Moscow again with that thing bucking like it did the last time, we're not liable to get back."

"Let us not speak of danger as though we were children." For the first time Schoeller's voice took on a hint of irritation. "If you good Christians are to die, do you not believe you will be saved by your Jesus? Me, I do not believe a man improves enough by dying to be worth saving. . . . But I am not afraid."

Damn your soul, Jack thought. The picture of Schoeller's face gloating over the radio broadcasts came swiftly before him. He kicked the brands of the fire aside with one angry sweep of his foot and stepped through them, looming over the small, still figure of the little German.

"I didn't start out to set up any airborne Fourth Reich, Max. I started with one silly idea and I even had little enough sense to put it into words. I wanted to save the world. Well, it took your twisted mind to set me straight. To make me see we really had set out to play God. Now look what we've done. The last war may be starting right this minute because we three—and Hank Alvin, too—thought we could do what Christ couldn't. Well, I've had it, Max. I'm through."

The great silence fell over them once again.

John Sloan broke it. "I guess that goes for me, too."

Jack moved a step nearer the silent, hunched form on the

ground, until he was looking almost straight down. "And it goes for you, Max. You're through, too."

"So?" Max said, the scar on his face suddenly flashing red like a fresh saber wound. "You are like all Americans. When all else is gone, for you there is always the bullying. Always the big talk."

"Call it what you want. Just believe I mean it."

"Well, now." John Sloan stood up, making an elaborate thing of dusting off the seat of his pants. "I don't see any point in all this pulling and hauling. The fact is, Max is outvoted and the two of you might as well both get off your high horses. There's a lot to do even if we have changed our plans. We've got to decide"—he sighed ironically—"the same old question we had to decide before we got into this scrape. What are we going to do with the brain child?"

The two men stared at each other through the darkness, no longer brightened by the puny fire. But each knew what was on the other's face, what was in the other's mind. And Jack knew what had to be said, even though it would have no more permanence than those brilliant fire brands one thrust of his foot had sent dying into the night.

"It's all right with me." Jack stepped back and Schoeller got to his feet. "Let bygones be bygones, Max."

"So," Max said. "We will see."

"Now then." Sloan became briskly efficient. He turned to Jack. "I personally don't think that shoring-up you fellows did on the bomb-bay brace is worth anything. And the rocket is certainly beyond the facilities here."

A wild joy sprang suddenly into Jack Baker's heart. Perhaps it was over. Perhaps it was truly over. Perhaps it could all go weightlessly into the past, becoming in the eyes of men one of those mysteries that dot the course of history. Perhaps it had not, after all, been a permanent step. And if not, he could go home to Sandy.

"So we'll have to go back to Nevada," Sloan said. "Fix the

old bird up and decide something once and for all. Eh, Max?"

But Schoeller was no longer with them. In the silence that followed Sloan's words, they heard his slow, precise steps going toward the *Argonaut*.

These were bad days for Henry Alvin, although he had become an accomplished conspirator and found his role simple enough to play. He followed with obvious admiration Johnson's quick mobilization of the country's tremendous sky-watching facilities, electronic and human. He listened with interest when Waverly confided that the American Ambassador in Moscow had been filled in on Pentagon thinking, which was completely sold on the idea first advanced by Johnson. It was, however, generally called the "Waverly theory." He searched the newspapers avidly as their black headlines announced the most severe Russian-American impasse since the Berlin crisis. He began, at Waverly's insistence, a study of the New York incident, developing all the information known or deducible about the craft and its "bomb," as preparation for a possible second visit.

But all this was window dressing. In his heart, he lived sickly. He blamed himself. A good man, John Sloan had said, a wise man. That was what they had sought in him, and he had responded with a scheme worthy of the most cloistered ivory tower. He had yielded to a romantic idealism which, like any idealism not firmly seated in probability, was deceptive in its simplicity. He had ignored the poignant lessons of a lifetime and had listened to a siren.

Four nights after the New York incident he sat alone in his apartment, staring at the John Marin water color above a heavy, straight chair. Behind it was his wall safe. That safe fascinated him. He could not look away from the picture, nor could he free himself from the question of what he should do with the papers Sloan had promised to send him, once they were received. Should he take them immediately to Waverly?

That could be absolution for him, but he rejected the thought. This did not seem to be the proper moment to bring the papers to light and thus confuse the situation further.

He knew from his daily conferences with Waverly's air defense group that time enough had elapsed for adequate intelligence to be developed in the Soviet Union, and that the Pentagon was now confident no immediate surprise attack was threatened. What the Soviets were concerned about, it was clear to inner circles, was the incredible new craft. They, too, knew it existed; and, knowing that, they were not likely to strike until they tried to appraise our strength with this new weapon. Their diplomatic storm had been raised to cover their own confusion, gain time and seek information. Several weeks from now, however, the situation could become extremely dangerous. The Washington administration, acting on this theory, was being cagey. It was not denying the possibility that its forces were in possession of a super aircraft; it was simply denying the demonstration over Moscow. Meanwhile, Johnson, acting as executive officer of what Alvin knew was one of the greatest electronic projects in history, patiently baited his trap.

None of this solved Henry Alvin's personal dilemma. He could not communicate with the men of the *Argonaut,* either to warn them or to dissuade them from their second venture. Nor, he felt sure, could he offer them protection by disclosing their identity. He stared gloomily through the swirling grays of the water color, his glasses hanging from his limp hand, seeing nothing of it but the imaginary outline of the safe it concealed. A tap at his door interrupted his heavy thoughts. He got up, taking a last look at the water color, and went to the door. A tall woman stood in the shadowy hall of the apartment house.

"Dr. Alvin?"

"Yes?" The woman came closer. She was blond and smartly dressed in a gray suit and a white blouse.

"You don't remember me, do you? I'm Sandy Carlson."

"From Crestview!" Alvin held out both hands, a fine web of wrinkles springing from the corners of his eyes. "Now I know I'm getting old and forgetful."

She laughed, putting her hands in his, letting him lead her into the apartment. "Well, that was a rather hilarious occasion. Anyone could forget a face from that night."

"Sit down, please." He indicated a chair. "I really do apologize. I just wasn't expecting such a pleasant visitor. Can I get you a drink?"

"Thanks, no. I'll come right to the point, Doctor. I . . ."

"You called me Hank at Crestview. After all, I think Jack and I told you things we wouldn't tell our own mothers."

"I hope you wouldn't!"

They laughed and he sat down, too. She was the first non-official person he had talked to since the night the courier had come for him with Waverly's summons, and he found not only her blond good looks and her long crossed legs pleasant but also the simple fact of a social presence. It was as though he had removed a tight uniform.

"I will come to the point," she said again. "Hank, how can I get in touch with Jack?"

My God, Alvin thought, as though things aren't bad enough. But he merely raised his eyebrows. "Why, in California, I suppose."

She reached in her handbag and took out a cigarette. Alvin leaned forward with a desk lighter. Above its flame her clear eyes met his.

"I might as well be honest, Hank." She leaned back in the chair, tossing back her head to blow a jet of smoke toward the ceiling. "Jack and I—saw each other several times after Crestview. He told me why the two of you met there."

Alvin casually put his hand to his mouth as his heart leaped. Sandy waved the cigarette impatiently. "I know I don't have any business saying all this, but I have to. He told me he was going overseas on an experimental project that he had arranged with you. No more than that. He couldn't say when he'd be back. He said"—she put the cigarette in her mouth, took it out without drawing on it and crushed it with one swift gesture in an ash tray by her chair—"that he might not come back at all if the experiment went wrong."

"That's all he told you?" Alvin noticed the bitter way one corner of her mouth curled down. A lifetime of personal observation had taught him to watch for expressions of personality and he prided himself that he could instantly distinguish between such a movement or look and a casual gesture.

"I—liked Jack Baker. He seemed to have something important on his mind. I was in Washington for several days and tried to call you. No telephone listed. No address. So I got my spies out and found you."

The scientist looked down at his hands. He did not remember from Crestview that Sandy Carlson had been an extraordinarily good-looking woman. But now, from the corner of his eye, he could see that she was very nearly beautiful. There was a vivid, eager light in her face. Poignant sadness settled on him as he thought of the misguided gallantry with which Jack Baker had marched off to his private war, leaving so much behind. He shook his head, suddenly exhausted for the first time since his crisis had begun.

"I'm not available to the general public. How did you find me?"

"I'm not the general public, Hank. Where is Jack?"

He reached across the incalculable gulf that separated them and took her hand. It lay in his, strong and capable but cold. "I would tell you if I could, my dear. I simply don't know."

She frowned. "Can you say—Hank, what do you think? Will he—be back?"

He looked at her directly, his eyebrows pulled together. "I can't tell you that, either. It's another thing I just don't know."

Something slackened in her. It was a disturbing sight, like

watching all the lights go out, one by one, in a great building.

"Is it so important then? Whatever it is he's doing? Is it worth so much more than he is?"

Alvin stood up and went to the cabinet where he kept his liquor. "If you don't need a drink, I do." He looked at her questioningly.

"A little brandy, then."

He poured for both and carried the glasses back to their chairs. She took hers without expression and drank it instantly.

"It's better if you sip it," he said, smiling as he stood above her.

Sandy put her glass down with a decisive little click. "I don't sip." She stood up and walked to the door, the corner of her mouth moving in a way that made him wince for her. "Drop me a penny post card at Elliott Freight Lines, Cleveland, if you hear from him."

He held the door for her, wanting to answer but not knowing how.

"If he comes back I'll let you know, Sandy. Security be damned."

"He won't; not in time. I think I knew that all along."

He frowned. "In time?"

"Never mind. I'll appreciate it if you'll tell me anything you can. I really will."

"You're going to be in town a while?"

"A week or so, off and on."

"Perhaps we could have dinner some night."

"You know," Sandy said, "I like talking to you. Would you like to pick me up tomorrow evening maybe? I'm at the Hay-Adams."

When she had gone, the great weariness was still with him. He closed the door and leaned momentarily against it. He had slept very little since the New York incident. He lurched across the room and fell on the sofa and slept instantly. He was still there when the courier awakened him at 4:30 A.M. and gave him General Waverly's summons to the Pentagon.

189

It was a bleak dawn ride across the city in the uncomfortable rear seat of the second-grade Air Force sedan. The driver's young neck rose rigidly in front of him, and it seemed to Alvin that the steel walls of the car were moving gradually in from all directions, like a room in a story by Edgar Allan Poe. He was almost glad to arrive at the great sprawling white building, ablaze with light, even though he thought he knew why he had been called.

Waverly was waiting for him in his private office, his feet cocked jauntily on his big desk, a huge cigar roving unlit between his pleased lips.

"Well, well, well," he shouted as Dr. Alvin entered. "There's my old space cadet himself. Hank, my boy"—he swung his feet to the floor and stood up, taking the cigar from his mouth with an expansive sweep of his arm—"it's all over but the shouting."

"All over?" Alvin felt his knees weakening. He leaned against a huge globe, feeling it turn slightly under his cold hand.

"Just about." Waverly came around the desk, pacing with his hands behind him, like a man who had inherited a block of General Motors. "Area Eight, my boy, has just called in the biggest, fattest, prettiest bogy you ever saw. Coming straight down"—he paused, winking—"somewhere in Nevada."

"Nevada?" Alvin put his entire weight against the globe.

"They picked it up at Wendover Air Force Base and tracked it right in till it fell off the screen. Practically the whole damned Marine Corps is on the way out there. One thing Marines are always good for is places like Nevada. They ought to turn up something by noon. Now what do you think of that?"

The scientist straightened. He looked carefully at the smooth surface of the globe, then at Dick Waverly's smiling, triumphant face.

"Well," he said, "that's what we were waiting for."

14.

Walking the earth of America again was like striding the streets of heaven, Jack thought. Above him, the great sky bowl was as vast as it had been in Australia, but at his feet the Nevada earth was more mountainous and forbidding. A bright blue sky seemed to merge into the barren hills. The underbrush was much thicker than in Australia, but it was much nearer to humanity and therefore less protective. He thought of Reno, not so far away, and of other places where people were unconcerned about the *Argonaut* adventure. But someone, with a stronger purpose, might come looking for them. This was not the back country of Australia. Although it was the heart of desolation in America, no place in the U.S.A. could be more than a few minutes from detection.

It was early in the day but a fierce desert sun was well above the horizon. Far away toward the west Jack could see the Ely and Quinn Canyon Ranges of mountains. Wheeler Peak to the north was gleaming freshly in the morning light. To the east was a monotony of small, rugged, crenelated hills. They look as though someone has been using the shears on them, he thought, rubbing his hand along his cheek and across his ragged, roughly cut hair.

This is home earth, home sky, Jack thought. They exerted the pull of a magnet, and he wondered how he had ever been able to contemplate leaving them. He thought of Sandy, far across the continent in Cleveland. Just being in America was like being with her again. It was odd, the way a man's loyalties got all mixed up between people and earth and abstractions. A man could never tell at any moment what was acting upon him most strongly, what might lie hidden but powerful behind the curtain of consciousness. Patriotism is the last refuge of the scoundrel, according to Dr. Johnson, but Jack Baker had known men who died believing they were dying for a nation.

Six feet in front of where he sat on a man-sized rock, a square section of the desert floor suddenly rose on oiled hinges. John Sloan climbed laboriously from the concealed trap door opening into their underground hangar. He stood up, breathing deeply of the fresh air.

"Good to be home," Sloan said. "I feel like I could sing a hymn and give a short prayer of thanksgiving. I tell you the truth, there were a couple of times when I wondered if we'd ever see America again."

Jack moved over and made room for him on the rock. "What do you think, Dud? Has Max said anything about his plans?"

Sloan shook his head, grinning a little. "Not a word. But I don't think he's convinced not to make the second run, if that's what you mean."

"A little taste of power, Dud. That's all he had. And look how he's changed. Look what it did to him."

"I don't know." Sloan tossed a pebble at a lizard. "Men his age don't change a lot. I reckon we had him wrong to begin with. I mean it must have been in him all the time and we just didn't see it."

"Look, Dud. Suppose we've really started a war. What in hell can we do?"

Sloan contemplated the silent desert. Heat waves were beginning to shimmer from its vast surface. "I don't think we've started a war, Jack. According to the radio, the Russians are talking big but they aren't doing anything. If they haven't started it by now, I don't believe they will."

"I can't understand it." Jack's shoulders slumped dejectedly. "Our idea wasn't *that* bad. Apparently they didn't fall for the men from space angle."

"How do we know what they're thinking? Remember, all

we hear on the radio is what they want the public to hear. For all we know, somebody might have found a part of your bomb and identified it."

Jack's face turned crimson. "No, sir. Not a chance. There couldn't have been anything left big enough to do them any good. Not if I did my work right."

"That's what I said." Sloan stood up, thinning his lips. "Maybe you didn't. God knows, everything else has gone wrong. Let's go get the final verdict on that engine from Max."

They found the little German hard at work on the rocket engine. He had not left the hangar even for a breath of air since their arrival from Australia, having given his attention first to the bomb-bay doors.

"What's the story?" Sloan and Baker crowded up for a look at the engine cone.

"The leak is much bigger." Schoeller wiped sweat from his forehead. "I think we can no longer trust any simple repairs we might make. We must replace the engine."

"Well, we've got a spare here." Sloan looked sourly at Jack. "That's a hell of a job, though."

Jack nodded. "But we'd better get on it. I'd hate to be trapped with the *Argonaut* crippled."

"Not much chance," Sloan said. "Even if they spotted us on the coastal radar, Max probably lost them before we got here. They'd have to search the entire area with helicopters and those electronic 'diving rods.' I'd sooner look for a needle in a haystack."

"So?" Schoeller said. "Yet I think Jack is right. We cannot rest easily while we are immobilized."

Jack began taking off his shirt. "Let's turn to it, Dud."

For two hours they worked without a break until the old engine had been removed and the new one uncrated. Finally Schoeller motioned for them to relax.

"We will rest for ten minutes," he announced.

The three men sat down wearily and leaned against the

concrete wall of the hangar. Jack and Schoeller lighted cigarettes but no one spoke. After five minutes Jack snubbed his cigarette on the concrete floor and stood up to stretch.

"I have an idea," he said. "Did you see that big satellite as we were coming over from Australia, the one our boys made so much fuss about getting up to three thousand miles?"

"Sure did," Sloan replied. "Just think of all the fuss the Russians made when they tossed that first little Sputnik up five hundred and sixty miles. Hell, this thing is ten feet in diameter and weighs six tons according to that radio broadcast in Australia. No rocket attached, either."

"Max," Jack said, "maybe they've got radar-tracking equipment in that one. Maybe they got a fix on the *Argonaut*."

"Maybe so," Max said without interest. His eyes squinted almost shut as he reached up with his left hand to remove the short stub of his cigarette. He looked at his watch. "It was orbiting over the Indian Ocean when we came down to Mesatron. Now we must go back to work."

"Look, Max, if you could push the *Argonaut* that high and pick it up, we might still save the men-from-space idea."

"That's asking a lot, Jack," Sloan said.

Max was on his feet now and had started toward the ship. He looked back at them. "Not too much for me or the *Argonaut*. If we rise safely through the ionosphere we can go to the moon and land there. With full-capacity rocket fuel we can accelerate to thirty thousand miles an hour or more if necessary. But satellites do not interest me. I think we may still decide to make the second run"—a devilish grin crossed his face—"after your nerves have settled a bit."

John Sloan looked him straight in the eye. "Not a chance, Max. Forget that."

"Very well," he said with a shrug and turned to Jack. "But I cannot capture your satellite. The bomb-bay doors are only five feet across when fully opened."

Three hours later they had the new engine in place. Then

Schoeller called a halt. The three men walked out to the small kitchen for a bottle of beer.

"This is as much as we need to do until I return," Schoeller said.

Sloan raised his eyebrows. "Where are you going?"

"You saw for yourself." Schoeller pointed to the old engine. "The fittings are badly corroded. The tubing is old. Why put on a new engine if we must trust to such materials?"

"Don't you have fittings and tubing here?"

Schoeller sucked at his beer bottle. "Not in this hangar, no. In the storeroom on the other side of our mining claim, yes. It will take me two hours to go and two more to come back. Perhaps three. I will have a load on the return journey."

Jack Baker looked at his uncle. He was careful to allow no expression on his face. What Schoeller said was true enough. He himself had helped stock the storeroom and the fittings were there all right. But the thought of Schoeller going off alone disturbed him. Since the night of their discussion in Australia, he had had the feeling that the wiry little physicist was waiting, biding his time, patiently holding himself in check until . . . And he knew Max Schoeller was not the sort of man to default on his own ideas or surrender his dominance without a struggle.

"Why waste your time rambling around the desert?" he said. "You could stay here and supervise Dud while the two of you get the new engine ready. I'll go get the fittings. I believe I'd make better time, anyway."

"So?" Schoeller shook his head. "Suppose you come upon someone? There is little chance, but we must consider it. The fools around here are used to me, the crazy old prospec-*tor*. They will think nothing. But of you . . ." He shrugged. "I will leave in five minutes."

"It would be better to let Jack go." John Sloan carefv̓̉ studied the concrete floor under his feet.

Max Schoeller chuckled. "Ah, my friends, you are

You think I will not return, eh? That I will hurry off with my secrets?" He chuckled again, studying their faces with an almost obscene glee. Then, abruptly, his face became blank as a wall. "I promise I will come back. I have no other place to go."

"Listen, Max." Jack put his hand on Schoeller's knee. "You and I—we worked like hell out there in that secret lab all those years. We got along when we ought to have driven each other crazy."

"That is so."

"Well, maybe we don't see eye to eye now. Maybe you want one thing and I want another. Maybe I talked pretty rough back there in Australia. I apologize for that."

"It does not matter."

"I hope not. But what does matter is the ship." Jack jerked a thumb over his shoulder toward the *Argonaut*. "The things we've done with that ship represent something, Max. There hasn't been any greater achievement since they set off that first A-bomb at Los Alamos. Your gravity reactors. The hull we built. The liquid air-cooling system. The safeguards against radiation from the atomic power plant. Why, man, you know we've solved problems the whole world is working on—you and I—Max, we've *got* to stick together now. We've failed once. That doesn't mean we don't have a chance yet to . . ."

"To save the world?" Schoeller's grin was almost satanic. Looking at it, Jack knew he had not gotten through to him, knew that he could never again trust Max Schoeller.

"We can't save the world, Max. But we've still got a good [...] the world something better than it has."

[...] igarette from his pocket, placed it be- [...]ps. "That is our job, eh?"

[...]'t it all men can do? Isn't it our only [...]tter aircraft—better buildings—better [...]hing?"

"But not better people?" The satanic grin again etched itself across Schoeller's face.

"That isn't our department," Jack said. "We're just people ourselves."

"I don't think you can make people better by scaring them, anyway." John Sloan struck a match on the concrete floor and held it to Schoeller's cigarette. His long white hair glimmered in the feeble light. "But can't we all agree that Jack is right, that the main thing is to use the *Argonaut* in the best possible way?"

"Precisely." Schoeller stood up. "I go now, my friends." The cigarette bobbed jauntily up from the corner of his mouth, reminding Jack fleetingly of those old wartime pictures of cavalier German generals with their long, flamboyant holders and their high boots. "I promise. I will come back."

But Jack's lack of confidence remained. Without speaking, he watched Schoeller slowly climb the ladder to the trap door and then disappear.

For nearly four hours Jack and his uncle puttered around the hangar, relaxing as much as possible in order to face more alertly the unknown problems that awaited them. By then it was late afternoon, but though they knew the desert sun would still be boiling down they went outside for fresh air. The close atmosphere of the hangar was heavy with the scents of oil and alcohol and their own perspiration.

"Maybe we should have air-conditioned this rattrap," Sloan said, as they mounted the steel ladder. He pushed back the trap door.

"I don't think that would have been smart." Jack followed him into the brilliant but waning day. "Old prospectors don't wander around the desert with air-conditioning equipment. We had trouble enough getting the equipment we've got in here."

This time they sat down on a rock that lay in the shadow

of a bigger boulder. All about them the desert stretched away, shimmering in the sun's blistering glare. But a breeze moved above its arid floor, brushing the tops of just such low hills as they had used for building the *Argonaut's* hangar. It touched them with fresh fingers, turning perspiration into cool trickles.

"That was some idea you had about picking up the satellite. Do you really think the *Argonaut* could do it?" Sloan said.

"I know damn good and well it could. Max was also right about going on to the moon with the gravity reactors, once we get through that area where the meteorites are piling into the atmosphere. We could do that vertically like a rocket without trouble, and we could easily catch up with the satellite in outer space where there's no friction—only inertia to overcome."

Sloan looked out across the desert thoughtfully.

"That might really bring people back to the spacemen idea. And it wouldn't scare anybody or hurt anybody, either. Why, Jack, we might even contact Washington by radio and ask them if they want us to set it out again on an orbit ten thousand miles up."

Jack laughed. "We could do that too—but I guess it's just another impractical idea."

"Anyway, I liked what you said to Max," Sloan said. "I think maybe you convinced him."

"Do you?" Jack was staring across the desert with narrowed eyes, his head turning carefully, like that of a trained lookout.

"He sounded pretty cheerful to me. Yes sir, my boy, you may be back with that girl of yours before you know it."

"Yeah." Jack's eyes moved carefully along the horizon.

"You're lucky." Sloan grunted. "Suppose you'd have wound up out there on—oh say, a planet of the star Capella. No blondes on the planets of Capella I bet. Suppose . . ."

198

"Dud," Jack said. "Get up slowly and keep bent down, then creep over and raise the trap door."

Sloan's body went tense and hard. "You see something?"

"I feel something." Jack glanced at his uncle, a frown pinching his brows together. "Let's get out of sight, Dud."

The hiss of a jet plane pierced the silence like escaping steam. Then its roar shook the earth around them. It swept past, low, less than a mile to the east. Clearly they saw the head of the man in the cockpit, and the U. S. Air Force marking on the fuselage.

"All right," Jack said. "No need to go now. Hug the ground if he circles."

But the plane whisked away in a straight line, its thunder fading gently into the interminable desert.

"Did he see us?" Sloan searched the hot blue sky for signs of another visitor.

"No way to tell. He came up behind that hill over there. He could have if he happened to be looking the right way "

"Well, let's get the hell below."

"Suppose he comes back? Maybe he wouldn't be suspicious unless he found we'd disappeared."

"If he comes back, he's looking for something." Sloan moved hurriedly toward the trap door. "And if he's looking for something and saw us the first time, he's already suspicious.

They went through the hatch into the clammy, fetid air of the hangar. Jack clung to the top of the ladder, the heavy hatch held open a half-inch by the top of his head. A minute later, the hiss and the thunder passed over them again. He let the trap door close all the way and started down the ladder.

15.

It was a good thing for Henry Alvin that in his position as a personal aide to General Waverly he was required to perform no duties during that hectic day at the Pentagon. Actually, Waverly himself had little to do with the faraway activity in Nevada. A gigantic cobweb of men and machines and electronics operated at his order and was his ultimate responsibility, but the details were left to others. All day and on into the evening he sat jovially in his office or bustled down corridors alive with excited civilian personnel or carried on long, loud telephone conversations with official cronies; and Alvin had nothing to do but stand by and be ready to answer questions. A steady stream of reports on everything from the weather to the latest positions of individual aircraft came to Waverly's desk. He read them all to his scientist.

"You and your spaceships," he said once. "Why, do you know, Hank, you almost had me swallowing that stuff?"

Alvin managed a grin; he was barely able to keep back an irritated frown. Loudmouthed ape, he thought, with a bitterness that was not characteristic. "Well, General, it seems to me that what's actually happening is more incredible than spacemen. Earthmen have built a spaceship! Why, I . . ."

"Yes, and they're going to be damn sorry." Waverly sat up straight in his huge swivel chair. "Bunch of Reds or something . . . Why the hell any loyal, right-thinking American would do a thing like this is beyond me."

"I mean just the building of it, General. Think of what a project it must have been for any group of . . ."

"Building it is one thing, Hank." He wheeled in anger. "Not turning it over to the Air Force is another thing. That's treason."

"Do you"—Alvin swallowed and picked his words with care—"are you going to try to capture them? Or . . ."

Waverly snorted. "We're going to get them any way we can. Alive, if possible. With their spaceship, or whatever it is, intact, if possible. But if not . . ." He shrugged.

"I hope you can." He hated his own weakness. He wanted to fling defiance in Waverly's gleaming teeth. He wished desperately that he had those papers from Sloan to cram down Waverly's throat. But what good would that do? "I'd like a close look at that craft of theirs," Alvin said in firm tones.

"So would I, Hank." The general took his unlit cigar out of his mouth and pointed it at the scientist. "But don't forget. Whoever these birds are, they damn near started a war."

Even as an anguished protest rang in his mind, Alvin knew that Waverly was essentially right. It made no difference what he and his associates had meant to do, what they had hoped for, what heady dreams had led them toward their splendid vision. What mattered was the fact they had been wrong, and all their hopes and all their dreams had gone to dust. But was it entirely their fault? Hadn't the very splendor of the dream carried them for at least a moment above the ordinary entanglements and ambitions of average men? Had there not been high courage as well as foolhardy optimism? And had not humanity responded only with suspicion and belligerence and violence?

We asked too much, Alvin thought. We asked human beings to be more than human.

At that moment a courier brought the news of a jet aircraft's sighting of two men in the suspected area of the desert.

"Now that," Waverly observed, after giving Hank Alvin the gist of the message, "looks like we're getting somewhere."

"You know"—Alvin stared at the message fluttering in Waverly's big hands—"they must be brave men—whoever they are."

"Brave men are a dime a dozen." Waverly chewed the cigar rapidly across his wide mouth and back again. "What these guys ought to have been was smart. If they had been smart, they wouldn't be in trouble."

Well, you're right about that, Henry Alvin thought. Whatever else we were, we weren't very smart.

"Yessir," General Waverly said. "In this old world the smart boys win. Every time, Hank. Every single time."

Jack spoke nervously. "He's looking for something, Dud. Maybe us, maybe not."

John Sloan lowered himself gingerly to the concrete floor. "I don't think it could be us. He wouldn't have any reason that I know of."

"Unless they *did* track us after we crossed the coast."

Sloan shook his head. "They weren't watching as high as we came in. And they don't cover this desert, so they couldn't have zeroed in on this place."

"Sure. But all that was before we dropped the bomb on New York. God knows what they're doing now."

"Remember, an *Argonaut* with one bad engine is better than any airplane in the business. We could fly her out to Australia when Max gets back and fix the engine there."

Jack unclasped his knuckles and frowned. "I sure hate to leave the good old U. S. A. now that we're back. But maybe you're right. I don't like that damn jet breathing down my neck."

Sloan sat silent a minute, rasping a hand across the two-day beard stubble on his lined, tired face, a pencil bobbing in his other hand. "Tell you what." He pointed the pencil straight at Jack. "You sneak out of here and go find Max. You know the way. Give him a hand with all that gear. Get back here as fast as you can and we'll shove off."

"He'll hurry back." Jack was pacing excitedly up and down the hangar floor. His lips were pressed together, his interlocked hands strained awkwardly. "He must have seen that jet. Hell, Dud, I don't want to leave you here alone."

"Why not? And Max can't know that flyboy spotted us. That is, if he did spot us. Go on and don't argue with me. The more I think about it, the more I want out of this molehill." Sloan gazed around uneasily at their concrete burrow.

Jack watched him closely. Then he made up his mind. "O.K., if you think so." He swiftly climbed the steel ladder to the hatch. At the top he looked back. "Keep an ear open. I don't want anything happening to you, you old goat."

The tired lines of Sloan's face and his lank, uncombed hair made him look older than Jack had ever seen him. But he smiled cheerfully and waved. "Old goats are tough," he said. "Get a move on, boy."

Jack carefully pushed open the hatch an inch or two. He listened for a long time. No sound disturbed the hot desert air. He looked back again. Sloan sat against the wall, his eyes closed, his long hands dangling over his drawn-up knees. He's too old for all this, Jack thought. I shouldn't have gotten him into it. He gazed at his uncle with affection for a moment longer, then crawled carefully out of the hatch, letting it drop back into place, and went swiftly on all fours into the shadow of the big rock.

Five minutes later he was crawling carefully up the hill just east of where the *Argonaut* was hidden. He knew the area well and he had a good idea of the route Schoeller would take. He kept close to the earth, moving as much under cover as was possible in the blistering desert, among the scrubby juniper trees and cactus. The slanting sun rays came down on his head and the dust made his throat and lips as dry as old paper. He looked carefully ahead, not wanting to pass Schoeller unaware, but the heat waves waves rising from the sand made visibility unsure.

Then he heard the helicopter. In that quiet air the sound gave him plenty of time to make himself invisible from above.

Ducking under the overhang of a boulder, he could barely crane his neck and see the craft as it came swiftly across the desert from the west. It was painted blue and marked with the insignia of the Navy.

That jet radioed the position back to base, Jack thought. He watched with eyes squinted against the sun and dust as the helicopter began dropping, its huge rotors whipping up swirls of sand far below on the desert floor. Then it began quartering carefully around the general area of the hill in which the *Argonaut*—and John Sloan—waited.

They must have divining rods, Jack thought, cursing to himself at how easily the instrument would be able to detect the metal mass hidden beneath the hollowed hill, now that their approximate position had been given away. If only they hadn't gone out for that breath of air!

Then he thought of John Sloan. *Dud!* Frantically he braced himself with his hands against the boulder. It was a physical effort to keep himself from dashing uselessly into the desert, toward that tiny opening beneath which the only father he had ever known waited calmly for whatever would come.

He knew, Jack thought. He must have guessed it was all over. That's why he sent me off. In spite of the heat and the glare of the sun, perspiration ran cold on his body. Tears grew bitterly moist in his eyes and rolled across his dust-stained cheeks. Grimly he watched the slow quartering of the helicopter.

Then it stopped. It was directly above the hill they had named Mesatron.

16.

John Sloan had watched the hatch close behind Jack with a certain satisfaction. There was a time in every man's life when he wanted to live more than anything, but sooner or later there were circumstances under which life would be worse than nothing. Besides, Sloan thought, getting up laboriously from the concrete floor, I'm not sure I'm going to die just yet.

He went to the steel ladder and pulled himself slowly to the top. Just as Jack had done, he opened the door an inch or two, letting its weight rest on the top of his head. Whatever happened, they would not catch him asleep at the switch.

Sloan knew that he was in desperate circumstances, much more so than he had indicated in his last conversation with Jack. His trump card—escape in the *Argonaut*—was risky, since one engine was totally out of use. His chance of surrendering the *Argonaut* was even more risky. Anything that moved in the area now would undoubtedly be shot on sight. Moreover, it would mean marooning Jack and Schoeller. But he was angry at the thought of leaving the craft where it was. He would not be pushed around.

His eyes carefully searched as much of the desert as he could see through the narrow opening. Nothing moved. Nor was there any sound from the skies. But they'll come, they'll come, he said to himself. Sloan thought with satisfaction of the packet of information his secretary would mail to Hank Alvin. Hank would have all the information the world would need to profit from their work, if his colleagues could decipher it. He would know what to do with it. He would even know, Sloan thought with a wry grin that hurt his dusty lips, whether to do anything at all with it.

A faint movement caught his eye. It was Jack, ducking along the broken terrain. Then he was out of sight again.

Sloan felt good about Jack. He did not feel particularly brave or self-sacrificing at having sent him toward a better chance for safety. He simply felt good that, in a world he might be about to leave permanently, this man he thought of as his son would still be aboard. A man wanted to leave something behind. If it were not for Jack Baker, there would have been only the business; a good thing in itself but hardly a fulfillment of his dreams.

Sloan saw Jack's careful movements once again and almost at the same moment he heard the helicopter. He saw it sweep by, then return, closer. He could tell that it was quartering the area. He closed the trap door and as he came down the ladder, he thought it had stopped directly overhead.

Sandy Carlson went slowly across the room and picked up the telephone, stilling its insistent ring. She stood a moment with the receiver in her hand, gazing out over Lafayette Square, watching the children romping along the concrete paths.

"Hello," she said finally, her voice uninterested. Cleveland was calling, the operator told her. Then a careful voice spoke her name.

"Hello, George," Sandy said. She looked back at the square, toward the green beauty of the trees in the afternoon sun, listening to the metallic voice from Cleveland.

"No," she said, "no, I told you I couldn't let you know till after my vacation . . ."

Jack Baker was not sure how long he had lain hidden under the boulder. To look again at the hill over which the helicopter hung, he had to inch carefully forward and crane his neck around a rough edge of rock. The helicopter hovered almost motionlessly, its rotors swishing up sand in great swirls. Occasionally, as the craft turned slightly, Jack could see the heads of the two men in its glass bubble. They, too, seemed to be unmoving. In all the desert the only things that moved were the great sweeping blades that had brought the helicopter to their hiding place; all else was still as death. In the western sky the great red ball of the sun sank bloodily toward the horizon.

Occasionally Jack would let his eyes sweep carefully along the rim of rock and broken hills. Beyond that lay the hidden storeroom to which Max Schoeller had gone—how many hours ago? He saw no movement, no flash of sun on metal that indicated a living presence, and he hardly expected to. Even if Schoeller had meant to keep his word about returning to the hangar—and Jack could not be certain that he had—he could hardly have missed seeing both the jet and the helicopter. Chances were that Schoeller, too, was lying somewhere near by, hidden from the eyes in the tiny glass cabin suspended from those circling blades fifty feet above the earth.

And Dud? Jack could hardly think of Dud. He buried his head in his arms. It was as though he literally took his brain in his hand and squeezed it, searching desperately among its tired, beaten cells for some solution. His uncle was too alert to need warning about the helicopter's presence, or its meaning. But could he do anything? Jack had had no real hope since the first sound of the helicopter had come beating up over the low hills of sand and stunted undergrowth, but he could not bear the thought of lying hidden, of watching helplessly while his uncle and the dreams of a lifetime were destroyed. He was wearing a .45 pistol at his belt and he thought desperately of working closer and trying to pick off the two men in the helicopter. Then he would fly out with Dud and the *Argonaut*. He contemplated trying to sneak back into the hangar through the hidden main doors and face it out to the end.

His mind wandered back to that cool green day when they had met on the wide lawn under the huge trees at John Sloan's Maryland place. How sure they had all been then that what they had done in creating the *Argonaut* was one of those giant steps into the future which civilization had seldom taken. How confidently they had dreamed of its presentation. What they had not perceived—John Sloan in his businessman's efficiency, Jack Baker in his artless dreams, Max Schoeller in his scientific preoccupation, Henry Alvin in his willingness to gamble —was that they had created a monster over which they could no more exercise control than a man on a tiger could guide his beast. The mere appearance of its flight track on a radar screen had doomed their chance of dictating the uses of the *Argonaut*. So it would all end here in this bitter desert, with the wind blowing its gritty laughter across the grave of their dreams.

Then he heard the throb of the planes. At first he did not look up, absorbing the sound through the sweating flesh of his arms. Slowly he raised his head. They were coming from the west, flight after flight of them, like great eyeless birds following an infallible leader. Jack counted them unbelievingly. He had not seen so many planes in one formation since the war. These were ancient flying boxcars, and even as he watched, the first paratroopers began to tumble toward the earth.

It was an incredibly beautiful sight. The vast sky quickly filled with the blossoms of silk, many-colored to denote the different types of equipment these men from the sky would need when they began to fight on earth. It seemed to Jack that they had hardly started to leap from the great planes before they were beginning to form up.

A slight wind drifted them away from his hiding place. The nearest paratrooper was a thousand yards off. Even so, he could hear their scuffling and shouting after the huge formation had roared overhead. He cradled his head in his arms, once again giving way to the despair that was like a funeral hymn in his soul. But immediately he felt a different throb from the arid earth. He looked up and scanned the horizon.

208

Far across the desert, just beginning to poke up into sight over the low hills, were mechanized vehicles. He could not yet hear their motors or the clanking of their endless tracks, but the earth and his wandering eyes had transmitted their presence to him.

Dully he turned his head back toward Mesatron. As he watched, the helicopter swerved away above the last of the descending parachutes. A line of skirmishers was already moving toward the hill. And far to the west he could see the white streams from a formation of jet planes, circling the edge of the vast desert basin.

The trap was complete. Heavy at heart, Jack rose to his knees and moved cautiously through the underbrush.

General Waverly had taken up a position in a busy Operations Room, far down in the bowels of the Pentagon. Dr. Alvin watched him hastily conferring with the lesser officers who were constantly bringing him reports. He supposed the great charts and electronic screens on the walls around him were recording the course of events in Nevada, but he could not watch them. He already knew more than any of these men, with all their equipment and training and skill. He knew more than any of them about what was really happening on that faraway desert. He watched Waverly coming toward him, his unlit cigar clenched in the corner of his confident mouth.

"Everything but the goddamn Navy's closing in on those birds, Hank." He chuckled, taking the cigar out of his mouth. "And if there was any way to do it, we'd run a battleship in there for good measure."

It took John Sloan longer than he had planned to make the *Argonaut* ready for flight. The useless new engine that could not be connected until Max got back with the tubing and fittings had to be secured. The scaffolding and other gear that they used in the repair work had to be cleared out of the way. And a good many adjustments were necessary because of the unconnected engine.

Sloan was not at all sure that he would be able to fly the craft in its crippled condition, but he intended to do so out of defiance, if he was really trapped. Schoeller had explained to him and to Jack how it could be done. In normal flight the *Argonaut* was easier to handle than an ordinary aircraft. But with all the thrust developing on one side Sloan knew he would have an extremely difficult time flying it in a straight line out of the hangar, and his speed would be greatly reduced.

At last he was ready. He was panting from his exertions and smeared with grime and grease. But he felt no panic. As he mounted the ladder to the escape hatch, hauling himself heavily hand over hand, he did not fear what he would find. He thought that he knew what to do, that he would be able to handle the situation. If he could not—well, there would be the satisfaction of giving it a good try.

At the last rung, he touched his sweating forehead for a moment against the steel of the ladder. It was cold and invigorating. He was tempted to rest for just a minute, but he realized a minute could not be spared. He lifted his head and carefully pushed up the hatch.

Immediately, in the afternoon's fading light, he saw the skirmish lines forming up. He could see only three-quarters of the horizon but he could tell from the activity that a great circle of armed men surrounded Mesatron. A continual drone told him that great fleets of aircraft were in the area, too. On the extreme left he spotted the tanks rumbling up a nearby hill.

He allowed himself not more than thirty seconds to assay the situation. Then he lowered the hatch and went swiftly back down the ladder. His brain, tired and lethargic a moment before, functioned as rapidly as it ever had. He went immediately to the *Argonaut* and strapped himself into the pilot's seat. Now, he thought, I must make a decision.

The nearest of the encircling men that he had seen had been almost a half-mile away. After all, Sloan thought, they weren't enemies, they weren't hunting for him, for the *Argonaut*— they were merely hunting for an unknown threat, just as men had hunted through all of history. Just as they always will, he thought.

Max Schoeller had seen the first evidence of jets approaching Mesatron long before Jack and John Sloan had seen the one which spotted them. He had been only ten minutes from the underground storeroom and he stopped to watch them screaming through the sky. He knew immediately what might happen. Almost as quickly he made up his mind what he must do.

Schoeller rushed to the storeroom and stuffed a knapsack with the essential fittings and provisions. As he hastened to leave, he placed a black, rectangular box under his arm. This transmitter could open the doors of Mesatron and trigger the miniature atomic bomb in the *Argonaut* he had secretly rigged—if necessary.

For almost two hours he walked rapidly, unmindful of cover, intent on reaching Mesatron before an alarm could be sounded. Then the jet which had sighted his companions shrieked almost over his head as he nestled into the thick cover of a juniper tree. Sharp anxiety was tempered with caution, and he began to pick his way more carefully over the broken ground. Twenty minutes later he neared the top of the hill just east of Mesatron and saw the helicopter approaching, far to the west.

Max's arms had been almost numb for the last hour from carrying the bulky transmitter, but he refused to give it up. Now his heart beat more rapidly and he no longer felt the dull aching as he turned quickly to the south and stumbled down the hill toward the dry creek bed where the undergrowth was thicker. Carefully he crept along the shallow gully, not knowing that Jack Baker was crouched under a rock barely two hundred feet above him. At last he rounded a corner where the dead stream had once swept out into the valley. Mesatron was just to his right.

Max knew it was only a matter of time until a greater power, of which the helicopter was the feeble outpost, would be launched against them. He moved close to the base of the hill to avoid detection. It was slow, painful work, particularly in those moments when he peered helplessly through the underbrush at the quartering helicopter as he sought his own outpost for destruction. Sweat blinded his eyes. He sank from exhaustion onto the hot sand, throbbing from head to foot. He lay there for many minutes like a feast for a passing vulture; then he awoke with a sharp new resolution, unmindful of the roar from many planes which filled the air. I will try it, he thought. I will try an open run for the main hangar doors. Even if I can't fly the ship out, I can destroy it there.

John Sloan sat in the cockpit wrestling with his decision. The frantic preparations of the last few hours urged the escape of the *Argonaut* as a natural sequel to their activity. He said to himself, If they don't return in time I will try to surrender the ship. I must trust America to use it wisely even if Max can't. He closed his eyes tightly. Still it would be better to fly it out, he thought. Jack and Schoeller must hurry. He realized that a delay of only two or three more minutes would find the emergency hatch covered by rifle fire from the troops, just as the hangar doors were probably covered now.

Sloan wondered whether to break through the emergency hatch, or open the great doors and hope that his fellow countrymen would withhold their fire. He decided to climb the ladder again. Jack and Schoeller might be approaching the hatch at this very moment. It was their only chance to enter the hangar.

Just as Max looked up from the ground the paratroopers began to spill from the lumbering planes. Too late, he thought, I cannot chance it now. Schoeller crawled vigorously through the scanty undergrowth. He watched their lines forming up. Then he took the black box from beneath his arm and set it on a high rock, extending the short antenna. He turned on the batteries and switched the knob to one of two settings.

The doors of the Mesatron hangar were barely perceptible to his trained eyes. He closed the switch of the transmitter. Nothing happened! Quickly he saw that the jut of a cliff was still between him and the receiver for the doors of the hangar.

Schoeller looked again at the nearest paratroopers. They were quite close with little cover between him and their location. But Schoeller clung blindly to his resolution. Now he had nothing to lose. He studied the contour of the land to make quite certain where the dangers lay, then ran for it. His run was good. He stopped behind a great rock above the dry stream, around the obstruction but well inside the line of soldiers, and extended the antenna of the transmitter.

There was no time to linger. The forces were advancing from three sides. One chance I will give Sloan and Baker, he thought, one warning. I will open the doors of the hangar as a signal for them to fly the ship out. I can give them only a minute longer.

John Sloan released his seat belt and stumbled quickly from the cabin of the *Argonaut*. He jumped to the concrete floor and ran for the ladder. As he grasped the first cold rung he realized that his chances of pulling this thing off were very slim. Was it realistic to hope that Jack and Schoeller could make it back? Could he really surrender the *Argonaut*? Perhaps he could get out of the hatch safely, but how could he attract attention without being shot in cold blood? Would he have time to take off his soiled white shirt and wave it in a feeble gesture? Would that mean anything in this moment of tension? He could not shout to anyone above the great roar that filled the air. Yet he kept climbing the ladder, deliberately. That is the chance I must take, he thought. I may die, but the *Argonaut* will fall to the government.

Just as his head pressed against the trap door John Sloan heard a noise behind him. He glanced over his shoulder to see the great hangar doors of Mesatron opening.

Max Schoeller's left hand rested on a button which would trigger the bomb in the *Argonaut*. He looked intently at the sweep second hand of his watch. Thirty seconds had passed since he had opened the doors. The second hand moved relentlessly to forty-five, fifty, fifty-five seconds. Schoeller took his eyes off the watch. Something burned within him. His thoughts were not of Jack Baker or Sloan. They were warriors just as he was, who had risked death and must now face death if they had lost. But he thought of the *Argonaut*, the only thing left in this world which bore the stamp of his genius. Then he thought of his vow to destroy it. It was this vow that had forced him to his blind resolution for destruction. He reconsidered it.

Schoeller looked at the front line of the paratroopers just coming over the top of the adjacent hill. They were running quickly but they had to run down a slight gully and up again before he would be clearly visible to them. The line behind them would likewise be running—over rough ground. They would be watching their feet, not the landscape.

With one quick gesture Schoeller cut the switch and hurled the transmitter at the rock he was standing on. He made a frantic dash for the open hangar doors.

John Sloan reached the bottom of the ladder just as Schoeller reached the *Argonaut* and heaved the sack of fittings and provisions through the entrance.

"Hurry, Sloan," he said gruffly, entering the ship. As he tightened his safety belt he heard the cabin door slam. Sloan poked his head into the cockpit.

"What about Jack?"

"We cannot worry about that now," Max replied. "Strap in."

The *Argonaut* rose gently a foot above the hangar floor. Max applied power to the port steering rocket and its nose turned slightly to the right. The single rear rocket fired at low power and the *Argonaut* moved slowly out of the dark hangar. At the moment the nose was free he applied full power to both the steering and the aft rockets. The *Argonaut* sped forward over the heads of the astonished paratroopers and suddenly leaped skyward. It appeared to be well out of range before the first shot was fired.

17.

It was after midnight when Henry Alvin came wearily back to the apartment he had left before dawn. The reports were all in from Nevada, and the puzzled General Waverly had immediately taken a plane to the scene.

Alvin lay down on the sofa. Only a small lamp burned near the window. The numbing fatigue of the night before was with him again but the unreality of the day was gone. His mind focused clearly and sharply and he thought of many things: of long-ago nights in Europe when he and a smiling boy had shared their hours and their ideas and the presence of death; of a night in the awful space above Pittsburgh when Max Schoeller had said, "That could be a bombsight"; of whether or not his friends might try the second run and plunge the world unalterably into war.

And he thought, too, that this could be his last night of freedom. His actions throughout had been technical treason for not reporting the *Argonaut* and the part he had played in its fantastic appearance. Certainly, for one in his position, they would seem to such men as Waverly to have been criminal. And he had no illusions that the government officials would make allowances for his good motives. He put his hands over his face. He had acted at all times with a clear knowledge of the consequences of failure. He had forced himself to go on with the deception when it seemed the most practical thing to do; yet, through it all, there had been a sly, maddening fear lying with him at night, tiptoeing at his side in the daytime. Now it must be faced. With the discovery of the *Argonaut* in Nevada he could no longer hide his secret. If I could only get those papers Sloan promised to send, he thought. Perhaps they will come. I must wait a few more days.

A knock interrupted the pushing flow of his thoughts. He got up and went quickly to the door, expecting to see another Air Force messenger. But Sandy Carlson stood in the hall instead.

"Sandy!" Alvin remembered their dinner engagement for the first time. "Listen—I just this minute . . ."

"Well, can I come in?" She was smiling and he saw with relief that her eyes were cordial.

"By all means." She went past him into the living room, holding a folded newspaper in her hand.

"Sandy—listen—I know this sounds awful but I just this minute got home. I haven't . . ."

"I know. I didn't even try to find you." She let the newspaper unfold, and he saw the black headlines of the special edition. "The minute I saw the paper I figured you wouldn't show up."

"But the least I could have done was to get in touch with you! The truth is—well, it just slipped my mind, that's all." Even as he made his apologies, his alert mind leaped ahead of his words. Had the newspaper stories made her suspicious? She was smart enough to put two and two together if a certain train of thought ever occurred to her.

"Please—just forget it." Sandy tossed the paper on a chair and sat down on the sofa. "I don't suppose the Air Force has this kind of excitement every day."

"It sure doesn't." Alvin shook his head. His face took on the old familiar cheerfulness as he moved swiftly to avoid any discussion that might make her think of the event in Nevada in connection with Jack Baker. "I'm sorry we didn't get a real look at whatever the thing was. I don't suppose we'll ever know."

"I suppose not." Sandy didn't seem particularly interested.

The scientist launched into a discussion of some of the facts the Pentagon had about the *Argonaut*. He deliberately disclosed some information that had not been released to the public, but not all that had been deduced. In doing so, he hoped to make Sandy think that he was preoccupied with the matter. He hoped even to pique her airman's interest, but to make it plain that he actually knew very little about the whole affair.

"That's fascinating," Sandy said, when he paused. "It must have moved at an unbelievable speed."

The scientist nodded. "That's why I'm sorry it escaped. It must have represented a tremendous advance in aircraft design. And our first reports, at least, say that the hangar is a most elaborate and modern affair. How any group of private citizens could manage a thing like that is beyond me. And there's another odd thing . . ." He talked on, becoming just a bit pedantic, until he could see her beginning to fidget. He relaxed. If he was boring her with the details he felt he could disclose, surely she was attaching no personal significance to the sensational headlines from Nevada. There was really no reason that she should, except by simply jumping to a conclusion that only he could suggest to her.

"But all that's no excuse for such rudeness, my dear." He held the lighter to her cigarette. "And I really do apologize."

"I understand." Sandy leaned back. In the dim apartment he could hardly see her face. "Now why I really came . . ."

"What?" A new alarm stirred in him.

"I know it's selfish of me to bother you with my personal problems. Especially when you're involved with—this sort of thing." She waved at the open newspaper. "But you've been very kind and Jack told me how much he thought of you. Hank, you're my only link with him."

Alvin got up without speaking and went to the window. He could not keep his face as emotionless as he wanted to.

"I can't say what he did for me," Sandy continued. "I just know I never felt toward any one else like I do toward him. Then he went away."

The room grew quiet, so quiet they could hear the muffled

sounds of night traffic from outside. Somewhere across the city a siren screamed.

"I had a call from Cleveland today." Sandy's voice was carefully expressionless. "From my boss. You know George Elliott?"

"I know of him."

"Hank, he wants me to marry him."

Alvin turned to face her. "He must be your grandfather's age!"

"But worth a few million dollars. I'll inherit his entire estate if I marry him. And I do admire him."

Alvin was shocked. He had read of such things in the newspapers, of course; yet, a bachelor himself, he had an almost naïve belief in romantic love. It was his conviction that lasting marriage was made in heaven and, perhaps because he had never known it himself, that love was a matter of fate, a thing one must never deny or impede.

"So I thought I'd tell you the truth, Hank. I thought perhaps if I did, you'd . . ." She shrugged.

Anger rose hotly in his blood. "You thought I'd tell you Jack wasn't coming back so you could go on and marry your rich old fool."

Sandy carefully snubbed out her cigarette. "I hoped you'd tell me he was coming back. I don't want George Elliott's money, but I respect him."

"Then don't take it."

"I don't want it *if*"—she wavered—"Jack's coming back to me. I want him more than anything else."

In that moment the scientist felt quite old. He felt that he knew nothing at all about people and, perhaps, that he had wasted a lifetime on lesser things.

"It's just that I've got to have *some* thing." Sandy impulsively put her hand on his arm. "If he isn't coming back, I've got to have—there has to be *some* thing to fall back on."

Then she leaned forward, her knees together, her capable

hands tense and white-knuckled in her lap. And in that moment he saw in her what he knew Jack Baker had seen: something tender and needful, something soft as love, strong, hardy, still unconquered. And even this was going to be destroyed at last.

It was her turn to search his face. Suddenly her iron composure was gone. He watched the flesh around her eyes and mouth crumple into a thousand tiny lines, and before she could hide her face in her hands, he saw the tears begin to spill from her eyes. She stood up and ran across the room to the door. He stumbled after her, striking his shin awkwardly against the coffee table. But she was already gone.

"Sandy!"

He called her name once. Then the slam of the door stopped his headlong rush. And as he waited by it, knowing he could not hear her footsteps in the carpeted hall but listening for them all the same, he thought that at last, truly, the worst had happened for her.

The days passed rapidly. General Waverly named Dr. Alvin to the scientific team which was to study the great hangar at Mesatron, and he flew there for a few hectic days. On his return to Washington, he found that the startling event which had demanded such huge headlines was already sinking into the limbo of old news stories. People were talking of different things, and even in the Pentagon the wave of busy excitement had slowly receded into the usual ripples of chatter and gossip.

Alvin even became, ironically enough, a signer of a "comprehensive report" that gave no indication of his personal involvement. Nor did it make any suggestion as to who might have been the builders of the awesome craft, except to question more than once how such a thing could have been done without the aid of the government. It strongly implied that some unknown origin for the craft seemed more acceptable than the theory of private citizens. The *Argonaut* became the greatest UFO in history.

Why, Alvin wondered, did they remain at Mesatron until they were virtually surrounded? If they had delayed just sixty seconds longer the paratroopers would have been at the doors of the hangar, regrouped and ready for the unexpected emergence of the *Argonaut*. This point had been made emphatically to him by the captain of the first-line troops when he visited Mesatron. In fact, the captain swore that the *Argonaut* had been hit by several bullets in the aft part, where they would not realize the damage that might have been sustained by the hull until they had sprung far above the earth in their frantic escape. Surely the slow leak of oxygen would suffocate them before they could recognize their mistake. Alvin shuddered at the thought and yet it was a real possibility, a most likely one if the captain was right. Perhaps their trail was truly lost. If they had died the gentle death of anoxia before the reactor motors had been stopped, they would have soared straight out into space and would be lost to this world forever. Perhaps he alone now had the burdensome responsibility of the truth. But he could do nothing about it except to confess his implication in their plan. That might help his conscience but not the situation. He knew that Baker and Sloan had covered themselves well by their plans for a trip to the far north, at least for a month or two. Schoeller was not likely to be missed by anyone unless it would be the immigration authorities. And even if their identities were uncovered, no trail could lead directly to Henry Alvin.

The bell to his apartment rang noisily. He stumbled from the bed and reached for his bathrobe, donning it clumsily as he walked through the living room. When he opened the door a messenger from the post office shoved a clipboard and pencil at him.

"Registered mail from California, sir."

Alvin signed his name with hesitation and almost drew

back from the large brown envelope which was handed to him. He closed the door against the lights of the hall and stood for a moment in the darkness. These are the papers, he thought, as he snapped on the light switch. Now there is no escape.

The heavy envelope seemed to sear the flesh of his hands. Suddenly he wanted to drop it and run away. Instead, he walked automatically toward the John Marin water color which hung on the west wall of his living room. He pushed it aside and exposed the door of the wall safe, which he opened quickly, cramming the envelope into the dark cavern.

Late the next afternoon the scientist walked slowly, with a slight limp, through the entrance of his apartment building and turned toward the elevator. They never need to know anything about me, he mused sadly as he got out of the elevator at his floor and went along the hall toward his apartment. Not if I burn those papers. The very thought gave him a flicker of release from fear for his own safety, that had grown progressively more intense since the *Argonaut* disappeared. But even greater, subduing his fears of personal security, was the dominant fear that no power could spontaneously create the atmosphere necessary for another presentation of the *Argonaut*. No power could suddenly twist human nature into accepting a point of view that would insure the use of this great development as a weapon of peace, not a weapon of war. Is mankind ready? he asked himself.

Alvin shook his head, inserting his key in the lock, opening the door. This chance to end it all with a sudden gesture was an idea he could not drive away. Until last night he had only thought of taking Schoeller's notes directly to Dick Waverly, if they were received, and of paying whatever price was necessary for his own guilt. But now he was tempted to take the easy way out by their destruction. He shook his head again, angrily, hating these impulses he was discovering in himself.

222

He slouched into his apartment, glancing automatically toward the water color behind which rested his safe and its terrible secret.

Jack Baker sat in the hard straight chair just beneath it. He watched Alvin collapse on the sofa to the left of the door, as though his legs would no longer support him. One of his hands came up in front of his face, pointing a shaking, incredulous finger at Jack, but he did not speak.

"I'm alive, Hank." Jack wanted to smile but he couldn't. He wondered how long it had been since he had smiled.

"Alive—and here." The words came querulously, high pitched, in the voice of an old man. "But I don't understand." Alvin closed his pointing hand and put it quickly in his lap, as though to hide it. "I thought . . ."

"Oh, it was simple enough." Jack stood up, thrusting his hands into his pockets. He stalked across the room, then back. "I didn't mean to startle you, Hank. But I couldn't be sure about what kind of surveillance you were under. I don't think anyone saw me come here except the maid who let me in."

"I'm not under surveillance, Jack. They don't know anything. Nothing at all." Alvin shook his head. "And, perhaps, neither do I."

Jack sat down again abruptly in the same straight chair and began to tell the story of the *Argonaut* in a quick, emotionless voice. He told it from the beginning, from that dark night when they had flown out of Nevada toward the Arctic Circle. Only when he described the escape did he falter.

"Dud thought we were really trapped but he didn't let on. He sent me out to find Max, and then the helicopter blocked my return. They were hovering right over the trap-door entrance. If I could have made it to the old creek bed on the south I might have sneaked around to the hangar doors, but there was no cover on that side of the hill."

"Then Sloan flew the ship out alone?"

"He must have."

"Where is Max?"

"I wish I knew." Jack put his hand to his eyes a moment, then looked straight at Alvin. "Dud can't make it alone, Hank. There were practically no provisions in the ship and Dud can't navigate. He could never find any of the bases."

"He might have landed somewhere."

"If it wasn't in Russia we'd know by now."

"Maybe Max is with him."

"Slim chance. I don't think Max ever came back to Mesatron—not after he saw that jet."

Jack buried his head in his hands. "Max changed," he muttered. "He became greedy for power. It came out all over him after that first run on Moscow. He insisted on the second run, Hank, even after all the trouble we'd caused."

Alvin got up slowly and walked toward the dim light of the window. "Maybe it's best he didn't come back if that's the case. Your second run would surely have caused a war." He turned sadly to look at Jack and walked back to the sofa.

There was quiet for a long time in the room.

"Why did we fail?" Jack asked.

"First it was the bomb you dropped on Moscow," Henry Alvin said in a matter-of-fact way. "Somehow they got hold of a part of the radio altimeter you used, and identified it."

Jack lifted his head and stared at the ceiling. When he lowered his eyes he could feel his flesh burning like fire. "Then I balled it up all the way around, didn't I? The bomb-bay doors nearly killed us. Because of that, the rocket almost got us. And because of that, Max had to pour on the power and ruin a sick engine that might have been repaired. So we had to come back to Nevada to change it. And, because my bomb failed, I suppose they were waiting for us. And then Dud took off to nowhere."

Alvin quickly told him how the radar network had been set up, how the watchers had searched for the vertical fall pattern, how Johnson's obstinacy had been largely responsi-

224

ble. "So I wouldn't blame myself too much, if I were you, Jack," he said kindly, gentleness filling his deep brown eyes. "I can see now we didn't have a chance to begin with."

"We were damn fools, Hank."

"Not that. We just chose the wrong thing to do." His face elongated sadly. "At least we had no malice."

Jack stood up again, lighting a cigarette angrily. "Men from the stars," he said. "There we were looking to the stars for help. And all the time we had everything we needed right here on earth." He went to the window. "We have intelligence; logical, penetrating minds. I don't mean just you and me. I mean most people, the Russians included." He paused, putting his hand wearily to his forehead. "We all have an emotional kinship. Fear, grief, ambition, selfishness, joy. Feelings must be about the same everywhere in the world and maybe in the stars. Hunger is hunger, want is want. At some particular time, a man in New York and a man in Moscow can look up and see the same star, Hank. For me the stars are the hand of God spread across the sky, which symbolizes the truth, but for most of us the stars are too high. The truth, like the stars, is so far above us we have little responsibility toward it, at least as nations. We grow unmindful of the fact that the truth must some day reach down and touch nations as it touches individuals; therefore we take liberties with it as though it were a harmless star many light years away. We shred the universal character from the truth and make it local to fit our own needs and ambitions. That's why it looks different to each of us—though it shouldn't. That's why no man from the stars or anywhere else is ever going to settle our troubles for us. Maybe we'd all be glad to have him do it, but no two of us would ever see him the same way. We've got to do it ourselves. Nations must come to recognize that the inexorable truth is the same for all men."

Alvin crossed the room and stood beside him. Jack Baker inclined his head toward the window, toward the city and the sky turning dark. His hands were clenched together. "We lost everything, Hank, even the *Argonaut*." Slowly he looked up.

It seemed to Jack that something calm, something resolute moved across the older man's face. Alvin went to the water color on the wall, pushed it aside, and then with quick fingers opened the safe. From it he took a large brown envelope.

"We didn't lose everything," he said. He tore open the brown envelope and handed the contents to Jack, who saw immediately that the inscriptions were in Schoeller's handwriting. Then he threw the brown envelope on the bare grating of the open fireplace and struck a match to it.

"Your uncle sent this to me. I think he was afraid of what might happen."

"He was a good one. He was the best." Jack studied the packet for a long time, while the scientist stood silently at his side.

"Open it," Alvin said. "Schoeller might have tricked us. It might be nothing."

Jack tore open the tight bindings.

"This is it, all right. I was with Max when he sealed this package. The Air Force ought to be able to put all this together if they can get the idea without having it spelled out. Max said the *Argonaut* was out of this world and he would use out-of-the-world symbols to describe it."

"Then you leave the rest to me. Go back to California. You can't help the cause now."

Jack had the sensation of climbing a long, sloping rock wall, up which he could only proceed a few feet before inexorably sliding back many more. For a moment the documents in his hand had almost given him hope, had almost shown him a way out. In that moment he had glimpsed his old world, his old life, and all of his mind had cried out for it. But as quickly as it had come, the vision was gone, and in its place he saw the pinched, unsmiling face of Max Schoeller.

"No." The word was decisive. "As long as he's loose, as

long as he's got this"—he tapped the papers—"in his head, I have to find him. You know I do. One Max Schoeller free in the world with this kind of knowledge—that's too many. I couldn't even trust the FBI to do it."

The older man paced up and down in front of the fireplace. "But what can he do?"

"I don't know. But he found a way one time. He can do it again unless I stop him." Jack handed the papers back.

"But—it's like a needle in a haystack. He could be any-where—anywhere in the world. How can you hope . . ."

Jack shook his head, jamming his hands decisively into his pockets. "Max will go home. I know him and I know he'll go to Germany. How he'll get there I don't know but that's where he'll go. And from there—hell, Hank, you know I have to find him."

"Well, we must at least call the FBI in on it, too."

"And how can we say we knew Max?"

"I received some information on him but nothing on you."

"Why spare me? I was behind the whole damn thing."

"You've done your job, Jack. And a big job at that even if it wasn't perfect. There's no need to throw your life away now. You could add very little to these papers, which I will give to General Waverly tomorrow morning."

"And how did you come into possession of these papers?" Jack asked with a tilt of his head.

"They were delivered to me anonymously." Alvin walked over to the fireplace and gazed at the last spurts of flame from the blackened envelope. Then he opened the small trap door below the grating and brushed the ashes into it. "That will take care of the postmark."

Both men fell silent.

"Hank," Jack finally said, "there's a million-to-one chance Schoeller did get out in the *Argonaut*. If he did, he will try for the second run, even if he has to overpower Dud. He's a fanatic, Hank."

"Then the quicker we get to work on the papers the better."

"Right! But not too quickly. Things have simmered down a bit now. Those papers won't make sense to the government unless they want them to. The government could just toss them in the back of an old filing cabinet. They've done that before with important ideas. Promise me you'll wait two weeks, until after the time for the second run. If it comes off, then they'll really get on the ball with that information."

Alvin gazed thoughtfully at the ceiling for almost a minute. He lowered his eyes and spoke carefully.

"I will promise that, if you will promise to forget Schoeller for two weeks."

"Why?"

"Because you have another job to do."

"What's that?"

"You have to find Sandy. She came here twice looking for you. That girl's in love with you, but"—Alvin looked at the tense, obstinate face of his friend—"you'd better hurry."

"Why?"

"Because old George Elliott asked her to marry him and she doesn't think you're ever coming back." He paused. "Neither did I."

It was almost as though his heart had stopped beating, had frozen in mid-stroke. That night in Cleveland when she had spoken of Elliott . . . Jack remembered the harsh things he had said, the fury with which she had turned on him. Now he tried to push that aside, but it rose again, gorging him; and he thought with horror of how little anyone could know of how another felt, what another needed.

"He's given her a sort of ultimatum. He wants her now or not at all."

"Where is she?"

"Cleveland."

Jack locked his fingers together and stared for a moment

at the floor. Then he walked quickly to the door and opened it.

"I promise," he said as he stepped into the hall.

The air of the apartment seemed heavy and oppressive. Alvin went to the window and turned the air-conditioning unit up too high. He also opened the fresh-air vent, then sat down on the sofa. His mind was confused. Did the *Argonaut* really make an escape or was it now an insignificant bit of cosmic debris? Was John Sloan buried with it, alone in the heavens, or had Schoeller somehow, miraculously, made an escape with him? And then his great concern reached up like an open hand grasping for his throat.

If Jack was right and they had escaped, then he, Henry Alvin, a gentleman of peace, might have contributed to the start of World War III. It was his sign in the sky that had failed. What a terrible gamble, he thought; what a terrible gamble I took for the world. But now he was helpless. He could do nothing more—at least, nothing for two weeks.

He turned on the radio and tried to relax. A news broadcaster was giving his humdrum spiel: "For the third day Sputnik VIII is circling the earth five thousand miles up. This four-foot globe, which could not be located even by radar without its radio beacon, is reportedly equipped with special scanning devices. It is Russia's latest propaganda bid to offset the launching of the larger U. S. satellite six weeks ago. One government official said, 'Satellites are now old stuff. The important thing is what is in them, not merely the fact that they are there.' In scientific circles, however, great interest is being shown in the new Sputnik. 'Our round-the-clock monitoring of its signal leads us to believe that the Russians have a new scanning device of importance,' said Dr. William . . ."

Henry Alvin snapped off the radio. He was sick at heart and no such idle chatter could distract him. Sleep is the best thing, he told himself as he moved toward the bedroom—if I can sleep. The telephone rang before he reached the door.

"Report to the Pentagon immediately," the voice said.

With aching fatigue he slipped on his coat and left.

General Waverly was pacing in a cloud of smoke when he arrived at the conference room. "This may be important, Hank," he said, and continued pacing. The room was half full of high brass who had hurried back to the Pentagon, supperless, at his bidding. In ten minutes the room was full. Waverly had not stopped pacing and puffing at his cigar since the scientist had entered the room.

Thirty seconds after everyone had arrived and had sat patiently at attention, General Waverly stopped pacing and spoke. "There has been a sighting by our radar minitrack station near Darwin, Australia. The object was at three hundred and fifty thousand feet and traveling west northwest at approximately three thousand miles an hour. The object appeared to be oblong and about sixty feet in length. That, gentlemen, in my opinion, is our elusive visitor from Nevada. Perhaps it is coming home—the long way around."

There was a rustle of interest, more from respect than excitement. Every man in the room knew of the dismay and disappointment which the escape of the UFO had brought to General Waverly. But few believed that the UFO would return to Nevada.

"Captain Johnson, are you prepared for our visitor?" Waverly asked with his old swagger.

"Yes, sir," Johnson replied eagerly. "We have stopped all air maneuvers except normal training to avoid suspicion on the part of the UFO, and we have alerted all West Coast missile areas. We have ringed the hangar region with our latest interceptor rockets."

"Just let that damn thing come back," General Strahan broke in, almost rudely. "We'll blow it to smithereens if it gets within a thousand miles of Nevada."

Alvin's heart sank at Waverly's first words. It's not coming back to Nevada, he thought. It's headed for Moscow, ahead of schedule. Should I tell them now?

The door of the conference room opened suddenly, without a knock. General Waverly snapped his eyes fiercely in the direction of the intruder, his jaws jutting ominously. A courier and his armed guard walked straight to the front of the room without waiting for recognition. The courier saluted and handed him an envelope.

"An urgent message, sir. I was told to deliver it without delay."

"This is a closed meeting," Waverly roared. "You should have requested admission."

"I was told not to stand on protocol, sir."

"Not stand on protocol!" Waverly rumbled. He signed for the message and tore it open impatiently. "What in hell are the armed forces coming to?"

He dismissed the courier and the guard abruptly and swaggered back to the center of the room. "That type of interruption will never happen again, I can assure you," he said as he creased the paper and held it up with annoyance. He began to read aloud, in his seething frustration, ignoring the all-important security regulation of reading it first in silence:

"Nineteen zero three, Eastern Daylight Time, Antarctica." He looked up from the paper and his eyes swept across his rigid audience. "Less than an hour ago. That's efficiency for you." A smug smile of satisfaction crossed his face and he glanced back at the paper.

"At 18:57, Eastern Daylight Time, while Sputnik VIII was being minitracked for triangulation fix with Russian radar station on other side of South Pole, a large, oblong UFO was seen to move in zero fix position and follow orbit for thirty seconds. The UFO then reversed position and moved rapidly toward Australia, accelerating to thirty thousand miles an hour. It was roughly estimated at sixty feet in length. The Sputnik trace has disappeared!"

General Waverly collapsed in the single chair which had been pushed back against the blackboard. His ruddy complexion was gone; sweat beaded his forehead. With trembling lips he spoke. "Maybe spacemen dug that hole in Nevada after all." His hand rose to his throat. "What are we going to do now, Hank?"

18.

Russia had reacted violently to the Sputnik loss. Strong notes of protest accused America of space theft. A technical war raged as to whether or not the Sputnik was over the American territory of Antarctica or over Russian territory at the time of the incident. A protest was lodged with the United Nations within forty-eight hours by Russia, requesting a definition of outer-space territory as international property, whereby any satellite or space vehicle sent fifty miles above the earth would be the property of the sender, irrespective of its position over another country or possession. The American Government countered with the claim that any space vehicle was the property of the nation over which it was passing. Some Washington officials advised that this was a dangerous position to take, but the pressure of the immediate problem gave strength to this short-sighted policy. Of course, it opened the door to the possibility that the United States might lose a few satellites as they passed over Russia, or that the U.S.A. might attempt to shoot down a few of the Russian ones; but that was considered a minor eventuality in the present dilemma.

A United Nations committee was formed immediately to study the requests. It was given the best of assistance from international scientists, mathematicians and geometricians, but the problem soon became insoluble. If, for instance, the lines were projected only a relatively short distance into space above the claimed territories of the various nations, they either shrank the domain to an insignificant percentage of the total area when extended perpendicularly from the surface of the earth, or they became hopelessly overlapped if extended at a slight angle. The area above Russia or America on the angle basis soon became greater than the total area of the earth itself. To many people in all nations a sense of relief was provided by the ludicrous dilemma in which these experts found themselves. To an important few a philosophical warning was given that man must change his whole way of thinking, now that he was faced with a cosmic challenge and not merely localized bickerings on this speck of energy ash.

It was very interesting to the American Government that the Russians had chosen to appeal to the United Nations at all. For several years, since their dramatic success with the first Sputnik and their temporary superiority with the ICBM, they had appeared sullen and uninterested in the United Nations, though recently they had probed the possibilities of disarmament more seriously. This new attitude was taken in official circles as good evidence that the Russians were genuinely concerned about the strange UFO—that it was not of Russian origin. The tone of their overtures, as read between the lines, confirmed the belief that this was not a master stroke of subterfuge on their part. Meanwhile, as world public opinion began to laugh quietly at the confused accusations of the two nations, the American Government turned its attention to the threat of the leaflets which had been dropped over the Bronx. Almost timidly a feeler was sent out through the American Embassy in Moscow to determine the Russian opinion of the leaflets. It had been officially confirmed that such leaflets were dropped over Moscow.

The next few days were torture for Henry Alvin. Every evening when he returned home a great temptation seized him. The third evening he walked to the wall safe, opened it and held the heavy bundle of papers in his hands. What a foolish promise, he thought. I had no right as an official of the U. S. Government to tie my hands with a pledge to Jack Baker.

Alvin threw his hat at a nearby chair, removed his raincoat and sat down heavily on the sofa. He had unwillingly made a bargain out of consideration for a friend. A delay of two weeks in reporting the papers seemed a reasonable gesture at the time he made it, for the chance it gave Jack to find Sandy. But now such delay could be critical to the government, not for the time lost in working on a prototype of the *Argonaut,* but for the influence the possession of such knowledge might have on national policy.

Alvin got up and walked to the darkened window. As he gazed out upon the city with its bustle of human activity, he was seized by a realization that a man must stick to his word, however painful. He picked up the papers and put them back in the wall safe.

Even though he had resisted temptation, he could not bear the thought of spending ten more days shuttling between his apartment and the Pentagon in this role of duplicity. Two days later he requested General Waverly to let him return to Nevada for a more detailed study of the hangar. He departed immediately when the permission was granted. After twelve days he returned to Washington and walked into the general's office unannounced.

"Well, well, Hank, glad to have you back. Did you find any blueprints for spaceships in Nevada?" Waverly had been taking his hat from the wall rack when Alvin walked in, but he stopped long enough to slap him on the back. "I'm just leaving for the State Department," he said proudly. "High-level conference with the Secretary."

The professor thought of Waverly's first comment and his heart leaped. "I have something here I believe you will want to look at."

"Perhaps later this afternoon," Waverly said impatiently as he stepped through the door into the hall. Then he turned with a look of curiosity. "What is it?"

The scientist set his large brief case on a chair and pulled a bundle of papers from it. "Perhaps it is just what you said; perhaps it *is* blueprints for a spaceship."

"Wait a minute, Hank, that's going too far." He hesitated a moment. A harsh, determined look settled on his face.

"Does it give any clue as to who these birds are, how we might find them?"

Alvin smiled. "They didn't leave any forwarding address, if that's what you mean." The general frowned. He was obviously too rushed for jokes. "Seriously, sir, this is most unusual. All of the writing is in strange symbols."

"Some crackpot probably planted them." He pulled his hat down snugly. "Meet me here at five—but I warn you, I've got a bellyful of this spaceman theory."

Alvin watched the heavy figure rocking down the hall. He realized that the problem was deeply involved with Waverly's personality. Waverly was his only avenue of approach to those who set the high policy. Until recently he had thought he knew the very skeleton of thought which motivated the general, but now he pondered the fact that there was much more to the man than even he could perceive. Waverly's disdain for spacemen was understandable. His embarrassment at that last conference when his ego overcame his judgment and he prematurely announced the Sputnik steal, could account for that. Still, even in that moment, the hard-boiled general had been emotionally honest. He believed the report from Antarctica and he reacted with the simple, frightened logic that "spacemen could have dug that hole in Nevada." But his very show of credulity, with its moment of frail disturbance, had brought forth the subtle and indirect criticism of others. Dick Waverly would stand up against the whole lot of them for the spaceman theory if he could prove it to his own satisfaction, Alvin thought. But one could only speculate in confusion.

At 5:26 Waverly walked into his office, hung his hat on the rack and went straight to his desk. Henry Alvin had been waiting patiently since 4:55. He was struck with the look of preoccupation on the general's face. Something unexpected had happened.

"What do you know about the Council of Eight?" Waverly asked bluntly.

The professor was taken aback. He lowered his brief case to the floor and kicked it under a chair.

"Sit down, Hank."

"I vaguely remember that group, something the last President set up by legislation several years ago, wasn't it?"

"Right. These people were appointed for life, given protection from the pressure of economics, politics and public opinion. I didn't think much of it at the time. It looked like just another committee to mess into things, and God knows we have too many now, but since they had no power, only an advisory capacity, there was little opposition. Anyhow, I was wrong. It has turned out to be a very far-sighted move."

"In what way, sir?"

"In a big way. The Secretary had them all there this afternoon and they damn near changed my whole point of view on the role of military strategy, as well as our national objectives."

Alvin was astounded. Even though he knew that Waverly, like most of the government officials, was groping for a new outlook with which to face the confusion created by the *Argonaut,* he could hardly believe that any government agency had remained sufficiently aloof from perplexity to provide a line of action, particularly one acceptable to the military. This can only mean a policy of strength, Alvin thought with trepidation: scrap the peaceful coexistence theme, the determent and second-strike theory, confine the Communists with a bluff. Can I sacrifice the papers for such an objective, he wondered, sitting rigidly, tight-lipped in his chair.

The general lit a cigar and seemed to relax a bit. "These people made a most unusual point and made it well. First they asked us to evaluate realistically the armament race of the last few years." He looked soberly at the scientist. "You remember we were discussing that one evening not long ago. It hasn't gained us security. The Russians have kept right on with their nonovert aggressions like Berlin, the Middle East,

237

etc., things we couldn't afford to start a big war about. And it's cost like hell. Then we took a look at the economic warfare. The Russians concluded several years ago that this was the place to make real progress and they've made it. They've kept us hopping from one crisis to another while they took over new markets, consolidated their position in the old ones. They confused the issue with disarmament talk and made political capital in a frightened world. The Communists have let us go right on thinking they were determined to rule the world by force, the old Lenin doctrine that capitalism must be destroyed, but for years they have had no intention of attacking us or starting a big war anywhere. They were getting what they wanted without it."

"But aren't they getting what we want as well?"

"Right. And how are we going to stop them? With more arms, more bluffs and threats that they know damn good and well we won't carry out—we never have done anything more than call their bluff."

"How can we halt this disastrous game?" the scientist asked, wondering what the general was driving at.

"Three things have entered the picture according to the Council," Waverly replied. "First, the Russians feel that they are well along in their program of expanding world markets. They have us locked out of Red China and most of Asia, except Japan; we are crippled in the Middle East where they are selling below their own cost and far below ours to keep us out; they are buying so much of South America's raw materials that we are having tough sledding there; and finally, our tariff walls against European goods enabled them to work out a bilateral trade agreement with the European bloc about six months ago, as you know. Naturally they would like to keep right on holding us at bay through crises and confusion but they aren't too worried about us as a competitor now, in view of our inflation and high cost of living.

"Second, they are convinced that this strange craft is of

238

American origin and they're afraid of it. They think it's a new weapon we have developed, and this of course puts them on the defensive and has forced them back to the old bluff and stalemate attitude, just when we were making real progress on a world disarmament scheme. They had apparently concluded that the time had come to freeze the status quo by cooperating with the United Nations to set up a world police force under the latest plan of checks and balances, which they believe will not only contain the menace of Red China, keep us from messing up their pretty picture by starting a war, but also will assure them the opportunity of beating hell out of us in the world market."

"How do we know, sir, that this is what they're really thinking?"

"That's the third factor, this Council of Eight. After these people had been in operation for about a year, they recommended setting up similar groups in twelve other nations of the free world. The Communists saw that these people were thinkers, long-range planners, not the kind of people they could confuse and distract by their short-range strategy. Since the free world governments were working closely with these groups in their policy making, the Communists figured they had better get in on the act, that maybe they could get more information from these councils than their spies were getting. Well, the results have been most interesting, I learned this afternoon." He looked squarely at the scientist. "I am disposed to take the Secretary of State's word for it.

"The free world groups invited the Commies to join with them on one condition, that they be permitted to accept or reject the individuals who were proposed for membership. Our government thought the Communists would say to hell with that but they swallowed it, and it's an essential requirement. From the outset our President insisted that if we were going to arm ourselves with brainpower, as well as weapons, not only the intelligence but the horizon of the people chosen was all-important. He set up criteria which I thought were foolishness. They were not based on college degrees, and specialized training or experience. They were based on the ability of the person to approach a problem with clear logic and intuition, to solve it with a rare degree of practical horse sense. That wasn't too bad—sometimes you can find a natural genius—but the other thing threw me. To test their horizon, one of the questions they were asked was their opinion of flying saucers. Those who said they couldn't exist and couldn't prove it were written off. Those who said they believed in them wound up the same way. They couldn't prove a damn thing, either. Only those made the grade who argued that ten thousand years from now, or less, such a thing would be quite reasonable as a possibility here on earth; that, in view of a minor cosmic happenstance, one of those billions of inhabitable planets in this galaxy that our scientists project, might be only a few light-years away and might easily be ten thousand years more advanced than we are. The tough thing for the scientist to accept is the thought that we may someday exceed the speed of light, just as we exceeded the speed of sound not too many years ago. Then travel to these planets might be reasonable. The candidates had to argue that assumption, and the winners maintained that although some unknown space characteristic may limit the speed of light, it may not limit the speed of a material body. These people didn't say there were flying saucers or that there weren't. They merely gave a good logical possibility for such a thing, and this defined their breadth of imagination and knowledge in the space age. And the fact that they had the guts to do so in the face of an official government condemnation of the theory, defined their independence of thought.

"So we had these councils of carefully chosen people in Moscow and in five other Communist nations, working closely with the free world groups in an atmosphere of candid communication like scientists between nations have done for so many years. They discussed openly the thinking of their governments."

"That's why this group wasn't blinded and taken unawares by this strange craft like the rest of us," the scientist said with a slight tinge of guilt. "They were prepared for the possibility of an intrusion from outer space."

"But not an invasion by private American citizens," Waverly snapped. "Those birds have damn near started a war."

"That is humanity's fault, sir." Alvin spoke firmly. "People who are frightened, suspicious and without a broad horizon of understanding have almost started a war."

The general looked at him sharply. "But *those* are the people we have to work with. The governments may listen to this Council of Eight and their buddies when things are going well and they recommend something which seems to be a logical, inevitable step toward progress, but not when you get a thunderbolt like this strange aircraft, which creates a real crisis." He knocked the ashes off his cigar. "Even so, I almost changed my point of view this afternoon. It had seemed logical to play the game of strategy skillfully, intelligently, by nudging the Russians along with the rest of us into a world police force under the U.N., instead of playing a clumsy game of power politics. Instead of trying to contain the Russians, I would have accepted their challenge of competition in the world markets. We can't create customers through force any longer and nobody can win in another war, so let's bury the hatchet once and for all if there's any practical way to do it, and fight them with our economic vigor. I'd get a job with the U.N. forces."

Alvin gazed attentively at the general. It was hard for him to believe what he heard, but he believed it was spoken in deep sincerity. Waverly, with all of his intractable determination, had a rare flexibility of mind, he recalled. He would fight like the devil for what he believed was right but he never got trapped in an emotional casket; he could alter his convictions in the twinkling of an eye if he found they were wrong or incomplete.

"Then," said Waverly, "when things were beginning to make sense, these crazy Americans cut loose."

"We shouldn't condemn them, sir, even if they were Americans, and nobody can prove that for sure. All we know is they have a most astounding craft and they did ask men to do the right thing. Maybe they didn't dare turn their craft over to anyone until they found out how man was going to react to their entreaty."

"Entreaty, hell," Waverly roared. "It was a damnable threat."

"Call it what you like, sir, but if they are not Americans with one lone craft—if they have fifteen or twenty of those ships and a stock of hydrogen bombs, or maybe something worse, they can damn well carry it out."

The old man looked very tired, Alvin thought. He watched him intently as he slowly turned his head and spoke.

"You're right. I just don't like to be threatened."

"But they made a 'sign in the sky,' as you said. That should put the fear of God in us."

"And all it did was put the fear of America in the Russians," Waverly replied bitterly. "Whoever it was really fouled up the strategy. Now the Communists wouldn't think of surrendering their autonomy to the U.N. and have us pull a ship like that one out of our back pocket."

"But we won't do that. We can't."

"Of course we can't and that makes matters all the worse. Now Russia is really belligerent and we're as defenseless as ever with our defensive philosophy. For the first time in over ten years they might strike first out of sheer panic."

The scientist had been biding his time with the papers since his first unhappy fear that he could not bring himself to disclose them. "What if we could make a craft like that, sir? What if we had the blueprints for one?"

"And where in hell would we get them?" Waverly asked with a sneer.

Dr. Alvin stood up quickly and reached under his chair. He hoisted his heavy brief case to the general's desk, opened it, and dumped out the bundle of papers.

"This is what you spoke of earlier," Waverly said. "I had almost forgotten it." He broke open the seal and unrolled the papers. For a moment he looked at them, then he glanced up.

"Are they a plant, Hank? I'll take your word for it."

"I don't know their true significance, sir, but I am convinced they were left behind by the people who escaped in that ship."

The general perused the papers for several more minutes in silence. Then he bundled them together quickly and stood up. "All right. We can't overlook that possibility. Come with me and we'll put them in the big vault for tonight. Tomorrow I'm leaving for Dayton. You'd better come along with me. I won't tell the Wright Air Force boys a damn thing—where we got them, what they're supposed to mean, whether they're old comic-book tracings enlarged or not. I don't know what they are. If those Air Force scientists don't take an interest or can't figure them out, they'll just get tossed in the back of a musty old cabinet."

He walked toward the door. "Come on, Hank," he said with a twinkle in his eyes, "you and I can't afford to get tossed in the back of an old cabinet. We might have another war to fight. The only thing that could really save the situation now would be for these birds, be they spacemen, or Americans, or someone else, to turn over that craft in such a way that we could prove our government didn't make it, so both we and the Russians could start even in presenting it to the U.N."

"Don't come in the kitchen, Jack," Sandy Carlson said. "You can help cook but I wash the dishes."

"O.K.," he called after her. "If you'll step back on limits I'll help you tie that apron."

Sandy came from the small pantry of her Cleveland apartment, trailing the apron in her left hand. She walked briskly toward him and threw both arms around his neck.

"You'll never get dressed for the dishes as long as *I'm* tied up like this."

"In a hurry?"

"To hell with the dishes." He gently pushed her head back and kissed her deeply, with a lingering fervor.

Finally she wriggled free and handed him the apron.

"I'll try that call again to Hank," he said as he finished tying the strings and gave her an affectionate pat. "Can't imagine where that guy has been for the last five days. Don't listen."

"I don't give a damn about your funny business with Hank Alvin or anybody else you've got to go chasing after," she called back, "as long as you don't spend more than one night at a time away from Cleveland."

"Can't promise yet," Jack shouted. "Anyhow, you do worse than that yourself."

"Yes, but I'm resigning next week."

"Then what you gonna do?"

"Get married."

"To whom?"

"A crazy guy from California if he ever settles down."

"And if he doesn't?"

"Marry George."

"Too late."

He heard the clatter of high-heeled shoes. She stuck her head through the pantry door.

"Too late, hell. He'll wait a couple of more months if I ask him to."

"Will you ask him?"

"Not if you sign up to get your business finished by then."

He stepped across the floor and kissed her with his hands behind his back. "Let me make the phone call."

"Go ahead, but you've got your ultimatum." Sandy walked back to the kitchen and began to stack the dishes.

"Call to Washington," Jack said as he sat on the edge of a large upholstered chair. "Station-to-station, Emerson 3-8745." God, I hope we get through this time, he thought. Schoeller's probably in Germany by now, but I must talk to Alvin before I start after him.

The phone on the other end rang for a full minute. "D.A.," the operator reported.

"Please keep ringing," Jack said in desperation.

Eight rings later someone picked up the receiver.

"Hank!"

"Jack."

"Where in hell have you been?"

"Out west. I just left Waverly."

"What's cooking?"

"A damn good deal, with one exception. He believes things would work out much as we had hoped if the boys come home with the Model A."

Jack recognized that he was speaking with caution. "Anyone there?" he asked.

"No one."

"I only hope both boys are with the old puddle jumper," Jack said with tongue in cheek, feeling that this extreme of caution was uncalled for, but not knowing for sure.

"Assume that they are."

"But what about the wild one?"

"Forget him. If he's on the loose he can do no damage now. What we need is to get the car back in the garage."

"That's the one thing we can't do anything about."

"And the only thing that will do any good, so relax. How's your love life?"

Jack slapped his hand over the mouthpiece. "Hey, Sandy. Hank wants to know about my love life." She came to the pantry door.

"More than I expected, Hank," he continued into the phone. "Almost more than I can take."

Sandy stuck her tongue out at him, raised a dripping kitchen knife in a threatening gesture and withdrew.

"Go on and marry the girl and make it legal" came from the other end.

Suddenly Jack seemed to slump against the back of the chair.

"You're sure about Schoeller. You're sure I shouldn't go after him?"

"Positive. It might even be better if he did show his hand."

"Hank. I'm still afraid the stars are too high. From the way people reacted, I can't really believe that they are ready to seek the truth."

"Maybe not, but there's more behind it than you realize, Jack, much more than I realized. I can't say for sure about the outcome, but we've done our work. Now it's up to powers beyond our control. I only hope the ship comes home without the second run."

"I hope so, too."

"Then get on the ball and marry the girl."

"I'll do it, on your recommendation. Sorry you can't be best man."

"Too busy with incidentals. My heart is with you both."

"Good night, Hank." Jack hung up the phone. His frown

turned into a smile. "Hey, Sandy," he called. "Where's the pencil and paper? I'm signing up to be available in two days, not two months."

The *Argonaut* hung motionless eight thousand miles above the earth. Occasionally Max would nose the ship into the deep shadow to blot out the sun and cool the hull. At this altitude the shadow of the earth was clear and well-defined; there was no twilight zone as in the atmosphere. Slowly the continents rolled beneath them.

"Things are going better than we expected," Sloan remarked.

"Yes," Schoeller replied laconically.

"Damn fortunate. Our rations are almost gone, and I don't go for that distilled water much longer. What day is it, Max?"

"Tuesday." Max fumbled a cigarette out of his shirt pocket but realized for the hundredth time that he could not afford to light it with their diminishing oxygen supply. "The forty-fourth day since we picked up the Sputnik."

"Do you really think we can parachute it back to Russia?"

"If the parachute opens. It is the large one you know, the one we had for equipment drops." Max tuned the radio dial impatiently. "I am more concerned about your Washington plan."

"But the way they've buried the hatchet and gotten together in searching for us. That's what we really wanted, Max. You shouldn't worry about giving the *Argonaut* to America now. Why they'd probably invite a Russian delegation over to take a look at it, just like they brought them over to inspect Mesatron. Both sides realize fully that they can't fight this thing, or fight with it, either."

"So," Schoeller said.

"Given a power like the *Argonaut,* men can't keep on making mistakes."

"Did we make a mistake,". the little German asked, his eyes flashing with devilment, "by stealing other people's property instead of dropping fireworks on them a second time?"

"We only borrowed it," Sloan bellowed in the quiet cockpit. "Your fireworks scared a lot of people and that pleased you. It might have scared some leaders, too, but not in the right direction. It made them grab at their holsters instead of laying down their arms. Things looked pretty serious for a while."

"You promised we could make the second run after the Sputnik steal, if I wanted to."

"Yes, and I challenged you to pick up the Sputnik. I appealed to your vanity. I told you it was something you couldn't do and you did it. O.K., if you want a real anticlimax let's make the second run."

Max screwed up his face in a frown. His lips puckered in contemplation. "Perhaps you were right about the Sputnik instead of the second run. I'll take a chance on your idea of giving the ship to America if you will include in your note to the Russians that we will land the *Argonaut* at Wright Air Development Center ten days after we send back the Sputnik. I can wait no longer than that to give them an even start."

John Sloan looked straight ahead at the brilliant stars. He had no fear of what would happen to him and Max if they were shot out of the sky by a barrage of rockets over Russia, or even if they were captured in America. But he still hesitated to risk knowledge of the *Argonaut* in the hands of the Soviets. It was an old fear, deeply lodged in his mind. Then he thought of the papers he had sent to Alvin and wondered if the leadership America had shown with regard to genuine coöperation stemmed from the security those papers afforded. If only the Soviets had a change in government, he thought. I don't trust the old-line Communists. He bit his lips until they were thin and hard.

"You went along with me, Max. If you think that's best,

and you can translate the message into Russian, I'll go along with you."

"I will translate it," Max said, getting up from the cramped pilot's seat. "I will sleep now for three hours. We will not need to move the ship back into the sun until I awaken."

There was no sense of time in this celestial void, no night and day. Only the uncomfortable lessening of gravity gave any sense of direction. It was annoying, but it diminished the burden of hovering on the gravity reactors. Sloan dozed restlessly, wondering if his last decision had been right. But I must have faith in all men, he thought sleepily. We took this gamble in that faith. Another thought crossed his mind as his head nodded: perhaps God withheld the *Argonaut* from man until he was ready to accept it for peace. But he was too sleepy to be startled or encouraged by the thought.

Two hours later Sloan was aroused when the sun peeped over the great ball of the earth. Max barely had her in the shadow, he thought. It was hard to realize the earth was moving around the sun so fast. He switched on the radio to keep awake until Max returned.

". . . This change in attitude may be recorded in history as more significant than the Bolshevik revolution of 1917" crashed into his ears before he could turn down the volume. Sloan sat bolt upright. "Three alternatives have faced the world for many years: hot war, cold war, or coöperation in rules of fair play among nations with an international body to enforce them. It took this mutual fear of the unknown to put two great nations side by side in facing the issues squarely. The older factions in Russia still suspect a trick despite the blueprints disclosed by Washington and the assurance that the origin of the craft has not been determined. They cannot forget the piece of American gear dropped over Moscow nor the hangar in Nevada. However, our government has pledged that if this awesome craft is found on American soil it will be turned over to an international police organization, provided that Russia will agree to the same proposition. This morning the Russian government announced its agreement. Our Secretary of State has made the solemn statement: 'If a lasting peace cannot be carved from this situation, it never will be.'

"This is Raymond Blakely speaking. I'll be back in one minute with more news of this situation. . . ."

Sloan spun the dial of the radio with excitement. He heard only music or commercials. As he was preparing to turn back to the first station, a voice interrupted a symphony broadcast. "Word has just been received on the Associated Press wires that Washington has sent an official note of congratulations to the Soviet leaders on their acceptance of our proposal to dispose of the craft. All that remains now is to find it."

Quickly Sloan spun the dial back to the first station. ". . . This will give you sure relief from pain and neuralgia. I return you to Raymond Blakely with his analysis of the news."

John Sloan rushed from his seat into the cabin. He shook Max violently. "Wake up, Max," he shouted. "It's time to haul anchor and get moving. Change that message to the Russians to read tonight, not ten days from now."

Max followed him to the cockpit, strapped himself in his seat, and put on the earphones. He listened to the radio for nearly two minutes, his face growing progressively intent. Finally he turned to Sloan with an incredulous look. "Perhaps men no longer need terror to rule them, only discipline."

"Perhaps so," Sloan said, as he tightened his harness. "Let's drop this Sputnik over the Moscow airport and then head for Wright Field."

Max touched a control button and the *Argonaut* plunged toward the earth.

AGNEW H. BAHNSON, JR. is an inventor and a manufacturer of machinery for textiles and other industrial uses. It is not surprising that he should have joined a group of outstanding scientists in exploring the mysteries of gravity. In regard to these experiments he says, "I was able to enlist the help of Dr. John Wheeler of Princeton University, and with the benediction of the University of North Carolina we succeeded in bringing Dr. and Mrs. Bryce DeWitt, two young and most highly qualified theoretical physicists to Chapel Hill early in 1956. About one hundred thousand dollars have been raised for these efforts, and during January of 1957 the Second International Conference on Gravitation was held at Chapel Hill with forty-two leading physicists in attendance. We feel that progress is being made on this most difficult problem." The spaceship in his novel is made possible by the perfection of a gravity-defying device. "Let us say," in the words of its fictional inventor, "that I have found a way, not perhaps to neutralize gravity . . . but to put it to work for us."

Mr. Bahnson was born in Winston-Salem, North Carolina, in 1915, and attended the University of North Carolina where he was elected to Phi Beta Kappa. After graduation in 1935 he went to Harvard for a year to study in the widely diverse fields of philosophy and business administration. Between school terms he made a trip around the world as an ordinary seaman and twice climbed the Matterhorn in Switzerland. He entered the machine shop of The Bahnson Company in 1937 and worked his way up through the ranks to its presidency.

Hobbies have always held an important place in his life. He has set to music the Elizabeth Barrett Browning Sonnet XIV, which was orchestrated and played by the Winston-Salem Symphony Orchestra; and has done an oil portrait of his wife Katherine. Of all the hobbies he has undertaken, however, he finds novel-writing the most interesting and the most baffling.